QUESTIONS T...
ANSWERS—AN... ELINOR HAD NONE

What was in the packet that Elinor carried and that she had vowed to guard at all costs—and which someone wanted badly enough to kill for?

What was wrong with the heart that Elinor had rapturously given to the maddeningly handsome Lord Foxhall—but that now quickened so disturbingly when the gruffly attractive, not-to-be-trusted Reeves came too close for comfort?

What awaited Elinor in Vienna, where she faced a duel of wits and wiles with a beautiful society vixen—and another kind of struggle within herself?

So many questions—and so much danger if they were not answered in time. . . .

The Duke's Messenger

SIGNET Regency Romances You'll Enjoy

The Duke's Messenger

by
Vanessa Gray

A SIGNET BOOK
NEW AMERICAN LIBRARY
TIMES MIRROR

NAL BOOKS ARE AVAILABLE AT QUANTITY DISCOUNTS
WHEN USED TO PROMOTE PRODUCTS OR SERVICES. FOR
INFORMATION PLEASE WRITE TO PREMIUM MARKETING
DIVISION, THE NEW AMERICAN LIBRARY, INC., 1633
BROADWAY, NEW YORK, NEW YORK 10019.

SIGNET TRADEMARK REG. U.S. PAT. OFF. AND FOREIGN COUNTRIES
REGISTERED TRADEMARK—MARCA REGISTRADA
HECHO EN CHICAGO, U.S.A.

SIGNET, SIGNET CLASSICS, MENTOR, PLUME, MERIDIAN AND NAL
BOOKS are published by The New American Library, Inc.,
1633 Broadway, New York, New York 10019

First Printing, November, 1982

1 2 3 4 5 6 7 8 9

PRINTED IN THE UNITED STATES OF AMERICA

Chapter One

Lady Sanford's smart black town carriage trundled up South Audley Street toward Portman Square. The last evening of the month of October, 1814, had turned chilly, and the older of the two occupants of the vehicle gathered her fur-lined pelisse close about her.

Euphrynia Sanford, having reached what she spoke of—when absolutely required—as "mature years" was not one to disregard her own comfort. Fortunately her late husband had thoughtfully left her sufficient funds to indulge her strong bent toward luxury. So it was that even on a ride of no more than half a dozen city blocks she was warmed, not only by her miniver-lined cloak, but by two lavish fur rugs tucked about her small feet.

She stole a glance at her niece. Her dear sister's child, Miss Elinor Aspinall, allowed her own cloak to fall open at the throat. When one is young, reflected Lady Sanford with some regret, high spirits take the place of warm wraps.

Not that Nell's spirits were exuberant, Lady Sanford decided. Indeed, the child had for several days fallen into the mopes, for no discernible reason unless it was the approaching end of her first London Season.

The function toward which the coach was even now carrying them was perhaps the last event of its kind before the *ton* went its diverse ways for the purpose of celebrating the Christmas holidays at their various country seats.

The ball was being given by the revered Duchess of Netwick, a lady noted for her fanatic adherence to ways now considered sufficiently antique to be quite laughable. Such amusement was exhibited strictly in private, of course. No one with any pretensions to respectability would take the haz-

1

ard of being removed from her grace's carefully pruned guest list.

"But," said Lady Sanford, as though continuing a conversation interrupted, "her *cachet* is excellent, and one must expect the supper to be palatable. I heard that Gunther's has a new shipment of ice, so the confections are bound to be better than those at Devonshire House. I particularly dote on his fruit ices. I vow I was in a mind to cut him entirely off, but then I remembered his fine sugar plums, and I cannot deprive myself of them, not even for the sake of principle."

Nell appeared abstracted. Lady Sanford realized that this alarming state of not listening, of suddenly absenting herself from present company in favor of long, absorbing thoughts of her own, was growing on Nell.

From Phrynie Sanford's own experience, such an air of otherworldliness was an infallible indication of tender passion—*amour*, one might say, as opposed to the entirely practical emotion whose aim was marriage.

She was strengthened in this belief, since a number of eligible suitors had appeared and made their offers, which Nell, quite kindly, turned down. There was Morrow, for example, whom Nell quite properly avoided, but Phrynie could not fault her in that respect. That family had more than its share of notoriously unstable eccentrics. It seemed clear to Phrynie that Nell was not willing to settle for suitability, or even a strong affection.

What more did she want?

With apprehension, Phrynie cast her mind over the eligible bachelors of whom they had seen much during the past six weeks, for somewhere in their acquaintance must lie Nell's sudden interest.

"Nell, dear," she probed delicately, "are you greatly disappointed in these last few months? Have you enjoyed London?"

"Aunt, I'm sorry. Do you think me ungrateful? Indeed, how could anyone be unhappy here? The Tsar's visit, and the Victory Celebration, and the parties, and the outings—I dearly loved Richmond—and the Tower menagerie—and such amusing entertainments . . ." Her voice died away. "Indeed, Aunt, I am most grateful."

While her aunt was entirely aware that Nell was not a raving beauty, the girl was entirely amiable and had a fine pair

of speaking gray eyes, fringed with long dark lashes that had
had a certain effect upon quite a few young men.

As though idly, Lady Sanford murmured, "Do you think
Soames will offer?"

"Oh, dear, I hope not! A veritable Tulip, Aunt! His collars
are so stiff he cannot turn his head, and his padded coats are
laughable. Morrow said the other day that he thought Soames
was merely a broomstick, held upright by his ridiculous apparel!"

"But," objected her aunt, "I shall hope you are not judging
a gentleman by his tailor."

"Oh, no, I am not—but one must admit," said Nell with a
trace of wistfulness, "that appearance does count for something. Surely one's appearance is a signal of one's intellect?"

"Intellect?" murmured her aunt in a bewildered fashion.
She was suddenly aware that she had seriously underesti-
mated her niece.

Phrynie had taken Nell under her protection for the girl's
first Season. It was a duty that for the most part she enjoyed.
Since the accident—when Nell's parents had succumbed to
the entirely mistaken idea held by George Aspinall that he
could feather a team to a peg around a milestone hidden in
frosty grass, even though the metalled surface was covered
with a new layer of freezing rain—there was no question of
Phrynie's clear responsibility.

Perhaps she would have been better advised to probe the
inner workings of this biddable young lady's mind, rather
than spending time in Henrietta Street choosing Irish poplins,
French gloves, and Indian muslins. Phrynie now suspected,
darkly, that Nell might prove to be a rather formidable person. For the first time, she felt a qualm about Nell.

"Not that I begrudge any of these past months, my dear,"
said Phrynie, clinging to known landmarks. "But I confess I
cannot understand your reluctance even to consider any of
the offers you have had."

Phrynie had, Nell discovered, the most disconcerting way
of swooping into a conversation by a side door, leaving her
audience to sort out whatever formal beginnings had been
omitted. By this time, Nell had become expert at filling in her
aunt's ellipses.

"Aunt, I am dreadfully sorry, but I cannot think you

would truly wish me to face Nigel Whitley over the breakfast table for the next forty years!"

"Hardly so long," murmured Lady Sanford. "The Whitleys have a weakness in the chest, which has a sad tendency to cut them off in their prime." She thought a moment. "Not that even their prime is to be admired, I confess. But you realize, do you not, that the Whitleys are possessed of sufficient wealth to make you very comfortable?"

"Yes, Aunt. But not Nigel. Indeed, he makes me vastly uncomfortable, with that lisp. Besides, his hands are damp!"

Fortunately for Nell, the journey was short. They were already pulling into the line of carriages stretching halfway around the square. "Later, Aunt. I am excessively grateful for your concern for me, and I do not know how I would have gone on without you. But as much as I wish to make a good match, I cannot think that my brother would approve of Nigel Whitley."

"That Tom!" explained Phrynie in a dismissing tone. "Why doesn't he make his appearance, then, instead of leaving you to make your way alone? Surely he should circulate in society to lend you countenance."

And, thought Phrynie, to allow me to gather my wits. She had, she realized, probably spent no more than a waking hour a day in her own home since April. Nell had, so far, not been known to refuse an invitation.

"Incidentally," she continued, "I should also like him to explain why he himself isn't in the petticoat line? The Aspinall name is likely to die out unless he comes up to the mark!"

Since this was not the first time Lady Sanford had unburdened herself on the subject of her wayward nephew, Nell did not find it necessary to respond. Taking all in all, she thought, Tom's absence was in the ordinary way more to be desired than his presence.

Tom was a law unto himself, as their aunt knew well, disappearing and surfacing again without regularity or explanations, but more often than not, with disconcerting effects on his nearest kin.

Nell recalled with a shudder the most recent occasion upon which Tom arrived at Lady Sanford's town house, accompanied, for a reason never divulged, by a rawboned tomcat of belligerent tendencies, which at once found expression in a spirited encounter with the Sanford poodle.

It was entirely possible that in Lady Sanford's vigorous reaction to that episode could be found the primary reason for Tom's prolonged absence from the capital. Nell missed him, but she understood that her brother followed pursuits of his own, and she had long ago ceased to ask questions to which the only answers provided were vague and evasive.

The town house of the Duchess of Netwick occupied half a block on Gloucester Place, just off fashionable Portman Square. The palatial house and vast grounds were surrounded by a high iron-grille fence, broken in the center of the Gloucester Place frontage by great gates into which were wrought representations of the heraldic beasts which formed a part of the duke's ancient coat of arms.

A broad avenue leading from the street to the house was no more than three carriages' length, illuminated on both sides by flaming torches in the manner of bygone days. The house itself was ablaze with candlelight from every window, and the entrance doors, in spite of the chill, stood open. Even through the closed windows of the coach, Nell and Lady Sanford could hear the shrill hum of many voices mingled with snatches of music.

"We are late!" said Nell, disappointed. "The dancing has begun."

"Nonsense!" said Phrynie. "This is only the arrival music."

Unsettled by an unwonted note in her niece's voice, she looked sharply at her. "Nell, you are not as a rule so anxious to be the first on the floor." Unless, thought Phrynie, you have already promised the first dance?

"We're almost at the door, Aunt," said Nell, avoiding unwelcome conversation. And on the instant, the door to the carriage was flung open by a footman, and the ladies were helped to alight.

The cool air struck unpleasantly after the warmth of the coach, and they hurried up the steps and into the foyer. Nell murmured, "What a squeeze!"

It was indeed, thought her aunt. Nell had upset her in a way she didn't quite comprehend. She studied her niece unobtrusively.

She was proud of Nell's appearance—her long black tresses dressed in a style improvised by Lady Sanford's most excellent maid Mullins, an arrangement doubtless to be attempted in many a boudoir on the morrow. Nell wore to perfection her new gown, in blossom pink crape over an underslip of matching sarsenet, pink satin ball slippers, and French kid gloves in the same delicate hue.

Not every woman could wear pink, even that pale hue that resembled a strawberry fruit ice, but Nell's complexion was fresh and delicate. Nell, thought her aunt fondly, could wear anything!

Halfway up the staircase to greet their hostess, the explanation of Nell's behavior came to Lady Sanford, somewhat in the manner of an exploding girasol. Nell's glance was brushing across the crowd of faces above on the stairs and below in the foyer, restlessly, as though seeking one particular face in the throng.

Lady Sanford, herself an experienced flirt, recognized in Nell that same questing look that she herself had often worn—with, she thought, a little more decorum than Nell displayed!

Nell's seeking glance was, without question, the anxious search of a woman in love.

Not that love was to be despised, not at all. Phrynie Sanford in fact spent much of her time enjoying the various permutations of the tender passion. But Nell, with a marriage still to make and a life to establish, must not throw her cap over the windmill. This of all times was the proper moment to keep one's eye on the main chance, although Lady Sanford would never permit such a vulgar phrase to escape her lips, There would be time enough later—Phrynie judged from her own experience—to explore the farther shores of love.

Promising herself to keep a more than watchful eye on her niece this evening, she promptly lost sight of her charge, being pleasantly distracted by the Marquess of Darnford, an old friend. More than friend, if the truth were known, but Lady Sanford had no intention of allowing that particular truth to out.

Darnford's eyes swept over her with unconcealed admiration. She was gratified that she had decided upon a new gown of cornflower-blue crape, cut daringly low across her bosom. The dress was fashioned to have a sweeping fullness in the folds at the back, providing a satisfying swing of fabric at every step.

The duchess received her guests at the top of the crowded

stairway. She was attired without regard for her spreading obesity in a green brocade gown and matching turban embellished with the enormous Netwick emerald. The jewel itself was remarkable, supposed to have arrived in England in the previous century hidden in the baggage of a Netwick general returning from the troubles in India.

Now that the Season was drawing to a close, and all political eyes were focused on the congress now gathering in Vienna, there was almost an air of nostalgia about the company. One last great gathering, so it seemed, before the gaily colored flock, feathered by W. H. Botibol, *plumassier* of Oxford Street, scattered for the winter.

Her Grace the duchess had not stinted on her ball. At least seven violins played from a bay artfully screened by masses of potted trees from the conservatory, and already waiters slipped swiftly among the guests, bearing trays of refreshments to restore the guests from the rigors of a three-block carriage ride.

Nell was among the first couples led onto the mirror-polished floor. Her escort in this significant event, Rowland Fiennes, Lord Foxhall, was recognized with varying degrees of dismay by many a young lady and many an ambitious mama.

Lord Foxhall had been the prime catch of five Seasons. He was handsome as the sunrise—which in fact he somewhat resembled, being golden of hair and rosy of complexion. Dressed in a superlatively cut black coat and black satin knee breeches, he placed Elinor Aspinall's hand firmly on his forearm and stepped onto the floor as the musicians bowed the opening notes of a mazurka.

Watching Nell, Lady Sanford was distressed. Her dismay was not caused by the sight of Foxhall dancing with Nell. It was, on the contrary, directly a result of the impact on Phrynie's sensibilities of the expression on Nell's face. To give the girl credit, she was behaving with impeccable decorum. But a knowledgeable eye would detect Nell's too intense concentration on her partner.

Phrynie's eye was not the only discerning one. Darnford spoke quietly in her ear. "Too bad your child has developed a *tendre* in that direction, my dear, for you know he is bound hand and foot to the Freeland."

"Nell is not a fool, Darnford," retorted Phrynie. "He could

do much better, you know, than that vinegar-faced ape leader."

"Dear me," he drawled, "such unwarranted heat! Ape leader?"

Phrynie was greatly irritated. "If Penelope Freeland hasn't dragged Foxhall to the altar in five years, then it is likely he is not quite so firmly tethered as you believe."

"I wonder . . ." mused Darnford. "You can't think she is still hanging out for that fellow Whern, now that he's got the title?"

"I care not in the least degree," said Phrynie peevishly. "I simply want Nell happy."

Nell was, to put it simply, ecstatic. Excessively aware of Rowland's fingers clasping hers delicately and completely *comme il faut,* she felt a trembling that reached as far as her toes. She breathed in the fresh violet scent of his shaving soap, and thought it the most delightful aroma she had ever known. Even the intimacy of thinking of such a private rite as the removal of whiskers from a masculine face shook her until she feared she would blush most dreadfully.

"The weather has turned chilly, has it not?" remarked the Paragon.

"Of a certainty," responded the lady.

Conversation lapsed. Nell finally lifted her magnificent eyes to Rowland. This was of course not the first time she had danced with Lord Foxhall. Indeed, she had spent one or two pleasant hours with him, if not alone, then at least in a tête-à-tête a bit removed from the company. A certain picnic at Richmond shimmered delightfully in her recollection.

But this evening seemed subtly different. To be his first partner of the evening surely meant he liked her, a little?

She had quite simply been stunned by her first sight of the striking Lord Foxhall. All of six months ago, that had been, and the presence of the unbelievably handsome Rowland Fiennes in her dreams, waking or sleeping, had vanquished any hope nourished by Nigel Whitley or any other serious swain.

How very handsome Rowland was! His features, distinguished by their resemblance to a head carved on an old Greek coin, were to be endlessly admired. His elegant figure was superlatively graceful, owing little to his tailor, and indeed he was fortunate enough, Nell thought, to possess no flaws whatever!

However, Nell could distinguish fact from fancy. She was well aware that Lord Foxhall was a cut above her, even though her breeding was as good as his. It was simply that he was kind to her, and so handsome that she was drawn to him, moth to candle.

Many another lady had swooned over Lord Foxhall, and yet the heir to an earldom had remained immune to all the wiles, subtle and not so subtle, that had been practiced on him. How could Nell be so rash as to think that she had a chance to snare this very elusive prey?

But he had in fact given her very discreet indications that she pleased him, and Nell was caught between two poles. At moments she thought that he was indeed fond of her, and the next moment she succeeded in convincing herself that he was simply an accomplished man of society, treating her with the same civility he would bestow on a cousin!

Nell stole a glance at the other dancers. Penelope Freeland was dancing with Charles Inwood, but her eyes were on Nell, burning across the distance between them, and their message was entirely clear. She wished Nell at the antipodes, and that, as speedily as her own guardian angel could arrange it.

The dance, all too soon for Nell, came to an end. Just before he led her back to her aunt, who was sitting with Darnford along the wall, Rowland bent to murmur in her ear, "Miss Aspinall, I shall hope to have the first waltz with you. At that time, I should like to say something very particular to you."

Nell smothered an exclamation. She was oblivious to her aunt's obvious curiosity and Darnford's odd glance.

HE wished to say something *very particular . . .* !

Chapter Two

Nell was forced to set her rosy speculations aside, for many dances were played before the old-fashioned duchess allowed a waltz. Even in 1814, a most advanced year, the waltz was far from accepted by the older members of society. It had taken dignified Tsar Alexander and the vivacious Countess Lieven to lend their *cachet* to the Austrian importation by tripping it gaily at Almack's five months before. Only then had society as a whole believed it proper.

After all, it was hardly the thing for a man to place his arm around the waist of an unmarried woman, the Duchess of Netwick pointed out. "In my day," she said inaccurately, "a gentleman would expect to be horsewhipped for taking such liberties, and rightly, too. I recall my own brother calling out young Whern for something much more trivial."

"Young Whern?" said someone in the duchess's circle, as he idly watched the excessively handsome couple now on the floor. "Foxhall, wasn't it, with the Incomparable Penelope? Looks like they're having a real argy-bargy."

"He was young Whern at that time," explained the duchess. "He's put his spoon in the wall since then. The heir—that's his grandson—not at all up to snuff."

"In the army, wasn't he? Blue-deviled by some lady, as I recall. Didn't he come back from the peninsula with Wellington?"

"He did, and he has not yet made his manners to me," said the duchess, "as he should, being my godson. He's gone very mysterious, hasn't even opened the town house on Duke Street."

"A hermit, no doubt," said a dandy, guffawing, but his laugh was cut short by the duchess's stony stare.

10

"No, he's not one of your Tulips," said Her Grace with a significant glance at him. "The duke—Wellington, I mean, not Netwick—thinks much of him."

The duchess was perfectly capable of carrying on a vigorous conversation, at the same time not missing much of what was transpiring in the middle distance. Having neatly disposed of the dandy, she commented with malice, "I wonder Foxhall hasn't confessed defeat. The Freeland woman's been after him long enough."

Some one in the duchess's circle murmured, "Wouldn't want her laying siege to me! She's a stunner, but any man who married her would be under the cat's foot in a month, I'd take my oath!"

The duchess laughed until her little eyes disappeared in wrinkled folds. "Her grandfather, old General Sir Robert Freeland, you know, never won a battle in his life!"

The conversation around the duchess moved on to other, even more frivolous subjects, and the mysterious duke was forgotten. But all eyes remained upon the couple in question on the floor.

Penelope Freeland was not enjoying her first dance this evening with Rowland Fiennes. She had been out for five years, and had indeed come to think of Rowland as her own. Her father the Right Honorable the Lord Chawton was on Castlereagh's staff and was expecting to be appointed ambassador to France, or Austria, or wherever there was an amusing capital. She would find it easy to persuade her father to require Foxhall to accompany them to their new position. Penelope herself, having been brought up, so to speak, in the Foreign Office, would make a wife *par excellence* for a rising ambassador-to-be like Foxhall.

While Rowland had not yet precisely offered for her, such an event was only a matter of time. So Penelope had believed.

But then onto the London scene had come Elinor Aspinall. Penelope was not pleased. The Aspinall miss proved entirely too magnetic an attraction for Lord Foxhall, especially in recent weeks. At least so far Rowland had been discreet, his falling away signified only by a lessened attention to Penelope's wishes and a sad failure to do her bidding with his usual alacrity. She was certain, however, that no one other than Penelope had noticed his preoccupation.

Even though she considered the burgeoning affair as merely a novel diversion for Rowland, she was determined to forestall any consideration of more serious possibilities.

Her dance with Rowland, therefore, was an exercise to that end.

"I expected you at my reception this afternoon, Rowland," she began, breaking a too-long silence.

"I must apologize. Affairs at the Foreign Office required me."

"Nonsense," said Miss Freeland briskly. "You're merely packing up for the journey to Vienna. Your people could have managed."

Pacifically he said, "I had to give them direction, you know."

"No, Rowland, I *don't* know. You forget that I am in my father's confidence, and I am as well informed on matters in the Foreign Office as anyone."

"Penelope, believe me, I do not forget that fact."

Rowland was entirely courteous, as befitted a man with ambitions in the diplomatic field in conversation with the daughter of a man with great influence in that same area. But he made no promises, nor, to be precise, did he even seem to listen to her.

Only Miss Freeland's rigorous training kept her smoldering instead of bursting into flame, but it was clear to the most casual observer that she was unhappy.

Nell, dancing with one and another whose identities she would not later recall, was not aware of the byplay that so beguiled certain of the guests. If her aunt had not been indulging—simply to keep her hand in—in a mild flirtation with her host, the ancient Duke of Netwick, she might have found material for thought, but she did not.

At last came the first waltz, and Nell saw, as through a rosy veil, the approach of Lord Foxhall. The insistent rhythm captured her as he placed his arm, most delightfully, around her slender waist and swung her into the whirling dance. Her feet seemed to move without her volition somewhere above the mundane floor, the music sang in her veins, and paradise itself was not far removed.

At the conclusion of the dance, Foxhall led her off the floor. In this side room, where she suddenly found herself alone with Foxhall, the duchess had succumbed to the craze for Grecian furnishings that had followed upon the arrival from Athens of the marbles under the aegis of former Ambassador to Greece Lord Elgin. Nell had not before received the full impact of a room walled with plaster caryatids, whose blank eyes stared at the two inhabitants of the room. Even Rowland's thrilling presence could not remove her strong distaste at what she considered the gross overpopulation of what was after all a very small room.

Lord Foxhall did not seem aware of any lack of amenities. Of course he was not sitting on the cold marble bench upon which he had placed Nell. Instead, the rising diplomatist, ill at ease, was standing before her, his tongue unable to utter a sound since it was unaccountably cleaving to the roof of his mouth.

Better a hundred interviews with Lord Castlereagh, he thought, than one with this small girl with the great gray eyes.

"You must surely have understood," he began at last, "my purpose in seeking you out these past weeks. You are not unaware, I believe, of my intentions toward you."

Nell put out a hand as if to protest. Her response was to a degree chaotic. "No, no, Lord Foxhall—I dare not—"

"So formal, Miss Aspinall? I should like very much your permission to call you Elinor. May I?"

She thought she nodded agreement. In fact, her wits were so scattered it seemed a miracle that she had not fainted from the roaring tumult in her head.

It was a curious thing, she discovered, that happiness was such a *noisy* state. She could hardly think above the racket in her ears.

His voice came to her as though from a far distance. "Miss Aspinall—Elinor, that is—I—I confess that I have never before put this question to any lady of my acquaintance."

When he did not speak for some moments, Nell prompted him. "Question?"

He drew a deep breath. "I should like your permission to call tomorrow morning with the hope of a private interview with you. Shall you object?"

Private interview! The phrase rang in her head. She was well aware of its significance, especially when coupled with the anxious look in his shallow blue eyes.

"Oh, yes. I mean, oh, no, of course I shall not object!" *However could I?* By good fortune, her last words were not spoken.

Nell slipped into a timeless rosy haze, pale plaster ladies forgotten. How handsome he was! His address was full of grace, his manners entirely faultless. What more could she wish for? ⸫

Foxhall lifted her hand to his lips and kissed her fingertips respectfully. Behind her inward sigh of bliss, she perceived lurking a wicked hope that he might—just for a moment, of course—be swept away by passion to the point of clasping her willing body to his chest.

Only a heightened color in his cheeks gave an indication that he was possibly struggling against making an improper advance. If so, he subdued the wayward impulse manfully—to her unspoken regret.

Nell, bursting with her secret, and excessively anxious to share with her aunt dear Rowland's intentions, was not best pleased when she was requested to make room for Darnford in their carriage.

But, when the marquess gave every indication of making a long visit, even at that late hour, Nell gave in with good grace. In truth, she was not reluctant to hold her delicious news to herself for a little while yet. She had not fully savored the incredible fact that Lord Foxhall would, in the morning, make a formal offer for her hand.

She went to bed, but not at once to sleep. Rowland's classic features slid from her wakeful thoughts into her dreams, and she slept at last with a smile on her lips.

Chapter Three

Nell wakened when young Polly timidly set down her early morning tea tray. Nell watched the maid cross to the windows and open the curtains.

"Polly," she murmured, emerging slowly from sleep, "what kind of day is it?"

"Dreary, miss," Polly reported. "Gloomy, like. Begun raining in the night it did, and dark you can't see the street."

Nell came fully awake. With a rush she remembered the astonishing event of the evening before. "Oh, Polly, you must be wrong. It's the most glorious day since I've been in London!"

The maid cast a cautious eye in the direction of her young mistress. "Very good, miss," she said quickly, and scuttled out of the room.

Nell leaped out of bed and went to the window. To an ordinary eye, she conceded, it might be gray, damp, and dispiriting. How many unfortunates looked out this very morning and saw only dreariness!

Nell considered herself the most fortunate of creatures. She alone was the recipient of Lord Foxhall's attentions.

He was coming to call—and Lady Sanford did not yet know!

She scarcely felt the stairs beneath her feet as she descended to take breakfast with her aunt. In fact, she was hardly aware that her aunt Phrynie was scarcely in a mood to receive confidences, being hollow-eyed from lack of sleep and with a tongue excessively furred.

Whitcomb the butler had every sympathy for his lady. With deft and silent motions he placed black coffee before her and forbore to offer ham or eggs. He considered toast and honey, but with a second sidelong glance at his suffering mistress, he decided against them.

When Nell breezily entered the breakfast room, Lady Sanford closed her eyes. Whitcomb winced in sympathy and favored his mistress's niece with a cold eye of warning. Nell, caught up in her own rosy euphoria, did not notice.

"Dear aunt!" she exclaimed as she paused to drop a kiss on Lady Sanford's soft cheek. "Wasn't it a perfectly splendid ball!"

Lady Sanford's response was more moan than articulate agreement. "I do not know quite what the duchess put in that punch," she said severely when she reached the bottom of her second cup of strong coffee. "Ratafia, she said it was, but I warrant you I will never again believe her."

Whitcomb reflected upon the empty bottle of brandy that had met his eyes that morning in the salon. Lady Sanford, having entertained her solitary guest somewhat lavishly after her return home, had no need to blame the duchess for her splitting headache.

Nell gradually became aware that her aunt was indeed suffering. Her own pleasure at the ball had taken place far removed from the scene at the punch bowl. But she was possessed of a kindly nature and lowered her voice at once. She heaped her plate with feather-light scrambled eggs and the most delicately flavored pink ham, brought especially from the Sanford country estate in Essex, and proceeded to indulge her hearty appetite.

Not until she saw her aunt reaching tentatively for a biscuit did she dare to engage her attention. "Aunt, I must tell you—"

"My dear child, must you? I confess I do not wish to hear anything this morning. Not even the juiciest titbit of gossip. Unless, of course, you have heard why the Fitzgerald woman has left Mount Street in such great haste."

"Nothing like that, Aunt. Something far better."

Phrynie Sanford was no stranger to duty. Now, visibly, she pulled herself erect and prepared to be, if not enthusiastic, at least civil. "Better? In that case, I should like to hear."

Suddenly shy, Nell did not answer at once. Now that she was invited to share her news, she was most unaccountably loath to do so. However, she was aware of her aunt's somewhat bloodshot eye commandingly on her and, like a winter swimmer, plunged into the water.

"Dear aunt, I owe it all to you. You're so generous, so—"

"So impatient," interrupted Phrynie, tartly. "Do you indeed have something to tell me? If not, I believe I shall lie down somewhere."

"Oh, no, Aunt, you mustn't!"

Her protest was met by a raised eyebrow. "Mustn't I?"

"You are to have a caller this morning."

Lady Sanford's nerves were not at their best. "Nell, I must warn you . . ."

"Aunt, Lord Foxhall is coming to call."

Lady Sanford stared at the tablecloth. Her fingers, apparently of their own volition, began to plait her napkin. "Dear me. That punch cup must have been insufferably strong. Nell, my dear, forgive me, but I thought you said Lord Foxhall."

"Yes, Aunt."

"Nell, I must inform you that if this is a species of japery, I shall be seriously displeased. I agree, this kind of mischief is much more in Tom's line. However, I am a bit too addled this morning to be tolerant of any funning."

Her aunt's reception of Nell's stupendous news boded ill. "Dear Aunt, pray believe me," cried Nell, nearly in tears. "He asked last night—after the first waltz, it was—permission to call this morning—for a private interview. With me."

"Good God!" said Phrynie, at last comprehending the situation. "Foxhall. No one will believe it. Precisely no one, not even me. Private interview with you? Then of course he will wish to see me. What shall I wear? Nell, you must send for me at once when you've accepted."

Nell was silent. Misgiving struck her aunt. She fixed Nell with a commanding eye. "Surely, Nell, *this* offer you will not greet with missish refusals? You will accept?"

"Oh, yes, Aunt. I will."

"But Foxhall," said Phrynie. "Coming to call. That means—of course it must, no question about it. We are not presuming too much, child. It means an offer!"

Aunt Phrynie's reaction was all that Nell could have wished for. Lord Foxhall was indeed a catch to addle wits even sharper than Lady Sanford's, whose perceptions in the ordinary way were not in the least dull.

Now she simply stared at her niece. The full significance of Nell's triumph was realized. "You sly puss."

Nell basked in her aunt's warm approval. "I hoped you would be pleased, Aunt. And to think I almost didn't want to go to the ball last night!"

Phrynie was too much a woman of the world, however, to take Nell's news at face value. Nell's information was indeed startling, not to say unbelievable. No matter how sincere the child was, thought her aunt, her inexperience might well lead her into a misapprehension of Foxhall's intentions. Now, noting well Nell's euphoria, she believed she had solved the mystery of the girl's recent abstracted moods.

Phrynie hoped devoutly that Nell would not be devastated when—that is, *if*—she learned she was in error over Foxhall's sentiments. Best to be prepared for disaster, she thought, and began to explore the possibilities.

Her thoughts ran swiftly over the previous evening. Lord Foxhall had indeed danced—in fact, *waltzed*—with Nell, besides standing up with her for the first set. "But what about the Freeland woman?" Lady Sanford spoke her thoughts. "She's been all but in his pocket this long time."

"Penelope Freeland," said Nell, somewhat stiffly, "has nothing to do with dear Rowland."

"To think," mused Lady Sanford, unfortunately aloud, "that he would offer in the end for you!"

Nell was stung. "And why not?" She bristled. "Surely he has a right to make his own choice, and it was not Miss Freeland. He—he has a *tendre* for me," said Nell, demurely. "And he is so handsome!"

Nell slipped easily into the dream that had kept her company since she had first seen Lord Foxhall at her aunt's ball, given in her honor when she first came to London last April. That first glimpse of dear Rowland, coming up the stairs to meet his hostess, had struck her as though with an arrow, and she still marveled at it. Her impression had been then that the god Apollo, the embodiment of physical beauty, had suddenly donned elegant evening clothes and arrived in some inexplicable fashion on her aunt's staircase.

Stunned by such masculine beauty, she had found in him the substance of secret dreams, both waking and sleeping. Nell's clear adoration of him, while not obvious to her aunt, was apparent to Lord Foxhall himself. He had to that moment expected to offer for Penelope Freeland, comfortable in the persuasion that she was more than willing to accept him. His certainty that she looked upon him with favor, coupled with her regrettable tendency toward tactless instruction, led him into dilatory ways, and he had not yet declared himself when he saw a pair of speaking gray eyes, fringed with long dark lashes, looking at him with adoration.

Lord Foxhall had moved slowly, but with deliberate intention, to make further acquaintance of this discerning miss, so different from Penelope, who was prone to point out to him his failings.

Nell's simple worship came as welcome balm to him.

"But you hardly know him!" objected Lady Sanford now.

Under judicious questioning, Nell, with faltering shyness recounted snatches of conversation held with Foxhall over the past weeks. Lady Sanford, past mistress in the interpretation of nuances, at length admitted that Nell, if mistaken, nonetheless had a reason to expect his offer—this very morning!

Now, Nell's dream had, quite miraculously, come true. The handsome Nonpareil was to be her very own!

"My goodness!" cried Lady Sanford, once more able to speak. "I must say you've done well."

Nell was suddenly practical. "Dear Aunt, pray find a gown more suitable. He may be here any minute!"

Lady Sanford glanced down at her simple poplin morning gown. "Very well," she agreed, "though it is not I he is concerned with. It will not matter what I wear." She considered the Incomparable Foxhall for a moment, then added, "A pity, of course."

"Aunt!"

"All right, child. I shall endeavor not to embarrass you. Though I will admit he is quite the handsomest man I ever saw. But handsome, Nell, is not all there is to be desired in a husband. Sanford was far from a Greek god, you know."

Nell was not interested in the uncle she had never met. "Do hurry, Aunt!"

Phrynie was caught up in Nell's impatience. She did reflect, as she hurried up the stairs to change, that she would not be in the least surprised if Nell had been enchanted by moonbeams and simply misunderstood Foxhall. It was quite beyond anything that a prime catch could be interested in a modest heiress like Nell.

Loyalty chided Lady Sanford. Nell was quite as well born as, for instance, Penelope Freeland, and there was no reason on earth why Nell did not deserve to become a countess, one day. Phrynie was a woman of the world, however, and she was aware of a lingering element of strong disbelief, not to say cynicism, in her apparent acceptance of the prospective betrothal.

Nonetheless, obedient to Nell's sensibilities, she changed into a gown of gray India muslin with pale green satin stripes, primly suitable for the occasion of speaking to a niece's prospective betrothed. She had just reached the entrance hall when Foxhall arrived.

Nell, peeping from the breakfast room, was gratified to see that Whitcomb, who had not turned a hair when announcing the flamboyant figure of the Prince Regent, was stunned by the exalted personage who was just now arriving.

Lord Foxhall illuminated the foyer. Handing his damp hat and gloves to a footman summoned by Whitcomb, he stood at his ease, his golden hair forming a kind of halo around his head. He was knowledgeable in the manner of presenting himself—not for the Foreign Office was the exotic cravat, the extreme cut of a coat lapel, the adaptation of the newest fashions.

Instead, Lord Foxhall appeared in public in the most costly but exceedingly conservative coat that Weston could prove. His neckcloth of superfine linen fell in simple folds, and Hoby's boots wore a mirrorlike polish.

"Is Lady Sanford at home?" he asked.

"I will inquire, my lord."

As Lady Sanford crossed the black-and-white-tiled foyer, she shot a conspiratorial glance at her niece, smoothed her own still beautiful features into a suitable expression, and passed through into the green salon to greet her guest.

After an agony of waiting, Nell was rewarded by seeing the salon door open and her aunt emerge. Lady Sanford's expression was unreadable, but her gesture was imperative. Nell hurried to her.

"Go in," said Lady Sanford. "Lord Foxhall—" She drew a deep breath, rallying from the interview just past. "He wishes to speak with you."

Nell floated through the salon door, Whitcomb closed the door softly behind her and, with the privilege of an old and valued servant, joined his mistress to wait the outcome in the breakfast room.

Nell was alone for the second time with her beloved Rowland.

"My dear Miss Aspinall. May I dare—Elinor?" said the golden Lord Foxhall.

Golden was the right word, she thought once more. His hair was the color of liquid sunshine poured down upon a nobly shaped head.

The Paragon took her cold hand in his. "Dear Elinor," he repeated, "I have sought your aunt's permission to make my offer to you."

When he did not continue, she looked at him with dismay. Her mouth was suddenly dry. "Surely my aunt did not disapprove?"

"Not at all," said Lord Foxhall, secure in the conviction that any mother or chaperone would not dare to refuse him. "But of course you realize that before I speak to you I must speak to the head of your family."

Her wits scattered down the wind. "Head? Surely you cannot mean Tom?" She had for so long not considered Tom seriously that it required a swift mental readjustment. "Of course, Tom."

She loved her older brother dearly, but she was fully aware that he failed in many ways to behave in a satisfactory manner. For instance, just now, of all times! She did not know precisely where he was.

This was not an extraordinary circumstance. More often than not, she did not know his whereabouts, nor when he would reappear with an insouciant smile and a regrettable lack of explanation.

"But Tom has nothing to say to the purpose," she said, just short of a wail. "It is my aunt—"

"Of course," said Lord Foxhall, gently chiding. "But we must do all in the most proper way, don't you know. I should not like to chance your good opinion of me by speaking to you prematurely. I am persuaded that any impetuosity on my part would lower me in your estimation."

She could not find words to protest. It is doubtful whether he would have heeded her, for he bored ahead. "I should not wish you to consider me as prone to follow my own wishes to the detriment of the respect I shall hope you have for me. If

I am to prove worthy of the great privilege I dare to aspire to—at the proper time, of course—I must convince you that I am worthy of your regard." He smiled gently and added, "I am sure I do not have to tell you that I must speak to your brother. When may I call upon him?"

"B-but I don't know where he is!"

A flicker of an undefined emotion could be discerned on Lord Foxhall's features. Probably, thought Nell with a sinking feeling, it was disapproval of such havey-cavey management of family affairs.

"Oh," said the diplomatist. "I regret that his absence must of necessity postpone any formal offer on my part, for I must depart for Vienna at once. Tomorrow, in point of fact. But I am sure you are aware of my deep regard for you, and we must trust that my position may be regularized as soon as possible."

"*Your* position?" echoed Nell. "Soon?"

She wished that her voice had not given her the appearance of pleading with him.

"As soon as I return from Vienna. That should not be above two months. We must get Europe settled, you know," he added with kindly condescension, "before we can pursue our own happiness."

He bestowed one of his more brilliant smiles on her, kissed her fingers, and was gone. She watched his elegant figure as far as his carriage standing before the door.

Only then did she allow the pent-up strain of the last hours to overwhelm her, and she collapsed into a chair and abandoned herself to the racking sobs of disappointment.

Her aunt, rushing into the salon almost before the outer door closed on Foxhall's back, was stunned. "You didn't refuse him, Nell? He did offer, didn't he? Nell, what happened?"

Finally, Nell recovered sufficiently to speak, not entirely coherently. "No, Aunt, I didn't refuse. In truth, he didn't precisely offer."

"He didn't? But he told me—"

"He told me too. He said—he said I was sure of his regard. He said that his position would be regularized when he got back from—from Vienna! But he didn't offer because he didn't have Tom's permission!"

"He's been too long in the Foreign Office. I vow they wrap themselves in red tape before they go to bed."

"He is so entirely proper, you know."

Lady Sanford struggled with disbelief. "Tom?"

"Of course not. Rowland. He does not wish to lose my regard."

Lady Sanford thought that she could detect the slightest hint of irritation in Nell's voice, with reason. It would be most unsettling to have one's expectations raised to the highest pitch and then see them thwarted over a trivial point of civility.

"Where is Tom?" wondered his aunt. "We must send for him at once!"

Nell could not agree more strongly.

Where, when she needed him most, was Tom?

Chapter Four

On that same rainy forenoon, John Darcy, Duke of Whern, stood at a window overlooking the miniscule back garden of his town house on Duke Street. The house had not been opened since his grandfather's day, not even when the present duke made his unobtrusive return from the Peninsular Wars at least three months ago.

Whern was a stranger to London society. He had not always been so, but what was correctly rumored as a broken romance, five years before, had driven him into the army, where Wellington found him an invaluable member of his staff, particularly in connection with ascertaining, by means that no one questioned, the intentions of the enemy.

At first, he had plunged into battle in the forefront of his regiment, expecting, even hoping to be killed. Daily he summoned to his mind's eye the features of the faithless belle who gave him every encouragement until a suitor more eligible came upon the scene.

Clearly, the prospect of an earldom once removed was more enticing to her than a thrice-removed dukedom.

Wellington had plucked him from the line to form a badly needed intelligence service. It was at that time that he learned of the unexpected demise of the two kinfolk standing between him and the dukedom, followed swiftly by the death of the duke himself.

Upon thoughtful consideration of whether he should by letter renew his suit of the lady in his dreams, he found he no longer experienced the slightest feeling for her. In fact, where his love and bitterness had mingled in him, there was left only an echoing emptiness.

Grateful for an exacting job, he plunged into the world of intelligence—also called spying—with renewed diligence.

Now, back in London, his devious habits of secrecy, acquired under stress, held him captive. He could not contemplate with anything approaching equanimity a return to what he considered a frivolous way of life. After all, when one frequently faces the strong probability of being blown apart in the next moment by Napoleonic grapeshot, one discovers a wonderfully altered philosophy of what is important.

On his return to London, therefore, he had not even called on the Duchess of Netwick. He knew where his duty lay, but he was reluctant to face his godmother's ungentle quizzing. Perhaps, when he finished this last chore handed him by his government, he would make his way to Gloucester Place, with the news that he was leaving the intelligence service and retiring to his Cumberland estate.

But not quite yet. There was the parcel on the table behind him to be dealt with first.

As he looked out at the silver rain slanting down on the gray and brown of the dead winter garden the duke appeared to be an unremarkable man. His stature was not above the average, nor was his figure unusually graceful. In fact, an observer might call him stocky and even recognize the great strength that lay in him.

His hair was light brown, his nose somewhat out of the straight thanks to a mischancy rifle blow somewhere near Salamanca. His eyes were his best feature. Humor lurked in their hazel depths more often than not.

This day, the first of November, his thoughts were as leaden as the sky. His hearing was acute, and his reflexes extraordinarily swift. The slight sound behind him caused him to whirl and drop his hand to his hip, glaring at the man who had just entered. Then, recognizing him, the duke visibly relaxed.

"How many times do I have to tell you, Arthur, not to steal in like that? Had I had my pistol . . ." He forced a laugh. "You are perfectly safe, you know. I do not intend to carry a pistol again no matter what the provocation."

Arthur Haveney, the duke's aide and friend, murmured shakily, "I suppose you'll never need to arm yourself again, now that the little emperor of the French is safely away on Elba. Although I must say I would rather see *you* armed to the teeth than take my chances with our county militia." He shuddered. "I understand from my father that Wolcott had the men from your estate marching up and down the green, shouldering their pikes and scythes in a most belligerent manner. I vow they would be more menace than Bony himself."

Whern laughed. "Just the same, they would have done the French a good deal of mischief, had it come to invasion."

Arthur Haveney looked at the other with concealed affection. Whern had saved his life, more than once, and Arthur had pulled him away from the battle lines when the duke was bleeding from nose and mouth and had lost his senses. But those events were the result, rather than the cause, of the bond that secured the two. Brought up together on the Whern estate, Haveney, the son of the vicar, and the heir to the dukedom took their studies together, and their pleasures as well.

Arthur, close as a shadow, had gone with John Darcy to the peninsula as though following his leader to a self-imposed exile. Their thoughts now running, as often they did, along the same road, Whern said, "Arthur, do you feel as sadly dislodged from society as I do?"

"I never was a member of the *ton,* you know."

"More fool the *ton.* But I meant civilization as a whole. Do you think we can ever fit in again?"

"We must, John, or remove ourselves to one of Captain Cook's islands."

"I believe they are quite attractive," mused the duke.

It was unthinkable, thought Haveney, that he would ever feel in the least censorious of John Darcy, who was closer than a brother to him. But just now it did cross his mind that his friend's exalted title meant duties that must not be shirked.

As though Whern read his mind, he said, "How much am I worth, Arthur?"

"W-worth?"

"I mean in income, idiot. Enough to snare some lady willing to wed me?"

"I should think so," said Arthur stoutly, mentally adding that any woman who did not leap at the duke's offer was more than a little pea-witted.

Whern turned from the window. His speaking eyes held a light that his friend deplored. Apparently the defection five years before of Miss Penelope Freeland had left a mark that would never be erased.

Arthur, standing by helplessly at that time, had all but sickened of worry over his friend's rejection. If Miss Freeland had known that the two hitherto husky males who stood squarely between Lord John Darcy and the dukedom would succumb, one after the other, perhaps she would not have turned his offer down. Arthur would not be at all surprised if the lady tried her hand with the duke again.

"There you are, Arthur. Title and wealth—that's what it takes. Do you suppose that . . ." He was clearly going to utter that certain name, but altered his direction in midsentence. "That any society miss would fetch water and powder to the guns?"

"The way they did at Valladolid?"

Silence fell, while both contemplated the subject of women. The duke in his cynical way allowed his lip to curl, while Arthur, remembering a smiling pair of liquid brown eyes in the face of a volunteer gun server, smiled in reminiscence.

Whern shrugged his shoulders. "Ah, well, not likely that a duchess will find much reason to slog powder to the guns in Cumberland, eh, Arthur? Enough of this at any rate. We've got to do this one last errand for the cause of freedom, and then we can retire to Cumberland."

"Retire, John? And then?"

"Don't tell me you will miss this—this hole in the corner of London?" He waved his hand, indicating the confined quarters that had been, in the ordinary way, merely a sitting room for his grandfather's servants.

"No, I shan't." Arthur chose his words carefully. "Shall you be content to settle down and breed Herdwick sheep on the fells?"

Whern laughed in genuine amusement. "As well as you, my friend. And it's time, you know, to put away this skulking business. While Wellington was carrying on, it was worthwhile. Our information saved the lives of our men many times over. And the opportunities for travel, Arthur! Although the next time I venture into France and Germany it will not be, God willing, in the guise of a skulking rogue following the Emperor's armies."

"Yet," Arthur retorted, "I cannot see you descending in

lordly fashion at exclusive hostelries. Handing one's gloves and cloak to your downtrodden valet . . ."

Whern roared. "I shall fix mine host with a supercilious air and demand that the inn be cleared of all rabble lest they affront my sensibilities." Suddenly he turned sober. "But I confess stealth does not suit in a civilian life."

Arthur nodded. "And yet the peace is vital to us."

"That's why we shall see that this parcel gets to its destination."

He pointed to the small parcel, a hand span in width and perhaps three inches high, lying on the rough surface of the deal table. He regarded it without pleasure.

"This is the—the object?" Arthur inquired.

"This is it. Why on earth they don't send it across Europe on a velvet cushion, in the charge of a platoon of Household Guards preceded by silver trumpets, I don't know."

"It does look impressive, doesn't it?" Arthur mused.

"And disgustingly official," Whern pointed out. "I wish I had the authority to unwrap it and provide it with a disguise."

Haveney lifted his eyebrows. He was a slender man, with ash-blond hair, long nose, and thin features, appearing more aristocratic than his superior. His aspect was coldly forbidding, until, on rare occasions, he smiled.

Just now, his lips twisted in amusement. "Authority, my lord duke? When did it become necessary for you to seek permission to do whatever it struck your fancy to do?"

"*My lord duke,* Arthur? I trust this does not mean you are displeased with me? Nevertheless, I am convinced that we can make this into an entirely innocuous parcel. The question is how, innocuously as well, can we get it to Vienna?"

"By diplomatic courier? Castlereagh has arranged for a regular messenger service."

"Upon no account. This—this grenade, so to speak, would not have come to us to deal with had it been an ordinary message. Don't, I beg of you, look at me in such a fashion. I have no secrets from you. This little bundle, looking as harmless as a spinster's love letters—a spinster, that is, inordinately fond of red sealing wax—carries in it a load of explosives."

"Something to frighten the allies? Men who faced down *Napoleon*?" Arthur regarded the object with awe and shook his head. "I cannot fathom what could be in it. Secret treaties?"

Whern shook his head. "I should judge the parcel not large enough. We are not told the nature of the contents, only that it must be delivered swiftly and in dead secrecy to Castlereagh." He added drily, "I did not ask why."

Arthur nodded. In their line of work it was best to know nothing, if possible, for then no form of questioning could elicit details better kept private. He prodded the object with a slender forefinger. "Not pliant, at least. Wrapped in wash leather?"

"Doubtless. But I can tell you this, Arthur. Castlereagh is in Vienna to settle the map of Europe. Britain wishes certain boundaries to be drawn, certain allies to be rewarded, and—ahem—certain other allies to be, if not punished, at least thwarted in what are after all excessively greedy, even, so to speak, covetous, demands and expectations."

Arthur smiled. "You sound like our esteemed foreign minister."

"Indeed, I was quoting him. But," Whern continued, reverting to his normal brusque tone, "it is a prime belief—based upon whatever facts I don't know—that Castlereagh, and therefore England, will have a decisive and vital negotiating edge if this very parcel reaches his hands by December."

"It is clear then," said Arthur deliberately, "that this parcel may be valued by what we may call the other side?"

"Excessively so," Whern agreed drily. "Cherished, I should say."

"How shall we get it there safely, then?"

"I don't suppose you—no, no," Whern interrupted himself, "that's not possible. Every undercover agent in Europe may know you by sight. No, we must seek another way."

Arthur looked up in a kind of horror. "Not you, John? If this errand is dangerous for me, it is much more so for you. Your face as well is known in certain circles, you remember."

"No, not I," said the duke, reassuringly. "I'm getting a little old to caper in disguise across half of Europe. Besides," he added whimsically, "I haven't time to grow a concealing beard. No, Arthur, I've done my last derring-do. And I'm not sorry. We've both stretched our luck too far."

Arthur could only agree. He thought for a moment. "Why

can't this parcel, after we disguise it, of course, travel with Foxhall?"

Whern shook his head. "That idiot couldn't find his way out of a rain barrel. Nor do we know anyone in his party whom we could trust. Besides, he is leaving at noon. We would hardly have time to make the necessary arrangements."

Haveney was in two minds. He wondered whether John knew that Miss Freeland was still unwed but had her trap set for Foxhall. Alternately, he speculated as to the advisability of informing John that Foxhall, according to Arthur's informative sources, was on the verge of offering—if indeed he had not already done so—for Tom Aspinall's sister, and therefore it was to be supposed that Miss Freeland might well be casting her eyes once more in the direction of John Darcy, now so much more desirable a *parti* than Foxhall.

Arthur dreaded the thought that his greatest friend might succumb again to her hardened attractions. The rejected suitor had suffered savagely, had fallen into the blackest of moods, and had more than once, to Arthur's certain knowledge, been driven by self-contempt to the edge of self-destruction.

Never again, thought Arthur, if he could help it.

In the end, Arthur mentioned neither. "But I could go."

The duke was firm. "You could not, Arthur. Your only function in this business is to provide me with a name. A man who can get this—this idiotic parcel screaming with official sealing wax and tape—into the hands of Castlereagh."

"That is my function," said Arthur, deliberately provoking his companion. "And what is yours?"

"Mine?" echoed Whern. "Mine is simply to rewrap this—this *thing!*—into an appearance of normalcy. That, Arthur, is my only function these days." He lapsed into thought. "Our last chore, Arthur. Can you bear thinking about being without employment?"

"I can sustain that eventuality better than the thought that we will have failed after all."

"Justly put. Now then, I suppose you have the right name to submit to me?"

"Tom Aspinall."

"Just the man," agreed Whern. "A more amiable fool

never appeared in this world—an excellent disguise. He's the one who can get through without suspicion."

Before long, thought Whern, I'll tell Lord Liverpool he can run his government without us. The prospect of idleness stretched like a dun and fallow field before him.

He smothered a deep sigh. "Well, then, Arthur, let us get this parcel altered and out of this office before it blows up in our faces. Where, by the way, *is* Tom Aspinall?"

Chapter Five

"Where is your brother?" demanded Lady Sanford, not for the first time. "I vow I have never been in such a coil! The offer of a lifetime from Foxhall, and Tom is not here to receive it for you. Nell, I do think—but then he never was accountable." Her voice rose to a wail. "What shall we do?"

Nell's nerves had been stretched badly since the morning when Rowland had declared himself. She had to bear up under Rowland's departure for Vienna and endure her aunt's querulous moods. She told herself that if things got no worse, she could weather this crisis in her affairs.

Now, she could discern, ominously looming, that the situation was about to deteriorate—rapidly. Her aunt had never before been clearly losing control of her emotions. Nell believed that she was one step from screaming hysterics. Nell herself resolved, in case of her aunt's collapse, to do the same and let Mullins sort it all out.

"Dear aunt," she said, striving to stave off disaster, "we've only searched for two days. And in any event, he could not now give permission for my betrothal, for dear Rowland must already have traveled beyond Paris."

"Suppose he cries off?" demanded Phrynie. "I have the gravest suspicions that everyone knows of his intentions."

"Oh, no! Do you think it?"

"I think it," said Phrynie severely. "And if he cries off, then I do not know how I will hold up my head. I would much rather have Foxhall bound by an announcement in the *Gazette* than simply trust that his affections do not suffer a change."

Nell, innocently secure in the recollection of certain words he had whispered to her, brushed aside such a possibility.

"His affections could not alter, Aunt," she said with an appearance of serenity. "But I confess I am worried about the journey for him."

Her imagination provided her with an assortment of dire images. Dear Rowland beset by ravenous wolves, for one. She had no very clear picture of the fauna of France, but surely she had heard that in very severe winters wolves invaded the streets of Paris, battening upon its helpless citizens?

Or, nearly as grisly, his carriage overturned on a mountainside, or attacked by bandits, or footpads, or thieves . . .

"Nell, for heaven's sake," said her aunt with vigor, "no need to fall into hysterics!"

"*I*? I am sure *I* am not, aunt. But the journey is full of hazards."

"No more than the accidents that can befall a gentleman on England's roads. Forgive me, Nell, for mentioning your parents' mishap. France must be as civilized as our own land. Besides, I understand there is quite a cavalcade traveling with Foxhall. Quite like a royal progress!" Lady Sanford entertained troubled thoughts for a moment and made up her mind. "Nell, do you know that the Freeland woman will be with Foxhall in Vienna?"

Nell took a quick breath. Stoutly, she protested, "But I shall not be at all worried about that!"

Grimly her aunt pointed out, "You're not a fool, Nell. Trust me, she will have her hooks into him before the year-end." She laughed ruefully. "She'd better take Castlereagh's place in Vienna—she's a better diplomatist."

The seed sown, Lady Sanford wished with all her heart that she could take it back. What need to worry the child? Time enough when Foxhall cried off. Phrynie, while not a gambling woman, would have bet a hundred guineas that, Penelope at hand, he would.

Nell, heedless of all but her own thoughts, had considered the question that burned in the minds of both of them. Foxhall must be brought up to the mark, ran Phrynie's thoughts, while Nell's, with a different point of view, followed other considerations.

Dear Rowland was quite indispensable to her continued happiness. There was no contemplating any alternative to marrying Rowland and settling down in a rosy life of paradisiacal bliss.

Lady Sanford thought, If only we could lay hands on Tom Aspinall and send him to Vienna to settle things with Foxhall! Almost like an echo to her own thoughts, Nell said, "Aunt, we must ourselves go to Vienna." Aiming with guile at Lady Sanford's weakness, she added, "Surely there will be magnificent entertainments, I should imagine, with such important people there. I have heard that the Emperor has made *palaces* available to the delegation from England. Only fancy!"

"Palaces or not, we are not going to Vienna," said Lady Sanford. Only those who knew her best, like Nell, could have detected a note of wistfulness in her voice.

Her aunt, still immensely attractive at the age of forty, had cut a wide swath in her day. Suitors by the score, so Nell's own mama had told her, and then, unaccountably, she chose to marry the most ordinary of them all, Lord Sanford. That worthy had, quite without fanfare, succumbed to an ordinary kind of congestion in the chest. As Nell's mama had said, "His taking off was quite in keeping with the rest of his life, which was distinguished most particularly by its obscurity."

Nell's mother, Phrynie's older sister, had been a notable belle as well, but had settled down happily in her marriage to Aspinall, produced a son, Thomas, the heir to his uncle's baronetcy, and Nell, as lovely a child as one could wish. Nell's wide gray eyes, fringed with excessively long black lashes, had something of her mother's charm, even though her coloring was her father's.

It occurred to Nell for the first time that her brother Tom might not be the harum-scarum that she had always considered him. There was something mysterious, and in a way deliberate, about his comings and goings. And while there had for the most part been no pressing need to reach him, she knew there were times when he disappeared for several weeks on end. He was not a gambler, at least that she knew of, and yet she realized there was much about him that he did not divulge. A womanizer? She did not think so.

She had never pried into his affairs, and she did not intend to start now. But she was developing a hearty irritation with his thoughtlessness. So much like her father, so Aunt Phrynie had pronounced. She resented such criticism, but she was forced now to admit the truth of it.

If her father had not, after a night of ancient port, believed himself a veritable whip and insisted that his adored wife come along to witness his prowess, Nell would not now be waiting for her wayward brother to emerge from whatever low dive he was enjoying to give his blessing to her betrothal.

"No, no, of course not," said Nell. "I know it is out of the question. I know I could never have gone on these last few months without your enormous help. Believe me, without you—I would never have set eyes on Rowland, and fallen so in love with him that very first moment!"

Lady Sanford allowed herself to be soothed. The past Season had indeed been difficult for her. She was accustomed to being the center of a ring of masculine admirers, singling out one or two for later diversions, and not at all surprised to find that the fashions she initiated caught on in the *ton* within hours.

Then, she had been forced by duty to launch dear Nell into society and for the first time in her life had to face the fact that she herself was no longer in the first flush of youth. Nell's freshness, her undoubted beauty, her charming belief that all of life lay before her like a delightful buffet to sample at will, and above all her unfettered and wearisome exuberance, had taken its toll on Lady Sanford.

She found it desirable at this point in her ruminations to look baldly at her own motives. Was she jealous of Nell's youth, Nell's boundless energy?

Perhaps she was. But on the other hand, she enjoyed the intricacies of attracting men of mature years. She reveled in her own deftness in pulling their invisible strings, and most of all, she told herself in all honesty that dealing with young men of little experience and an overweening sense of their own worth was tiresome in the extreme.

"Vienna?" she murmured, dreamily. Then, briskly, she continued, "No, no. It is quite impossible. Foxhall would not thank us for following him eagerly across the Continent."

"You think not?" said Nell, frowning. "I should not like to embarrass him."

"Depend upon it, Nell. If we two went after him, to keep an eye on him so to speak, he would cry off within the hour." Returning to her primary source of grievance, she went on, "I can't believe your brother is such an idiot! When did you see him last?"

Nell reflected. "I think it was at the Victory Celebration. I recall he was near the pagoda when the bridge went up. Do you remember, Aunt? He came to tell us about it."

"But how totally irresponsible! That was August, and now it is November."

"So like Tom."

"So like your father!" retorted Lady Sanford with spirit.

Nell allowed herself to think ill of Tom for a moment. She adored him, and never thought of condemning him for his incomprehensible ways. He was dear Tom, and there was no more to say.

In the meantime, the search for Tom Aspinall was thorough and unavailing. The Aspinall servants, even more familiar with their master's proclivities than was his sister, returned empty-handed.

It was difficult to impress upon Lady Sanford's agents that Tom must be found without confiding too many details of the situation as it existed between Nell and Foxhall. It was not to be contemplated that the servants' hall be abuzz with speculation on the outcome of Nell's almost offer. Indeed, there was a strong possibility, which must be quelled at the outset, that given the intense interest in Nell's affairs, there would be odds offered and taken on several headings. . . . Mr. Tom's reappearance; his likelihood of allowing Miss Nell to accept the suitor, considered by the under footman to be too much of a sour apple; and, most disastrously, the possibility that Lord Foxhall might, if Mr. Tom's presence were not speedily felt, cry off.

Lady Sanford would not condone such impertinent behavior in her servants. But Tom's nearest kin were not the only persons who felt a great need for his appearance. There was considerable bustle on Duke Street, in the back rooms of the Duke of Whern's town house.

Arthur Haveney gave instructions and inquiries were made, very discreetly, in dives, in Crocky's gambling den, and in certain haunts in the shires where Aspinall lands lay and Aspinalls were cherished. There was no recent sign of Tom. Arthur decided that there was nothing for it but to inquire of Tom's own family. Surely someone must know where he was!

So, the next day after Nell's conversation with Lady Sanford, Mr. Haveney was announced. Whitcomb, in response to broad and monetary hints from the visitor, made sure that Miss Nell was alone.

"A Mr. Haveney to see you, miss."

Nell, caught up in gloomy thoughts, said absently, "Lady Sanford is not receiving."

The butler was wounded. He knew, and he made it clear to Nell, that she need not tell him his job. "Mr. Haveney asked particularly for you, miss."

Nell opened her eyes wide. "For me? Do I know him?"

Whitcomb, still resentful, said, "I cannot say, miss."

"Of course you can't, Whitcomb. Forgive me."

The apology itself was handsome, the butler had to admit, but the smile that accompanied it completely restored his sensitivities.

"I put him in the small salon, miss," said the butler, with the ghost of a smile. She understood that Whitcomb had made his own assessment of the quality of the caller. Well-known visitors were placed at once in the green room, mere acquaintances in the gold salon. But the small salon was reserved for persons with an appearance of respectability but without other recommendation.

Mr. Haveney was waiting patiently. He rose when he heard Nell enter. All his long training was called upon when he saw her. She was far from the most beautiful lady he had ever seen, but he was conscious of a charm that threatened to overset his wits. Whether it was her expression of bright interest or the intelligence lying behind her remarkable eyes, he could not have told. All he knew was that he must make an effort to keep his mind on his errand.

"Mr. Haveney?" said Nell. "You wish to see me? I'm afraid I do not know quite how I can help you."

"No, Miss Aspinall," said her caller regretfully. His voice sounded in his ears as unnecessarily harsh. "You do not know me. But I shall be grateful if you could tell me the whereabouts of your brother, Mr. Thomas Aspinall."

"Oh, dear, Tom's not in trouble? I do hope you are not expecting to reclaim gambling debts? Although I must admit I have never heard that he played at all deep. Tell me, are you a bailiff?"

Mr. Haveney was enchanted by her frankness. "No, Miss Aspinall. Not at all. I am simply—an old friend, shall we say, who truly does need to know where he is."

Nell kept her eyes fastened on his. The man had not yet convinced her that his aims were honorable. She continued to regard him hopefully. When he did not at once continue, she nudged him.

"Why?"

"Why?" he echoed.

"Surely you cannot expect me to tell you my brother's whereabouts simply because you ask me? Even if you are not a bailiff, you may be something else quite devastating, you know. I do hope you are not distressed because I speak frankly. Truly, I have often been told I am too direct, especially when I wish to know something. But you must realize that my brother and I are very close"—this was not quite the truth, but adherence to fact was not always a virtue—"and I do not recall his mentioning your name to me."

Arthur was taken slightly aback. He had expected, from what he had heard of Tom's sister, to find a timid, country-reared miss out of her element in the city. He should have realized, he thought now, that the source of his information was Tom himself.

It was of course impossible for an older brother, particularly one with several years' seniority, to accept the idea that his sister had grown, as this one obviously had, into an attractive young lady.

This older brother's opinion clearly was wide off the mark. If Foxhall had indeed offered for the lady, his taste was impeccable. Arthur felt a sense of loss for himself. Had he had more to offer than his friend's bounty, the bestowal, perhaps, of a living in the duke's gift, he might entertain ambitions above his station.

What he faced now, not to put too fine a point on it, was a bewitching young lady with formidable wits and the directness to pursue wherever they led her.

"I am quite sure my name never came up," agreed Arthur. "But perhaps the name of a man with whom both your brother and I deal will mean something to you. I have no hesitation in telling you that I am not of sufficient importance to engage your attention. But the fact is . . ."

Almost too late he realized that he was about to confide more than he intended in Miss Aspinall. He could not reveal that her brother, whose most flagrant sin in her eyes seemed to be gambling, had served often as a secret and resourceful messenger for the highly secretive intelligence service called only "Whern's business."

Even though there was no reason for Tom to be abroad now on the duke's business, the habit of secrecy held him in a strong grip. If Tom wished his relation to be made privy to his secret employment, then Tom would have told her. Clearly Miss Aspinall harbored no suspicions. It did occur to Arthur that Tom was lacking in his responsibility to allow this veritable child to travel at large in London! No wonder the young lady was looking in Foxhall's direction. Arthur shared the duke's view of him.

Arthur reflected. He would give nothing away, he decided, by simply mentioning the duke. Besides, Whern's was an honorable and highly respected title, even though the present incumbent was something of a mystery to his peers. However, Arthur was forced to rely on the *cachet* of that title to elicit the information he needed.

"I am here," he said in a manner designed to impress, "on behalf of His Grace the Duke of Whern."

Nell's bright expression did not alter. She said simply, with obvious honesty, "Who is the Duke of Whern?"

Chapter Six

Nell went up the stairs to her aunt's sitting room, where she found her recovering from the emotional turmoil induced by the unrewarding search for her nephew by reading *Mansfield Park*, Jane Austen's latest novel which had come out in the summer.

"Aunt," said Nell without preliminaries, "do you know aught of the Duke of Whern?"

"He's dead."

"He can't be. He's looking for Tom."

"Nonsense, child. I know he is dead." She added with humor, "It seems that Tom is in great demand, if even the departed are searching for him."

"Dear aunt, be sensible."

"I am, my dear. I know the Duke of Whern is dead, this three years at least. What would he want with Tom now?"

Nell was impatient. "Of course he wouldn't want Tom if he were dead. The duke, I mean. But this man—a gentleman, I don't doubt, from his address—called and said he was from the Duke of Whern, and he wants Tom."

"Don't we all!" exclaimed Lady Sanford. "All right, Nell, I shall not exacerbate your feelings further by repeating what we all know. Tom is failing in his duty to his family, and I wash my hands of him. If you lose Foxhall, then on your brother's head be it. I can do no more."

"Aunt, you have done so much. I'm sorry you are troubled by Tom's unfortunate absence. But I feel I must tell you that I shall not lose dear Rowland. He is strongly attached to me."

"Attachment is not always paramount in a gentleman's mind, you know."

"Indeed, I am sure that Rowland will honor his undertaking. But at any rate, I intend to marry him, whether Tom comes up to the mark or not."

Lady Sanford gazed at her, wide-eyed. "My dear Nell, will you kidnap him?"

Nell was suddenly struck by a thought that would, when explored, possibly make her way clear before her. She would consider it later. "No, not precisely. But there must be a Duke of Whern extant, Aunt. Pray try to remember."

Obediently, Lady Sanford set her mind to the problem. "The Duke of Whern—let me see. He died, but his son and grandson died before him, I am sure. Let me think. Was there a nephew?"

She thought to such purpose that she dredged up from memory the image of a small boy, John Darcy by name. "An odd one. His mother died when he was born and the old duke raised him. I saw the lad once, when he was eight. Unprepossessing, I must say. He was not near the succession then, of course. Could it have been a boating accident that took them? The direct heirs, I mean. No matter now, I suppose. Anyway, what does the duke, whoever he is, want with Tom?"

Nell could not inform her. Mr. Haveney had reached the limit of discretion in time, so that he had given her only the vaguest hints of his reason for seeking out Tom. But the gist of his information caused the burgeoning of a scheme in Nell's mind. This was the thought that she had, only moments ago, put aside for later consideration. But suddenly the scheme was clear in her mind, details quite defined and of a nature to promise a favorable issue, if it were presented to those involved in a certain light.

There was, Nell had gathered, a small parcel that must be taken to Vienna in the very near future. Haste was of the essence, so she had gathered, and since Tom was not likely to be at hand in time, there seemed to Nell no reason in the world why the parcel could not be transported by an Aspinall, even though the hand were feminine rather than masculine.

Nell was not an implicit believer in Providence, but she was also not one to overlook an opportunity as it arose. She was excessively anxious to be at the side of her dear Rowland. The near presence of Miss Freeland in Vienna, no matter how she had dismissed the danger in speaking to her aunt, nonetheless cut deeply into her thoughts. While Nell could not have managed the journey to Rowland's side by herself, it was more than reassuring to perceive that His Majesty's Government itself was taking a hand in her behalf.

She set herself, without too strict an attachment to the truth, to persuade her aunt to her scheme.

"It seems, Aunt, that the Aspinalls are once again being asked for a service to the Crown. You know it has been three generations since Great-grandpapa fought with Lord Clive in India."

"And a sad job of it he did, too," remarked Phrynie. "He was Clive's right-hand man, but Clive received all the honors. Baron Clive of Plassey—and it could have been Baron Aspinall."

"But now . . ."

Phrynie had not finished her complaint. "And riches, as well. He could have been wealthy as a nabob, you know. Look at that garish emerald of the Netwicks! In impossible taste, I have always thought, but it does bear witness to a certain enterprise on their part."

"But now," Nell said firmly, "we have a great opportunity."

"Nell, pray do not go on in such a foolish fashion. Next you will tell me that the fate of our country is in the hands of the Aspinalls. Fiddle!"

She regarded her niece with growing suspicion. Not for naught had she had the girl under her wing for six months. She had learned, to her cost, to mistrust mightily that remarkably innocent expression that she now noted. Once Nell donned that guileless demeanor, the world was well on its way to being turned upside down.

"Nell," she said in a minatory tone, "whatever it is, I forbid it."

"Dear Aunt, I'm persuaded you have the right of it. It's such a shame. Such a small matter, after all."

"I hope so, my dear. For neither of us shall indulge in it. Whatever it is."

Nell moved to the window. She was not certain of the wisdom of her first plan, to confide totally in her aunt. Lady Sanford could, at times, be surprisingly indiscreet. If Nell could manage without betraying the whole of her scheme, it was much to be desired.

"Such a gray day," said Nell with an air of inconsequence. "And you know London is no longer exciting. No one's in Town now." With a grand sweep of her hand, she dismissed four millions of people, earning their wages, preparing their meals, educating their children, sweeping the crosswalks, handling world shipping. "The Town is dead!"

"I agree that London is not precisely in the swing of things," said Phrynie with caution. "But I am persuaded that the holidays which we will—without question, Nell—spend in Essex and not in Vienna will be most enjoyable."

It was perhaps unfortunate that Lady Sanford's features were to such a degree open to analysis. Nell was not deceived for a moment. Her aunt loathed the country. The bucolic amusements appropriate to the area and the season had less than no appeal to her.

With enthusiasm, Nell agreed. "Of course, you are right, Aunt. From a child, I have always enjoyed the holidays in the country. Can you ever forget the great Christmas tree in the entrance hall, and the Yule log? I wonder if the carolers from the village still come, to sing, you know, and drink their wassail. My mother always held open house, and there was a party for the children—"

"And the front door stood open to the elements while the infants stood shuffling their feet in the doorway and the cold drafts sent smoke billowing into all the rooms." Lady Sanford's tone lacked enthusiasm for the coming events.

Satisfied, Nell moved on to the next step. "I wonder what Vienna is like. Have you ever been there?"

"When I was a girl. Your mother and I were taken by our grandmother, whose dear friend Lady Cornwell was the wife of the ambassador. All I remember was the divine music. And of course hot chocolate, and such wonderful whipped cream. Now, of course, I wouldn't dare to indulge. I vow all I have to do is look at sweets and I gain so much weight my clothes refuse to fit."

Lady Sanford claimed to be engaged in constant warfare to keep her figure, but she was still slim as a wand and willowy, possessed of an incomparable grace of movement. Nell envied her that indefinable but unmistakable allure.

"But, Aunt, if we could make our way there . . ."

"Elinor. I have told you, have I not, that I shall not allow you to leap across the Continent in pursuit of Lord Foxhall.

Such a jape would undoubtedly ruin us both for life. And Foxhall would fall into Miss Freeland's grip, once and for all."

Nell quailed. Was it true? Could he in fact mistake her sincere devotion for unseemly pursuit? At that moment she almost gave up.

But the perfect features of Rowland Fiennes swam before her vision. In truth, she must not confess defeat. If Miss Freeland, by mere propinquity, were able to attach Rowland to herself, Nell would quite simply die.

Nell had, in such a short time, moved beyond simply contemplating the marvelous thing that had happened to her. No longer was she innocently trembling under the wonder of Rowland's smile, his tender regard, his incomprehensible surge of emotions that led him to wish to marry her.

She had left what she could now only believe to be naiveté behind. She wished to marry Rowland, and he wished to marry her. Therefore, this deed would be accomplished, no matter what was required of her. She would prove worthy of her affianced husband. Almost, that is, affianced, she amended.

"Nell," said Phrynie in true curiosity, "does being with him mean that much to you?"

"Not at all," rejoined Nell airily. She added, without truth, "I suppose we should not even see him."

"Not see Rowland—in Vienna? What is this mad scheme? For you have one, I am persuaded. All this talk about Vienna, and then not even see Foxhall?" She regarded her niece from under fair brows, only slightly darkened by discreet use of a pencil.

Nell relented. "Of course it does not make sense, Aunt. I long to see Rowland, more than I can tell you, but you are right. We cannot go alone."

Phrynie was not satisfied. "Come now, Nell. The truth—the entire truth, if you please."

Nell told her all she knew on the subject of Mr Haveney's errand. "And there is no reason why we cannot go on a mission for the government, Aunt. Surely dear Rowland could not think we had come to Vienna merely to seek his company."

Nell was eloquent on the variations she improvised on her basic scheme. Her aunt's features moved from disbelief to dismay, to utter rejection, and then, as Nell mentioned once again that she longed to enjoy the entertainment furnished by the splendid Habsburg court, to an inward look at what must appeal to her pleasure-loving nature.

"But to go off alone," Phrynie protested, "on a harebrained errand of such doubtful provenance, Nell! How can you think I would permit such an escapade?"

"It was only that I thought to oblige the government," explained Nell. "They are asking Tom to take the responsibility, and we cannot find him. I should not like to think that Tom's credit would be lost for want of a little exertion on my part." She spoke carelessly, but later she would remember this remark.

Phrynie said tartly, "Tom can gain little credit for simply carrying a couple of forgotten documents to Austria."

Then Phrynie, all unwittingly, made a remark that would have consequences undreamed of in her sitting room in her Grosvenor Square town house. "If we could find Tom, then I might reconsider."

Nell fell silent. Had she misgauged her aunt? Had she even misjudged her own feelings? When she thought about the projected journey, she entertained a few misgivings of her own. France had been a closed country to the English for more than twenty years, longer than Nell's own life, and her knowledge of the land was minimal. Her governess had touched lightly upon the subject, and Nell retained an impression of pleasant scenery, abominable roads, and an ignorant peasantry.

Surely the Revolution must have disarmed the footpads and slaughtered the wolves? It did not seem illogical to her that she feared for Rowland but not for herself. She had not the slightest doubt that she could travel through Europe, if not in pleasurable sight-seeing, at least unscathed.

Just the same, Nell could not travel alone, with only her coachman, armed outriders, footmen, and two maids for company. Not, that is, if she wished to retain any reputation at all. Her aunt had spoken with finality on the subject of their going alone. Downhearted, Nell left her. Lady Sanford picked up *Mansfield Park* again, but it was a long time before she returned to the story.

A short period of concentrated consideration of the problem altered Nell's thinking. Of course, her aunt was correct.

Two women were restricted by convention far beyond their desserts.

But Phrynie's innocent remark bore fruit. Nell was not the descendant of the right-hand man to Baron Clive of Plassey for naught. Considering the matter in the light of logic, as was her wont at serious times, there was but one way remaining to accomplish her desired end. She must find Tom.

Struck by the brilliance of the idea that had come to her, she sat down abruptly and allowed the scheme to flourish. She must find Tom—or at least seem to find Tom. If her brother did not materialize, then she would simply have to make do as best she could.

The smile that flitted across her piquant features was not an ordinary one. Indeed, anyone who knew her would be quite sure that the part of wisdom would be to leave the immediate vicinity.

There was one arrow left in her bow. Since Tom had not been located by any of the ordinary means, it occurred to her that he did not wish to be found. In that case, she believed she knew where he was. He often retreated to an obscure little manor in the Cotswolds, given to him by his grandmother. The hunting was excellent, and Tom, at heart a countryman, reveled in the outdoor life without the cumbersome trappings of the Aspinall manor.

In no time. Nell had penned a note to him and entrusted it to Grigg, a footman she had brought with her to alleviate the strain on her aunt's household by her own requirements.

"You must deliver this, Grigg, directly to my brother at Oakcliff. It is of the utmost urgency, and if he is not to be found then I don't know quite how I shall go on."

She would have sent word to Oakcliff before, when it was desperately to be desired that Tom receive Rowland's offer for her. But it would take two days at the very least for Tom to reach London from the Cotswolds and Rowland had departed the next day. Urgency had ebbed, therefore, only to return with Mr. Haveney's parcel.

Grigg, brought up in the Aspinall household, adored Nell. He straightened his shoulders, clearly ready to brave polar regions if that were required of him, or even, if Miss Nell wished, track down Lady Hester Stanhope, last heard from three months before at an outlandish place called Meshmushy.

In truth, the footman did not return when Nell expected him. But she had every confidence, if not in the footman, then in Tom's own curiosity about Mr. Haveney's request. Once he learned that exciting news waited for him, he would travel to London without even penning up his cattle.

Chapter Seven

While Nell waited the return of her footman, she raised her plans on the foundation stone of Tom's arrival. She must be ready, for if Tom were to take this mysterious small parcel across Europe, she must make it inevitable for him to include her and Aunt Phrynie as part of the expedition.

Mr. Haveney's presentation of his need for Tom indicated that the parcel must be carried without fanfare to Vienna. Surely, Nell reasoned, if camouflage were desired, what better than a simple family group traveling for their own pleasure?

If a traveling family party were required, Nell would see that one was provided. Lady Sanford proved less recalcitrant than Nell had expected, and in the end she was surprisingly easy to persuade. Clearly, she too felt the lure of lights and music emanating from far beyond the horizon, and as she said privately to her maid Mullins, "Even Tom is better than nothing."

Even though Nell heard nothing from the messenger sent after her brother, she had wrought such a change in her aunt that on the morning of their proposed departure Phrynie was out of bed even before her first cup of tea, harrying Mullins over her attire.

"What makes you think I shall wear that puce traveling suit? You know what traveling does to my complexion, and puce is the last thing I should wish to wear. Take it away at once, and lay out the Persian-green one. I declare, Nell," she added, turning abruptly to her niece when she entered, "I don't know why we are doing all this. I told you we would not travel to Vienna."

"That was before you knew that Tom was going with us," said Nell serenely, even though she had had no word either from Tom or from the office of the mysterious Duke of Whern. She had written to Mr. Haveney to inform him that Tom was returning posthaste to London and would be prepared to receive the parcel and deliver it to Castlereagh. "Now, Aunt, we must be ready to leave the moment Tom gets here."

"Which will be hours late, if I know anything about him." Something in Nell's attitude aroused suspicion in Lady Sanford's breast. "Nell, are you conniving?"

"I don't know what you mean, Aunt."

"You know very well. To be quite plain, are you planning some nefarious scheme? Where is Tom? And what makes you certain he will allow us to accompany him to Vienna? I have not so far seen any sign of his amiability in ordinary matters, let alone an affair of such moment as a veritable expedition." She eyed Nell with misgivings. "I have the strongest feeling," she declared, "that he will simply tell us we are to stay at home and be gone before we have an opportunity to convince him to take us."

Phrynie touched an echoing chord in Nell. However, Nell had taken certain precautions of her own. "The carriage is ordered for an hour from now," she informed Phrynie, "and Stuston is prepared to drive us all the way. Samuel is coming with us and another footman and a groom as well. And Mullins, who will make you comfortable, you know. Should you think these were sufficient servants? I am sure that Tom will have a man or two with him. So you see we shall be well equipped."

"I confess I have grave misgivings, Nell. I cannot think why, for all seems *convenable*. I wonder whether there is any merit in premonitions?"

"Nonsense, Aunt. I am persuaded we will go on excessively well. Whitcomb has sent ahead to take rooms for us this night at the Ship Inn and has arranged our passage across the Channel. Don't worry, dear Aunt. All is in train."

All except Tom, she told herself. But she could do nothing about her brother now, and she must turn her thoughts to the messenger who would bring the parcel. She recalled her exact words to Mr. Haveney—her brother would arrive during the night just past and would be on hand to receive the mysterious parcel at the earliest convenient hour this morning. She had not precisely told an untruth, for she was not informed that he would *not* come.

It was already past the earliest hour convenient to Nell. She could only conclude that Whern's office kept late hours.

But, a half hour later, when Nell was ready to climb the maroon velvet draperies and scream in an attempt to relieve her taut nerves, the messenger from Mr. Haveney arrived.

She had dreaded the likelihood that Mr. Haveney himself would come. It was in the highest degree probable that he would make difficulties over the preparations, which could not be concealed. The traveling chariot before the door, vast amounts of luggage strapped on the back and even encumbering the roof, Lady Sanford's coachman ready to swing up to his seat—it must be obvious to the dullest intellect that Lady Sanford was taking to the road.

If Mr. Haveney demanded the actual presence of Tom Aspinall, Nell was undone.

Just as she began to sink below the surface of depression, Grigg reappeared, grubby and breathless, having ridden far into the night before and taken to the road again before dawn. Like a faithful retriever, he handed Nell an equally soiled and ill-written note. Tom's formal education had slid off the surface of his brain like water over a smooth rock. With some difficulty, she made out the sense of his missive.

> *Sorry, Nell, I'll be a little late. Tell Whern I'll get there as soon as I can walk. Fell off a sorry hack that Charlie Puckett sold me, nothing wrong, just a bruised knee. Isnt he a grate fellow. Whern, I mean. Not Charlie.*

Nell's spirits, not at their most vigorous just now, were dashed completely. She had not fully realized how much her scheme depended upon Tom's immediate presence. She was prepared to anticipate his arrival, even to the point of falsely informing Mr. Haveney that Tom was still abed upstairs. But now that she had word from her brother that he was not now even on the road to London, her heart failed her.

If Tom could not come in the next hour, then her entire project was in vain. Her aunt would never again trust her, nor would she consent to postponing their departure for several days. Besides, Nell, always honest at least with herself, recognized that if urgency were required, Tom could much more easily travel swiftly without the cumbersome addition of his family.

In addition, Nell saw clearly that if Tom came to London to do Whern's bidding, then he was perfectly capable of going directly to Whern, obtaining the parcel, and, realizing that time was of the essence, sending word to his sister from Paris that he was on his way. Alone.

Already three days had been lost waiting for him, and who knew how many more would elapse before his knee would serve him?

For want of a nail, she remembered, the battle was lost.

Not Nell Aspinall's battle.

"What did Tom's note say?" demanded her aunt.

"He'll be along soon," said Nell, distorting the message slightly, but scrupulously adding, "his hand is all but illegible." Then, rejecting half measures, she continued, "He says we should take the parcel and begin the journey. He will overtake us at the Ship Inn."

"But," objected Phrynie, "where is the parcel? I wish to meet this Mr. Haveney. Do you think that the duke himself will come? I have the liveliest curiosity about him. I wonder, do you know, whether he might not be a better catch even than young Foxhall. The old duke was a veritable nabob, and clench-fisted at that. I never met him but once." She sighed. "Too late, of course."

Nell said, primly, "We are not apt to meet the present duke either. At least, he sent Mr. Haveney in the first instance. But don't trouble yourself over Whern, Aunt. I am perfectly satisfied with Rowland. I love him, you remember."

Drily, Lady Sanford commented, "What does *that* signify?"

Whern's messenger arrived within the hour. To Nell's great relief, it was not Mr. Haveney. The note handed to her on his behalf was brief.

Urgent business came up. The bearer of this parcel is instructed to place it only in the hands of Thomas Aspinall. Aspinall in his turn is to deliver the parcel directly into the hands of Lord Castlereagh. Any violation of these instructions will be gravely dealt with.

Nell bit her lip. "*Gravely dealt with.*" It was almost, she thought, as though Mr. Haveney had read her mind and found it necessary to warn her against carrying out her devious plot.

Impossible that Haveney knew what she was planning!

Even though her scheme rested firmly upon Tom's presence, she was not averse to improvisation. Besides, she had gone too far to be intimidated—at least at present—by the probable nature of the threatened "*grave consequences.*"

She smiled dazzlingly at the messenger, a red-haired boy of no more than fifteen, and without great effort was soon possessed of the parcel.

In short order the Sanford chariot rolled away out of Grosvenor Square to South Audley Street, heading toward Great George Street, the nearest way to Westminster Bridge. It was barely out of sight before the messenger realized that he had allowed the parcel to leave his hands even though the designated receiver was nowhere in sight.

He had failed in his mission. His mind whirled with visions of the unpleasantness that would be his lot, he believed, when his lapse became known. It did not occur to him to call upon his masters to retrieve the parcel from illegal hands.

He walked aimlessly toward the river. He had no intention of ending it all, but he could not bring himself to face Mr. Haveney, to say nothing of the duke. Instead, he thought only of delaying his punishment as long as was possible.

The luckless messenger was sunk in despair, rising in intervals to contemplate the lovely lady who had led him—or rather his parcel—astray. At odd moments he was visited by the recollection of Mr. Haveney's definite instructions, along with a veiled suggestion of punishment to follow deviations from duty.

But then he remembered the very ordinary look of the parcel. Big enough so that he must hold it in his hand as he traveled from Duke Street to Lady Sanford's, it was wrapped in plain paper as though it were merely a bundle of letters. If it had been wrapped in tape and sealed with red wax, it would have been important. By degrees, the boy convinced himself that Mr. Haveney was simply returning personal missives. Why should he be overwrought if his messenger simply told him the truth—that the young lady had taken them with a promise to deliver them to her brother?

Eventually, he believed that wherever the fault lay, it was

not with him. Nevertheless, twilight was blanketing the city before he returned to his employer.

For want of a nail was a myth. But for want of an early warning, the Sanford carriage was allowed to trundle on toward Dover without hindrance.

As they left London behind and moved steadily out on the Dover road Nell settled back against the blue velvet squabs with a contented sigh. She had succeeded so far. Her aunt was in the carriage, committed to the journey to Vienna. Nell had no fears now that Tom would go on his own, bypassing his family, to Austria.

After all, Nell had the famous parcel tucked safely away in her own jewel case!

Chapter Eight

When Nell saw Lady Sanford's blue traveling coach unloaded from the ferry on the far side of the Channel, she began to relax. Even though Mr. Haveney by now had learned the truth from his pliable messenger, there was little that he could do. The storm that threatened as they left the Ship Inn for the ferry had worsened, and theirs was the last vessel to cross for a while.

There was no way, other than by a private yacht with a foolhardy captain, to set anyone from England down on the French shore.

The Channel crossing had been very trying. The November seas, driven by near-gale winds from the North Sea, had risen in tumult, tossing the ferry unmercifully. Lady Sanford, never a strong traveler, had taken at once to her bunk, moaning incessantly.

Since Mullins was, if possible, even more prone to respond disastrously to the motion of the waves than her mistress, it was left to Nell to tend them both, until their heartfelt pleas simply to leave them to die had driven her up to the deck.

This journey was Nell's very first crossing, and she was gratified to find that her sea legs—such a vulgar expression!—were strong, and she truly enjoyed the rowdy winds and the tossing waters.

Lady Sanford found that one night's rest in the Blue Dolphin, the small but comfortable French inn where they lodged, was not sufficient to restore her to health. No matter how anxious Nell was to place more distance between them and Mr. Haveney, she could not but feel sympathy for the patient in the back bedroom of the inn. When Lady Sanford was ill, so it seemed, she expected the world to stop and commiserate with her.

The proprietors of the Blue Dolphin found that the new influx of English tourists, after the famine resulting from the Revolution and the belligerent tendencies of the Emperor, brought prosperity beyond their wildest dreams. Certainly the advent of this English milady and her *ah si belle* niece, accompanied by an equipage and staff of some opulence, was welcome custom, and the landlady had promptly installed the ashen-faced milady in the best bedroom, looking out upon a garden now winter-dead. *Tisanes* which were guaranteed to restore her from the rigors of the crossing were furnished hourly to her.

While Mullins had been equally indisposed on the ferry, she felt the pull of duty in addition to a well-developed sense of martyrdom. By the second afternoon on land, she was able to totter downstairs and take a little gruel.

Nell entered her aunt's bedroom. "How good it is to see color in your cheeks again, dear Aunt."

"I shall never again set foot on a vessel of any kind," declared Phrynie. "Never."

"I shall hope our French improves, then, for we shall of necessity not return home again."

Phrynie, quite properly, ignored her niece's remark. "I should have simply insisted, Nell, on refusing to embark on this—this mad journey." She lay back on the down pillows and closed her eyes. "I must say that even the word 'embark' makes me queasy."

Nell silently blessed the *mal de mer* that afflicted her aunt—heartless, of course, but at least there would be no question now of returning to London!

Nor would there be for the moment any probing questions on the subject of the nonappearance of Tom Aspinall. Lady Sanford would soon enough notice that Nell's assurances of Tom's imminent arrival were not fulfilled. But, thought Nell, buoyed by her success thus far, she would deal with her aunt's renewed suspicions when required to do so.

"Now, child," said Lady Sanford faintly, "go away and let me sleep. I have not the slightest doubt that my looks have faded entirely away, and I shall not wish to see a mirror for days."

Nell had no hesitation in leaving her aunt asleep in the

care of the fawning but competent landlady while she set out for fresh air and to explore her first French town. She of course had a thorough grounding in French, and had at the outset had little doubt that she could make herself understood. But speaking the language in the schoolroom was a different affair from being fluent in the streets of Calais.

Nonetheless, the lure of the exotic and unknown drew her, and without fear but with commendable caution and mindful of the conventions, she took Mullins with her. "Besides, Mullins, you've been indoors too long. I cannot understand why you loathe fresh air so much. It is beyond all things health giving. Get your shawl, Mullins."

The maid, fearing for her life if she set foot on a French street, made clandestine arrangements with the footman Potter to follow them at a distance.

"These frogs would soon as not cut a throat," Mullins informed him, "and my throat suits me the way it is."

"Aye," responded Potter, "and a purty throat it be, too!"

"Mind yourself," retorted Mullins loftily, "my throat's me own, and not for the likes of you to gaze on!"

Properly, but not seriously, chastised, the footman followed his mistress and the abigail as they set out for the waterfront. The Blue Dolphin was only a short way up a side street, and there was little there to attract a pedestrian.

The waterfront was a broad street lying parallel to the quay. No trees lined its edge, but because of the recent storm an abundance of fishing vessels tossed at their sheltered anchorages. Innumerable masts moved back and forth in stately fashion. If she watched them long enough, Nell suspected they might exercise a strong hypnotic effect on her.

Here in the harbor the ferocity of the seas was tamed, even though the lingering swell was sufficient to lift the decks of the smaller vessels at times above the level of her eyes. Imagine going out on such small boats to find fish, of all things! Yet she was intelligent enough to realize that if this were all one could do for a living, it did not behoove one to complain.

The storm, while subsiding, was not over. The wind blew hard, driving the rain nearly horizontally before it. The water deepened on the cobbled pavement, sudden gusts piled it into miniature seas, and she and Mullins were soon drenched to the knees.

Nell herself did not complain. Brought up in Essex, in

what was after all a domesticated neighborhood, she considered herself an outdoors person, a veritable country-woman. She had loved London's giddy whirl and manifold entertainments, but now with the fresh wind buffeting her, she knew that living in the city was not the goal of her existence.

She wondered how Rowland would consider the question. His duties of course would keep him in London, if they did not lead him to stations abroad. She felt a pang of dismay. She believed she could live a contented life in the city, if he were with her. But her distress stemmed from the fact that she did not in truth know what Rowland thought about a great many things.

She was willing—even eager—to put her future into the hands of a man she knew nothing about. But, she told herself stoutly, he loved her, and between them they would sweep away all misunderstandings, all conflicts. . . .

She clenched her fists in her pockets. The thought of conflicts between them was a completely unwelcome, unwarranted intrusion on her state of bliss. She was too tired, that was all.

She became aware of a voice whining in her ear, above the wind.

"Miss Nell, can't we go back?" panted Mullins, her breath taken by the gale. "Bain't nothin' to see here anyway more'n what we seen already on the boat. I had enough of that."

"All right, Mullins," said Nell, philosophically adding, "it won't do us any good to come down with a congestion on the chest."

They turned their backs on the wind and the waterfront and started back toward the inn. They had taken only a few steps when feet pounded behind them, and Potter burst out, "Oh, Miss Nell! Come quick!"

Nell stopped short. "What—oh, it's you, Potter. What are you doing here?"

"It's Stuston! Come, quick!"

"Where is Stuston? I thought he was—Never mind, Potter. What about Stuston?" The thought came to her that Potter had garbled the message. "Is my aunt all right?"

"No, miss. I mean, yes, miss. It is *Stuston*! He's *dead*!"

Nell breathed, "Oh, no!" Potter was a fool, he must be, to alarm her so. But a second look at the footman's ashen face told her he was in deadly earnest. She spared a thought for the appropriateness of the word that came to her before she demanded to be taken to her aunt's coachman.

Potter hurried before her along the waterfront to an area nearer the main body of the fishing fleet than she and Mullins had reached. The elderly coachman was stretched out on the wet cobbles, one leg twisted beneath him, his face as gray as the pavement and streaming with the falling rain.

The little knot of jersey-clad fishermen that had gathered apparently out of nowhere moved aside to make way for her. Absently she noted the strong residual aroma of their latest catches as she knelt beside Stuston.

He was not dead. His eyes were open, even though they seemed at first not to recognize her. "Stuston! What is amiss? Are you ill?"

Recognition came to his eyes. He made a convulsive movement to rise. "Please, Miss Nell, I'm sorry. I just don't know rightly what came over me. I'll be all right and tight. Just give me a jiff, by your leave, and I'll get my breath back."

His eyes closed. Nell caught her forefinger between her teeth in a gesture of extreme dismay. How would she get him back to the inn? She looked wildly around at the faces of the fishermen, set in lines of compassion or skepticism according to their various temperaments. Suddenly Stuston opened his eyes wide and cried out, "I must 'a been pushed, that's what!"

She heard the voices of the men surrounding her, speaking in a patois she did not fully understand. "Fell, didn't he? Came all over sudden. Nobody near him. That *garçon* there, he was. Didn't see him pushed, *vous savez*. Only tried to help, that's all I did."

Nell knew there was no help to be had from them. Mullins was worse than useless, and Nell thought she would do well to deal with only the coachman and not have to drag Mullins back as well.

Stuston struggled to rise. The movement of his leg forced a groan of pain from him and he fell back, this time mercifully unconscious.

"Pushed, did he say?" said one of the men. "Going to make trouble for us, is he? Nobody saw him pushed, did they?" The speaker glanced around the group, sending them a clear message. In a body, they removed themselves from the scene as quickly as they had come.

"Wait!" cried Nell, "*s'il vous plaît!*"

Only one of the roughly clad men lingered. Her eyes went to him in mute appeal. She saw that he was a man of somewhat stocky build with irregular features—his nose seemed awry as though it had at one time been broken—and a general appearance of having slept in his salt-encrusted clothes for a sennight. His grizzled hair and his manner put his age at around fifty, she guessed.

"*S'il vous plaît?*" she ventured.

His voice was husky, but to her vast relief he spoke in native English. "This gent's yours, miss?"

"He is my aunt's coachman. Do you think—it's serious?"

"Bad enough," he grunted. His hands, surprisingly clean, moved competently over Stuston's supine body. "Nothing vital broken, as it seems, miss. But that leg's not right." He looked at her from under thick eyebrows. "What shall I do with him, miss?"

Nell bit her lip in frustration. "We're staying at the Blue Dolphin, just up that street. Can we get him there? I could take one foot, and Mullins—Mullins, where are you?"

She looked around for her aunt's maid. Mullins was standing well away from them, clearly torn between her duty to stay with Nell and her strong desire to run on tottering legs back to safety at the inn.

"Don't count on her," said Nell's companion, "we shall be fortunate if she does not give way to hysterics."

His comment was so at variance with his appearance that Nell could only gape at him. His eyes glinted oddly for an instant before he seemed to gather himself together and attend to the task before him. When he spoke again, it was with a strong flavor of English countryman. "Tha'd best see him to his bed." Then, with a sidelong glance from under his heavy brows, he added stiffly, "Miss."

Suddenly the balance of authority seemed to shift. Nell was, in spite of her misgivings, quite willing to leave the next step in the rescue of Stuston to this man. To quell her doubts, she simply told herself that she had not heard correctly.

"Can you—would you help?"

"Yes." He glanced around, and caught sight of Potter, lingering beside Mullins and wearing a helpless air. "You there, come here. Off with your jacket, lad."

With Potter's help, he slid the jacket underneath Stuston's

legs, carefully moving the injured one to lie parallel with the good one. Handing the jacket sleeves to their owner in the form of a makeshift sling, he ordered, "Hoist 'im up. I'll take the shoulders. Now, then, miss, lead the way."

Obediently Nell turned and, gathering up the tearful Mullins, led the way across the waterfront while the two men carried Stuston the short distance to the Blue Dolphin.

Chapter Nine

After they had put Stuston to bed and the surgeon had come to examine him, Nell waited for the doctor in the parlor. The coachman's rescuer had disappeared for the moment, but when the surgeon came to report to Nell, she was glad to see the stocky figure just behind him.

"The leg, mademoiselle, is *mal, très mal*," the doctor pronounced, proud of his uncertain grasp of English. "And even if I encased it, *vous savez*, the man cannot go on. Two ribs are also damaged. Much pain. I have given the laudanum. As well, the jolting that even Madame's well-sprung carriage will of necessity provide this poor man"—clearly the doctor was on the side of the downtrodden populace liberated by the Revolution—"will of a certainty put a hole in—how is it, puncture?—what you Anglais call *les lumières*. Is it not?"

Nell's features reflected bewilderment. Lamps? Her schoolroom French failed her, not for the first time since she had arrived in Calais. Mystified, she turned automatically to the man who had followed the doctor into her parlor. She raised an eyebrow, and murmured, "Torches, perhaps? I do not quite understand."

The stranger translated, "Lights, miss. Damage to his breathing lights."

"Oh. Lungs. I see. Of course he must not travel." With words of thanks and reassurance as to the proper care of the patient, she paid the doctor's fee and bade him farewell.

Thinking that Stuston's rescuer had left with the doctor, she thought herself alone. Eyes filling with unwelcome tears, she turned blindly to the window, trying to control her sudden longing to throw herself on the settee and howl in disappointment.

All her scheming had come to naught. To give her credit, she was much more distressed at the moment for the harm that had befallen Stuston, through her, than she was over the sudden disruption of their journey to Vienna.

"All my fault," she scolded herself. "I should never have conceived this dreadful scheme."

A slight sound behind her caused her to turn swiftly. The man from the waterfront was standing just inside the door, watching her.

"I thought you had left with the doctor!"

"No, miss. I was wishing to speak with you, by your favor. Miss."

"Not now," she told him. "I must go to see Stuston."

She was halfway up the stairs before she realized he was just behind her. She half turned to bid him go down, but she was certain that he would not obey. Setting her chin and firmly resolving to put the man in his place, she climbed to the attic room where the coachman lay in a clean bed, propped against pillows no whiter than his face.

"Dear Stuston," said Nell affectionately, "I am sure you understand the doctor's instructions. We cannot allow you to travel until you are quite well. You will stay here in the Blue Dolphin."

"But, Miss Nell, I ain't leaving you in the lurch, pardon my expression, miss, but you can't go across Europe with only the footmen and a groom to do for you. I'll be up and about in the morning," he insisted, his words becoming slurred as the laudanum took effect, "sure as—my name—Stuston."

Nell turned to Stuston's rescuer who had followed her up to the attic room, but not in time to notice a sudden alertness in his hazel eyes.

Had she seen that expression and coupled it with the odd unevenness in the man's speech, which veered from broad countryman to educated English, she might not have been so relieved when, later in the day, the man returned to the inn, his fisherman's beret in hand, and sought an audience in the small sitting room that had been placed at her disposal.

"I am glad you came," she told him, "for I should like again to thank you for your timely assistance. I cannot reward you as is your due, but certainly—" She rummaged in her reticule for coins.

He protested. "Nay," he said in a gruff voice. "I did not come for blunt. I'm sorry about your man. Lucky I was on the spot."

"I truly do not know what I would have done," she said, still hunting for coins.

"Mebbe my luck's still in."

Something in the tone of his voice caught her attention. She looked up quickly. "And what do you mean by that, pray?"

"Begging pardon. I meant only that you don't have a coachman and I don't have a job." As an afterthought, he added, "Miss."

"But you're a fisherman!"

"Am I? A'course. I have druv horses afore, though, miss. Noth—naught to it."

He puzzled her. His accent was rude, as was his voice. He was not a gentleman, judging by his clothing. Even his features spoke of a rough and ready, not to say violent, past. But his hazel eyes looked steadily at her, without humility, and she was visited suddenly by a feeling of confidence. This man was competent, as revealed by his immediate authority with Stuston. If he said he druv—I mean drove, she corrected herself—horses, then she was sure he could.

Not like herself, she thought, who says I can do many things that I cannot do and trusts to learn them before disaster comes.

Yet she hesitated. He spoke English without a French accent, but his speech was oddly variable. She finally decided that he must often have been in contact with those of the upper classes, and being ambitious, had tried to ape his betters.

"But you have no references?"

"Nay, miss, but then you see, we're not in England."

"How very convenient for you."

The man waited in the public room until Nell gave him the news that he had been hired. He said only, "Call me Reeves, miss."

She had not, remembering the level look in his eyes, expected any obsequious phrase of gratitude. But she had not quite reckoned with his easy acceptance of his new employment. Indeed, when he added, "What time do we start in the morning?" she was quite put out. *We* indeed! She and Reeves were in no sense of the word partners in this expedition. He was merely a coachman, hired because accident had befallen old Stuston.

It occurred to her dimly that perhaps she would be glad of Reeves's ability to manage affairs before they reached Vienna. Their company was becoming sadly depleted, since Samuel was to stay here in Calais with Stuston. When they had left London, Nell was content to travel lightly. One cumbersome chariot, providing space in the interior for Lady Sanford, Nell, and Mullins, seemed sufficient for their needs as well as enabling them to travel more swiftly.

Accompanying them at the start were a minimum of servants—Stuston and Samuel, Potter, and young Hayne as groom. Now the company had dwindled by half. Only the footman Potter and the groom Hayne, both young and without experience, remained. Reeves was clearly a worthy addition. Nell had no reason for the uneasy feeling that remained with her, but she was acutely aware that its source was the new coachman.

Reeves remained a vivid figure in her thoughts the rest of that day.

It had been a much easier task to convince Lady Sanford to employ the stranger than she had expected. She was prepared to use her not inconsiderable powers of persuasion and would have pointed out that in two days they would reach Paris, where they could, with the advice of the ambassador, seek out a coachman of more reliable background.

Her arguments were not needed. Lady Sanford was still too weak to care inordinately. She was only mildly distressed to hear about Stuston, saying only, "They'll take care of him here. And he was far too slow a driver. I feared we would never, at his rate, get to Paris. I do hope your protegé will really put them to it."

"I thought you did not wish to make this trip, Aunt?"

Lady Sanford dismissed her about-face with an airy gesture. "Now that we are started, it seems foolish to give it all up. After all, Tom will be along shortly."

Nell hoped he would indeed.

"And besides," continued Phrynie, "everyone I know has traveled to Paris since May, and I felt quite out of it. There may be some excitement at court, although I have little hope of it. In truth, Pamela Wright said that ditch water wasn't in it for dullness. But the Bourbons did once know how to live, and one can only hope that the present king has not forgotten everything he knew."

Enlivened by her speculations, Phrynie threw the covers aside. "Call Mullins, my dear. I do not choose to lie abed any longer. Go hire your man, Nell, and let's be on with it."

She had done her aunt's bidding and then, stricken by the realization that she had neglected Stuston too long, made a visit to the attic room.

He made an ineffectual effort to rise when she entered. "Pray do not disturb yourself, Stuston," she told him, "for I am persuaded movement gives you great pain."

"That it does, miss, for a fact. And a' course, the leg don't move less I take it in hand, so to say."

After a word of commiseration, she said, "I have not heard just what happened to you, Stuston. Pray tell me."

She nursed a secret suspicion that perhaps Reeves, who spoke confidently of his luck, might have given that luck an assisting hand. After all, Reeves alone was to profit from Stuston's mischance.

But a few words from Stuston put that suspicion to rest.

"It's only, miss, that I've always had this longing, you might say, to go to sea. It was like the ferry put me in mind of old times. I know it's a hard life, for my father and his father afore him sailed afore the mast. Not an easy life, like the one I got now."

He hesitated, clearly fearing to jeopardize the easy living that was his. But after a glance at his mistress's niece from under tufted gray brows, he bumbled on. "So it seemed like, having the chance, I had to go down and look at all them little boats. Not so grand as His Majesty's fleet, a' course, I know that. But there's something about them tidy little vessels that says summat to me, you might say. And I was watching them, thinking, don't you see, how it would be to straddle the deck and feel the sea pushing up from under."

He fell into silent recollection. At last, Nell ventured, "Stuston, you did say that you were pushed. Do you know who did it?"

"Now *that* I don't remember, miss. Did I say pushed?"

"Yes, Stuston, you did."

"I must 'a thought a man could stand on his own feet less

he *got* shoved. But I reckon I was a bit off me head for a bit."

"There was no one near you? A stocky man, for instance, with a navy-blue fisherman's jersey? A man with a crooked nose?"

"Ah, now, miss, I see which way you're thinking, if I may say so. It's the gent that got me back here and into bed, right? I don't recollect seeing him afore, and that's a fact, miss." He shook his head. "Maybe I got shoved and maybe I didn't. Maybe I slipped and maybe I didn't. But first thing I knew, that is first thing I'm *sure* of, I was flat on my back and that fool Potter yelling his head off his shoulders, and that was it, miss, until you come." Shyly, he added, "And I thankee."

She cut short his apologies about putting them to inconvenience by his accident. Hesitating, she told him about his replacement. "But he is only temporary, you know, until we get to Paris and can find another coachman."

The old man shot her a look of surprising sharpness. "It's not for me to say, miss," he began, going on after all to say, "but I'd rest easier in my bed if the man—Reeves, you call him?—kept on all the way. He's not apt to want my job in the end, so I read him."

She considered his remark thoughtfully. "I'm not sure but what you have the right of it." Suddenly she felt a deep need for reassurance. "Stuston, pray tell me the truth. Do you think we can get along? Can we succeed in getting all the way to Vienna?"

She was hanging on his answer. The accident to the coachman had shaken her badly. Another accident might well reduce their numbers to a perilous few. And yet she was reluctant to ask her aunt to hire additional outriders, for one unknown servant at a time was quite sufficient.

"Nay, miss, I don't wonder you're fair diddled. But best call to mind that Mr. Tom is coming along ahind us, and he'll not be traveling alone, I'll be bound. Now then, just you count on Mr. Tom. He'll not let you down."

How misguided Stuston was! Tom was certainly far from the rock of reliability that the coachman thought him. She started to give him the benefit of her considered analysis of her wayward brother. "He—" She stopped short, realizing that the man's pain had come back with vigor, and his every breath was troubled.

"Didn't the doctor leave you dosage?"

"Aye, he left me summat," he gasped, "but I thought not to take it for a bit."

"Nonsense," said Nell stoutly. "Take the medicine at once. You'll be better more swiftly if you can rest. I'll send Potter to you. My aunt has it in mind to leave Samuel here to keep you company. And don't worry about your job. My aunt cannot do without you." She smiled sweetly at him, watched him take his dose, and left him.

With Stuston provided for, the new coachman hired, and her aunt quite clearly looking forward to their arrival in Paris, there should have been nothing to keep Nell awake that night. But unaccountably she could not sleep.

Summoning up her recollection of Rowland Fiennes, she tried to concentrate on his admirable features. Guiltily, she realized that the entire day, to say nothing of the day before, she had not given him the slightest thought. Now she would make amends. It took an effort of will to put aside the clamant calls of the day's business on her attention. The object of making the journey had vanished in the details of simply getting on.

With determination she dwelt upon Rowland's face—not weak, but more classical than even the angel Gabriel. Straight nose, not crooked—she itemized—piercing blue eyes, a firm, even stern expression that spoke of devotion to duty, and ambition.

For some reason, a remark came to her which she had overheard several months before in the retiring rooms at Almack's. She had been in London only a fortnight then, and while she was keenly aware of Lord Foxhall's identity, she did not know then who spoke in such carping fashion. But the words came to her now. "Foxhall? You can't warm that piece of granite!"

Granite? Impossible to believe Foxhall was hard as stone when she remembered the glow of admiration in his eyes, the softening tenderness when he looked at her. Anxious to keep him blameless, she dismissed any lurking criticism of his adamant adherence to the letter of custom, delaying his offer until he had spoken to Tom.

Even were he a cold man, she believed, like many another

young woman, that she could change him from a man whose duty was his life to a person of more unbending charm. It was of course, her aunt would say, not the first time that a bride thought she could change her new husband. But then, Phrynie was notoriously cynical when it came to men.

Firmly she fixed Rowland's dear features in her mind, expecting to fall into dreams of delight. It was too bad, she thought in the morning, that the only dream she could recall was woven around the figure of the new coachman.

Such a dream held no significance at all, she told herself. Not until later, much later, did she wonder whether that dream had in fact been a warning. Did it foretell, for example, that Reeves, of the crooked nose and the speaking hazel eyes, would turn out to be quite the worst choice for coachman that she could ever have made?

Chapter Ten

It was late afternoon of the second day when the heavy traveling chariot lumbered into the environs of the French capital. They moved less swiftly now, for the horses were weary, Reeves having put them to it as Lady Sanford wished.

They passed along the forest roads of St. Cloud. Through the bare trees, Nell could catch a glimpse of the palace where Napoleon had been stunned to learn that his armies for the first time would not obey his commands.

The allied armies had overrun France, she knew, under the leadership of Tsar Alexander and General Blücher, and joined forces with turncoat Talleyrand to depose Napoleon. Foxhall had explained the situation to her—at Richmond, wasn't it?—and said, "We must do all we can to keep Talleyrand in check, for if he is disloyal to his Emperor, who gave him honors and wealth, then he may turn against his new masters."

Yes, Nell remembered, it had been Richmond, for that day was fine, warm with a gentle refreshing breeze, and she had worn her almond-green India muslin and a matching chip hat tied with ribbons under her chin.

"My dear," commented Lady Sanford, "I remember riding along this very road when the King was still alive. My grandmama had brought me to Paris when I was young, on a visit." Lady Sanford paused, calculating whether the actual date of this episode conformed to her publicized age, and added, "Very young indeed."

"Did you see the Queen then?"

"Oh yes. Such a foolish woman, the Austrian! I can still hear the cries in the street, although I did not know all the words they used. Quite vulgar, I am sure. But there was no mistaking *L' Autrichienne* when one saw her! You know they brought all their trouble down on their own heads. Louis was so besotted that he could not hear a word against her."

"How nice"—Nell sighed, her thoughts on Rowland—"for a man to love his wife."

"Well, there were reasons, you know," said Phrynie in a lowered voice. "He was not quite—he had a disability—dear Sanford could hardly speak of it even to me—but the Queen overcame his fear of the knife, and then it all went well."

"It? Aunt, what do you mean? Something terrible, I expect? And romantic?"

"Well," said Lady Sanford drily, "not romantic at all. Quite disgusting as a matter of fact. And I shall not say another word until after you are a married woman." When, added Phrynie to herself, if Providence is gracious, you will not be curious about certain abnormal aspects of the connubial state. "I shall hope," she continued, not entirely irrelevantly, "that our unheralded arrival in Vienna will not completely revolt Foxhall."

"Aunt, your doubts do me no credit," said Nell. "I assure you again that he will not alter his mind. If I did not have such trust in his steadfastness, his integrity, I should not love him so much. Dear Aunt, we are bound fast to each other in affection."

"That is fine, my child," said Phrynie, "and your devotion does you great credit. I wish I could be as certain as you are."

"If you truly fear the outcome of this—this journey, why did you consent to come?"

"I had hoped the question would not occur to you. I shall only hope that Tom will be able to explain satisfactorily to Foxhall that he considered us necessary to the safe delivery of the mysterious parcel."

"Rowland will not need such detailed explanations, I warrant."

Secure in her perception of Rowland's strong *tendre* for her, Nell smiled. Lady Sanford noted the smile and wondered without pleasure what it signified. How far had Foxhall gone with the child? He had offered, of course. But Nell was an impulsive child, and her devotion to Foxhall, painful to see, might make her all too willing.

Phrynie was conscious of strong doubts as to the suitability of Nell's intended marriage.

How would Rowland deal with his bride? Much as oil deals with water, she suspected. For Nell was gay, impulsive, bewitching, and too fond of her own way, having been coddled by her parents in a fashion that Lady Sanford, having no children of her own, considered outrageous. On the contrary, all the Fiennes family were noted for a cold sense of duty and strong ambition, coupled with a shocking sense of conservation that could be, and by their enemies was, termed closefistedness.

Nonetheless, the match was made, if not in heaven, then certainly among the upper echelons of London society. In a material way, Nell could do no better, so it seemed.

And yet, Phrynie dreamed, if Nell could find the happiness that she herself had experienced—but regrettably not with Lord Sanford—then she would be content. Just now she could not recall which of her many suitors had provided that happiness. More than one of course—Lord Fenwick, for one, and dear Darnford . . .

"Didn't I hear," she mused, not realizing at once that she spoke aloud, "that Charles Bolesley had come over in May, when the embassy reopened?"

Nell did not know. "But we will shortly arrive at the embassy, dear Aunt, so you will soon be able to inquire."

The carriage moved across the bridge and into the city itself, toward the embassy. It did not occur to Nell to wonder that the new coachman moved with such certainty along the smaller streets and the broad avenues to their destination. If she had asked him how he had become familiar with the city, he would have told her that he had made Paris a stop on his return from the Peninsular Wars.

Whatever Nell expected of Paris, the reality was far different. Peering from the windows of the coach, she learned that at least at first sight it was a city of contrasts. Some of the streets she glimpsed as they passed were squalid, dirty, altogether frightening.

Clearly, there was reason, for although the mobs of the Revolution no longer roamed the streets regularly, there were signs that they had not been forgotten. Shops selling wine or bread, for example—marked by a garland of grape leaves or a loaf painted above the entrance—still had iron gratings ready to draw across the door, if such a measure became desirable.

At the embassy, the welcome given Lady Sanford left nothing to be desired. Lord Westford himself came down the steps to envelop her in a warm embrace. The ambassador was a bluff, red-faced man with graying side whiskers, the clear embodiment of a country squire. It was difficult to imagine how he could represent England in this sophisticated capital until one saw the shrewdness in his eyes. There was much naive heartiness in his manner, but suddenly Nell was quite sure that very little escaped him. In a way, she wished he were not so acute of understanding. Her conscience was far from clear.

Their host swept Phrynie up the steps and into the foyer without a glance at Nell. She looked ruefully after her aunt. How like Phrynie, she thought, surrounded once again with the adulation to which she was accustomed, to forget her niece completely.

Once again Nell realized how much of her own life her aunt had sacrificed to see that she was well launched into society. It seemed even more desirable now to marry at once and release her aunt to her own concerns.

Nell's spirits sank a little lower. Already the excitement engendered by their arrival in the city of enchanting reputation was waning, leaving her lonely. If only Rowland were here to show her around the city, to explain and instruct her! But, with a feeling of disloyalty, she knew that she did not welcome instruction from him. A glimpse came to her of the long arch of the years ahead, including Rowland speaking often with a touch of condescension as he endeavored to educate his lady wife. The prosy prospect did not entirely please.

She stood on the pavement, pondering. Reeves came to her. "Shall I send all the luggage within?" Noticing her start, he added, "For a long stay, I mean, miss. *All* the luggage?"

"Oh, yes, Reeves, thank you. You must think me moonstruck not to understand at once," she continued, impelled to explain where no explanation was needed, or even desired. "We shall wait here for a day. I expect my brother to join us, you know. We are on our way to Vienna to join my fiancé, Lord Foxhall."

Reeves's expression did not alter. "Yes, miss."

She blushed. One did not explain oneself to a mere coachman, especially one so newly employed. She lifted her chin.

"Hand me my jewel case, Reeves, if you please. It is there on the seat, where Mullins left it. I shall carry it myself."

"Very good, miss."

His formerly rough speech, she noted, had given way to the ways of an upper servant. Whitcomb himself could not do better. He handed her the jewel case, his fingers brushing hers as he did so. Quite by accident, she thought, and entered the building, leaving him staring after her with an odd thoughtfulness in his hazel eyes.

Not until she was installed in the delightful guest room assigned to her, next to Lady Sanford's, with a dressing room between that contained a tiny cot for Mullins, did she feel the flush receding from her cheeks. How stupid she was, to let a mere servant distress her in this manner! Reeves was only temporarily in her aunt's service and was quite uncouth, to judge from his touching her. No more to be considered than a crossing sweep to whom one's escort tossed a coin.

However, the thought of traveling across half of Europe with such an unsettling man, who was eminently capable of dealing with cattle as well as dealing out silent rebuke, did not add to her comfort. She was not even sure now she could tell him to his face that his services were no longer required.

Perhaps the ambassador could furnish them with one of his own coachmen and even dismiss Reeves himself on her aunt's behalf. But, were she to ask Lord Westford for this favor, she might have to explain herself and her purposes more fully than she thought wise.

She came face to face with the essential dilemma of the journey. Her own need to join Rowland could not be acknowledged without throwing her reputation to the winds. However, she could not explain their ostensible reason for traveling—the mysterious parcel—without revealing the secret that Mr. Haveney had entrusted to them.

The only possible explanation that could be given to the ambassador, or to anyone inquiring closely, was that they were sent on ahead by her brother Tom, who was following directly on their heels.

She hoped with all her heart that somehow this would become the truth before she fell into disaster.

Dinner was a welcome change from the dreary sustenance provided them in the inns they had recently patronized. Not every French cook, it developed, was a master of cuisine.

Lady Sanford wore one of her newest gowns, a blue Italian silk that made her blue eyes as brilliant as the sapphires around her throat. The skirt was in the newer narrow style, with rows and rows of matching thread lace adorning the hem. She was in her element—a diplomat to charm, a diplomat's wife to put in her place, and a foreign city to explore on the morrow.

Since Lady Sanford was enjoying herself, Nell, not required to fill conversational lapses, could indulge in quiet meditation.

Hardly noticing the sautéed fillets of fowl à la Lucullus set before her, and *fricandeau de veau* to follow, she fell prey to all the doubts she had brushed aside. Now she could not return to England, could not renounce the journey itself without confessing her machinations. Clearly Tom was not following them, as he had promised. They had been five days or more on the road from London. The chariot, even in Reeves's hands, moved far more slowly than a solitary horseman. If Tom had started at all, he should have overtaken them by now.

She longed to be with Rowland, to bask in his warm glances, to foil whatever schemes Miss Freeland concocted to ensnare the handsomest man in England. This impulse—nay, far more than impulse—this *need* to be with her dear Rowland had blinded her to all else. She noted without surprise that the removes had vanished, and before her sat a Savoy cake and coffee creams in cups of almond paste. Mechanically she picked up her fork.

She could not go back. Nor could they wait long for Tom to come. If he did not arrive in two days, she would decide what best to do. There was the overwhelming fact of the parcel just now reposing innocently in her bandbox. She felt tied to the parcel, yoked to its urgent secret requirements.

Five days to Paris—it gave one pause to think. She knew little about the geography of Europe, but she had dark suspicions that the way ahead might be much longer and more wearisome than she had thought. Now, with no bridges behind her, she had no choice.

They would have to travel to Vienna, no matter the consequences!

At length the evening was over and she could follow Phrynie up to bed. She went on to her own room, but her aunt followed her almost at once.

"What a perfectly delightful evening!" she cried. "I quite look forward to our stay in Paris. Even though His Excellency tells me that the court is beyond all things dull, I cannot quite credit him. How can a court be French, and Bourbon, and not be in the highest degree elegant?"

"Will you be presented to the duchesse, the King's niece, do you think?"

"We shall both be presented. I shall insist upon it. Fancy coming to Paris and failing to pay our respects. After all, it was due to England that the King is again on his throne. It is only right that he should have the opportunity to return our years of hospitality to him, you know."

Nell sighed. She was suddenly overcome by the weariness of indecision. It had always been her way to make up her mind at once, whether on the question of one gown or another, or on the weightier problem of refusing Nigel Whitley's offer or of accepting Rowland's.

It was tedious in the extreme to be so unsettled.

"I shall be glad," she said plaintively, "when we are on our way again."

Lady Sanford gave her a shrewd glance. "Never mind, Nell. If the Freeland woman is to subvert Foxhall, she will have done it by now. One more day or two will make no difference!"

When Nell was alone, she sank into a chair by the hearth. It was perfectly clear that Phrynie was looking forward to an extended stay in this city of light. And haste was essential, because of the parcel.

She glanced toward the bed. How tired she was, and how inviting was the high feather bed. Her nightclothes were laid out neatly for her. . . .

She sprang up with a smothered exclamation. She had forgotten the high level of service that the ambassador's lady commanded. The maid had unpacked Nell's bandbox. Had she also unpacked the parcel?

The bandbox was empty, standing on the floor of the wardrobe. The clothing it contained was hanging properly on the rod. And the parcel was nowhere in sight.

Nell's head began to throb. The parcel, stolen!

She looked in the dressing-table drawers. Under the pillow. In the bandbox again. She sank into a chair and put her head in her hands.

Then she remembered. Once again she had moved the parcel, as she had done daily since leaving London. This time, she had changed its location from bandbox to jewel case. Hadn't she?

The case lay on the dressing table, locked, the keys tucked into her reticule in a drawer. Anyone with a larcenous bent and any degree of initiative could have found the keys! She was certainly not trained for this kind of covert activity! With shaking fingers she fitted the key into the lock and opened the jewel case. Her knees grew faint with relief. The parcel was still safe!

She did not know why she expected it to be stolen. Mr. Haveney had spoken of the importance of delivering the parcel swiftly to its appointed recipient. If an object were valuable or important, then it followed that its removal by unauthorized hands was a likely hazard.

All at once she wished she had not been so blithe about overlooking the perils involved. She was in bed before the thought occurred to her—was the parcel precisely where she had put it? Or had it been moved from the right side of the case to the left?

She had moved it so frequently as she transferred it from bandbox to jewel case, and even when she had this evening taken out her amethysts to wear with her lilac crape, that by this time she could not precisely remember its most recent location. But the case was locked and the key was in the place where she had put it. It was only imagination that made her envision a maid poring over the contents of the jewel case and moving the parcel.

After all, even Nell did not know the contents of the parcel. How much less likely that a maid in the embassy might seize upon it with a glad cry and spread the word to her confederates!

Nell closed her eyes. She had quite simply read too many Minerva Press novels and taken them to heart. Life was fortunately not filled with moldy chateaux and evil dukes and dungeons and pilfering maids. Any doubts along those lines were merely the product of several exhausting days of travel.

She slept at once.

Chapter Eleven

At breakfast the next morning Lady Sanford gave evidence of her intention to linger in the capital for some time.

"I am looking forward," she informed Lady Westford, "to seeing dear Paris again. I was but a child—a very young child, of course—when I was here last. But my mother often told me how exciting it was, with such magnificent balls, fabulous gowns, and fantastic jewels. Excursions into the countryside as well. My mother was the Queen's guest at Versailles, you know."

Lady Westford smiled sourly. Where the ambassador was hearty, his lady was acidulous. She was thin and pinched, as though placed in the sun to dry and left too long. Having been born into a county family of some standing and gentility, she was stunned when she found herself moving into the upper reaches of the diplomatic service. Convinced that the task set for her was beyond her grasp, she took refuge in complaint, as though by showing herself superior to her surroundings, she would not be expected to deal effectively with them.

She was not, therefore, loath to disappoint Lady Sanford's hopes. "I fear you will find it sadly altered, as my dear husband told you, I believe, last evening? The King is so obese that he can barely manage affairs of state and leaves all the events at court in the hands of his niece the Princesse. A sad affair, that. I do hope I know my duty, and I have offered many times to assist Her Highness in any way she wishes." Lady Westford's thin lips tightened in unpleasant memory. "But I shall not trouble her again."

Lady Sanford murmured, "What a pity."

"However, since you wish it, I have ordered the carriage,

77

and we will drive out. I do not believe the Princess is receiving, but we shall at least see the public rooms in the palace."

As soon as Nell had a moment alone with her aunt, she whispered fiercely, "Aunt, you know we must not linger here. We must be on our way at once."

Lady Sanford was not pleased. "My dear child, I cannot understand you. I understood that we were to wait here for your brother. Did you not tell me that Tom was following at once?"

Nell, caught in a snare of her own devising, agreed. "But just the same, whatever progress we make now is that much less to be made after he overtakes us."

"I cannot fault your logic, Nell. Although in truth, I am not sure that logic plays any part whatever in your thinking. But we shall stay here for a bit. I have not suffered this long journey only to go on without seeing Paris. Now change your gown. We must not keep our hostess waiting."

Nell lifted her hands helplessly. She hoped that Tom would be following hard on their tracks at this very moment. But she could not escape a strong urge to move on. Logic told her that Phrynie had the right of it. To wait here in comfort for Tom was quite the best thing to do.

Nevertheless she knew she would not be easy until they were on their way again. It was the burden of the parcel that moved her, she told herself, and not the quite impossible vision of Penelope Freeland arm in arm with Rowland Fiennes. She had no doubts of Rowland's constancy.

The three ladies, plus coachman, groom, and two footmen up at the back, set out from the embassy on a morning's drive about the civilized city. Lady Westford proved to be an endless wellspring of information, if a somewhat muddied one.

"We were here, you know, even before Louis was restored. In April, there was a great deal for the ambassador to do. Talleyrand took it upon himself to negotiate with the Emperor—although I must not call him that now. My husband would be most displeased. He has instructed me, you know, not even to mention the name of the usurper."

Phrynie made an appropriate comment and added, "But I do not recognize some of these scenes. I suppose that arch there—"

"That is the Place de la Concorde," Lady Westford interposed. She had an unfortunate habit of not listening carefully. Instead she waited, so Nell surmised, until the other's voice halted, perhaps to take breath, and then went smoothly on with her own conversation. "That is where Madame la Guillotine stood. I have heard that the tumbrils—those carts filled with straw and prisoners, you know—lined up every day from the Bastille to this place." She shivered. "But that is over, of course, and there will never be another such atrocity. Fortunately, civilization has conquered at last."

Soon Lady Westford's thin voice continued. "I count my attendance at the entry of His Majesty into Paris as one of the high points of my life in the diplomatic service. His snowy hair, his kindly smile, riding down the boulevard to his palace, he looked quite like a father returning home to his wayward children."

"Very touching," said Lady Sanford, her expression without guile. "The King must be most gratified to regain his throne."

"As well he should be," the ambassador's wife said with some acerbity. "Not by his own efforts, I may tell you. If it hadn't been for the English, he would still be sitting in that little house on the outskirts of London."

Nell could not gaze her fill. She caught sight of one small fountain, and before she could do more than glimpse its perfection, they had passed and another object demanded her attention.

"The gardens must be beautiful in season," she suggested. The space before the Tuileries, toward which they were now progressing, was broad and treeless. The pavement before the palace was wide, and even in the chilly morning air people were already strolling, much at their ease.

Beyond the promenade could be seen walkways leading in intricate design into each other, separated by geometric figures of gray, frosted lawns and darker, turned earth.

"It is hard to believe," said Lady Westford, "that the French are so callous. I told you that the King's niece, Princess Marie-Thérèse, might not be receiving. It's been more than twenty years since she was last in Paris, but the French are so cruel. I was told that her coachman, when she entered the capital for the first time, drove her directly over the spot where her parents were killed! She could not speak for weeping." She paused to consider the Princess's plight. "I am told she weeps much."

Due to Lady Westford's prestige and a certain amount of strong persuasion, they were admitted to the public rooms of the palace. The carpets, to Nell's surprise, appeared worn and faded. Even the red velvet draperies hung in dispirited folds.

The Bourbon lilies were strewn on the curtains and over the carpet like fallen leaves. Her foot caught at the edge of one fleur-de-lis, and she looked down. The edge of the woven medallion curled up where she had inadvertently torn loose the threads that had attached it to the floor. Underneath the lily, woven into the carpet itself, was revealed the golden Napoleonic bee. The tacked-down lily was indicative of the haste with which the Bourbons reclaimed their throne, but perhaps it was also a symbol of the transitoriness of their reign. It would be the work of only hours, not days, to remove the lilies if the impossible proved possible and Napoleon appeared again at the palace door.

The Princess was indeed not receiving. An aide whispered in Lady Westford's ear that the lady and her nonentity of a husband, her cousin the Duc d'Angoulême, had quarreled bitterly the night before, and Marie-Thérèse did not wish to be seen with tear-swollen eyes.

So much for viewing royalty, thought Nell, basely relieved by the Princess's domestic difficulties. Now at least tomorrow we can be on our way.

But tomorrow arrived and still Lady Sanford made no move in the direction of resuming their journey. When traveling on was suggested, in fact, Lady Sanford said simply, "I see no need to hurry away. And in truth, I see more than one reason to stay. Are we not to wait for Tom to arrive?" She made a moue. "Not that I particularly enjoy our quarters here. I should think that our embassy ought not to be quite so shabby."

"Aunt, they are only newly in possession," Nell pointed out. "There will be improvements."

"If that woman has them in hand, then I am sure I shall take a dislike to them."

"You have diverted me. Aunt, we really cannot delay longer."

"Why must we? You are truly becoming tiresome on the subject. Perhaps you can inform me, my dear Elinor, why we must hare off into the wilds when we can wait for your brother here in some degree of comfort."

How dreadful, thought Nell. When Phrynie chose to call her niece by her full name, she was seriously displeased with her. It would in all likelihood tax Nell's persuasive powers to coax her back into a reasonable frame of mind.

"But, Aunt, you know we cannot remain as guests of the embassy forever?"

"I am sure we have not yet worn out our welcome. I certainly am not so ill bred as to overstay when we are not wanted." Lady Sanford's eyes narrowed. "I cannot avoid thinking that I have not been placed *au courant* with affairs. There seems to be a lively undercurrent to this journey. Elinor Aspinall, are you bamming me?"

Nell faltered. "B-bamming? Of course not."

"Kindly do not attempt further to deceive me. Did your nurse tell you many fairy tales? I know mine did, and you would be quite surprised were I to tell you how often they prove illuminating."

"Fairy tales?"

"One of my favorites was the tale of the little girl who told lies. Do you recall that one? It developed that every untrue word she spoke turned into a toad. How extraordinarily exciting it was, at my age then, to envision toads leaping about the room. I fear the moral was lost on me, for I do recall telling lies deliberately, but I never spat out any toads. A grave disappointment."

"Aunt," cried Nell, exasperated. "What do toads have to do with anything at all?"

"Why, child, when you stammer in that fashion, I know you are—I should not quite like to say *lying*—but I sense a certain evasion of the truth. Now then, Nell, I may as well tell you that I shall not move another step on the road until you tell me in what havey-cavey business you have involved me?"

Lady Sanford sat in one of the velvet chairs beside the hearth and imperiously pointed to the other. Nell sat opposite, as she was bid. She made one more attempt, without hope, to divert Phrynie.

"How can you tolerate Lady Westford any longer? And not a ball in sight to relieve the tedium. Everyone of importance has already gone to Vienna, you know."

Lady Sanford was thoughtful. "I agree," she said finally, "but the prospect of entertainment in Vienna does not cancel the opportunity for you to tell me—and tell me *now*, Nell—exactly what our situation is. Is this all a scheme to join Foxhall? If so, I warn you, I shall be seriously grieved with you."

"No, Aunt. I may have started out—indeed I did—with the intention simply of being with him, for in truth I am desolate without him. But there's more to it now."

Her aunt's gaze grew even sterner. "I think you must agree, Nell, that it is time for a complete confession. It may do little for your conscience, but I should like to know exactly what to expect."

Nell resigned herself to the inevitable.

"It began with Mr. Haveney and his parcel. The one he wished Tom to deliver to Vienna. From what I could make out, Tom has done this kind of thing before, though goodness knows he never made much of it, and I confess it is most unlikely that anyone with any sense would entrust anything to him, as dear as he is to me."

Phrynie made a small gesture as though to interrupt but thought better of it.

"But Tom wrote that he would come to London to meet Mr. Haveney and pick up the parcel. And I made sure that if Tom were presented with us, the chariot packed and all made ready to travel, he could not refuse you, dear Aunt."

"Flattery!" pronounced Lady Sanford, not pleased in spite of herself. "However, since Tom did not arrive to view us in such a state, I must assume there is more to the tale."

"Well, you see, Aunt, Tom did say he would come right away—as soon as he could walk."

"Walk!"

"Charlie Puckett sold him a hunter—Oh, what does that matter? Tom can't walk for a little, but he is coming as soon as his knee is better."

"And when will that be?"

"I don't know."

"Well, then, perhaps the omniscient Lady Westford can find us lodgings in Paris, and we will send word—Nell, you are still blue-deviled. I am persuaded I have not yet heard all."

There was no way out, and in truth Nell was seized with a longing to unburden herself. Not in the ordinary way untruthful, the carrying on of an involved web of deceit had taken its toll on her.

"The parcel that Tom is to bring, when he overtakes us—"

"The parcel that provides our *raison d'être* for this entirely questionable journey?"

"The same parcel. Well, to put it without frills, Tom will not be picking it up from Mr. Haveney."

"I am not sure I wish to know the explanation for that odd statement."

"We ourselves have the parcel."

Phrynie stared, unbelieving. "Elinor, you have misappropriated government business? I cannot believe it."

"Not exactly misappropriated," said Nell scrupulously. "But the messenger from Mr. Haveney did expect me to put it at once into Tom's hands. As I would do, of course—if he were here."

Nell had expected, at the least, that the ceiling would fall on her head. Alternatively, she would be given orders to return to London at once and return the parcel to its rightful hands.

Neither eventuality happened. Instead, Lady Sanford laid her head back on the chair cushion and laughed. When she was genuinely amused, as appeared to be the case now, her laugh was like a cascade of silver bells, very pleasant to hear, especially just now.

"I suppose, Nell, you bewitched the messenger into forgetting even his head?"

"I did not precisely tell him an untruth," Nell said primly.

"I wonder whether you stammered."

Nell grinned reluctantly. "At least there were no toads on the pavement."

"Well, my dear, I am glad you told me everything. I suppose you have no more surprises for me? Good. I assume Tom will appear in due course, and in the meantime we must get the parcel to its destination. I did not think to launch out on a new career at my time of life, but perhaps it will be interesting after all. We shall leave early in the morning."

Nell sprang to her feet and hugged her aunt. "How wonderful you are! I wish I had told you from the beginning."

"No, you don't. For we would, in that case, still be in London."

"I'll send Mullins to you, shall I, to begin packing? I shall hope that 'early' does not mean afternoon?"

"*I* shall hope," retorted Lady Sanford with immense dignity, "that by noon tomorrow I shall have eaten my last meal to the accompaniment of unasked-for, and indeed highly unattractive, education at the hands of the ambassador's wife."

Chapter Twelve

So far, thought Nell, so good.

She had been required to give up the secret of her deception, but she had won her aunt's agreement to leave Paris. The next step was one she approached with misgivings but with determination.

She had planned to discharge Reeves in Paris and hire another coachman. She felt no compunction about leaving the man on his own, for he had only to return to Calais. She would of course pay his fare as well as his wages. She would not then be required to travel to Vienna in the company of an elderly man who knew all too well how to register his disapproval.

She did not reflect on the reasons why she felt so sharply the disapproval of a man she scarcely knew. After all, Stuston had not been blind to her faults, nor had Whitcomb. Nor had either been in the least backward about letting her know his opinion.

Halfway down the stairs to the foyer of the embassy, she paused. Suppose she could not find another coachman on such short notice? She could not properly ask the ambassador to provide them with one of his own staff. The sudden recollection of an adage of her governess, a long time ago, came to her. "A bird in the hand, my dear, is worth two in the bush. That means, of course—" Nell forgot now the tedious explanation of that moral.

But the fact was true. Better, perhaps, the evil she knew than one she did not know.

She realized all at once that she had not informed the coachman of their intention to leave in the morning. She set out to find him. She ran him to earth in the servants' dining hall. She stood in the doorway watching him, unable to believe what she saw. This was a different Reeves. She had thought him on the far side of middle age, gruff and soured, without humor. This man looked to be in his early thirties, no more. He was laughing, and clearly something he had just said had put the entire staff into an uproar. "And then—" he was about to continue.

One by one the servants caught sight of the elegant Miss Aspinall in the doorway, and one by one they fell silent. At length, alerted by the alteration in his audience, Reeves turned and saw her. The change in his expression would have been ludicrous, she thought, had it not been somewhat unsettling. She had been mistaken in him. She felt he had played her for a fool.

"Reeves," she said, frost edging her light voice, "I should like a word."

He nodded briefly and rose from the hard wooden chair. By the time he followed her down the corridor to a small room which was probably reserved for the housekeeper, he had suffered a sea change. He stood before her now, slightly bent, head somewhat bowed in an attitude of humility. She must have been mistaken—this man appeared to be in his fifties. It must have been a trick of the light, back there in the dining hall.

"Reeves," she said firmly, "I hope you can assure me that you will continue in your position with my aunt until we arrive in Vienna?"

He nodded. "I giv my word back yonder in Calais," he said, "and the word of a Reeves is aye as good as the word of a—" He wavered. She was sure he was about to deliver himself of an indiscretion. The light in her eyes warned him, and he finished lamely, "The word of any gentleman."

"Very well, Reeves. Then since you know my reason for going to Vienna—my only reason," she repeated carefully, "to be reunited with my betrothed, then you will understand it is of importance to me to be on our way. Lady Sanford will be ready to leave in the morning. Early."

"Not meaning no disrespect, miss, be ye sure?"

Fully aware that he was recalling departures from Calais and other inns, she said briskly, "Yes, Reeves. Leave it to me." Then, completely on a tangent, she asked, "What part of England do you come from, Reeves?"

He was not prepared for that question, and for a fleeting moment there was an expression of something very like dismay in his eyes. His eyes, she thought inconsequentially, were a remarkable color, like water over brownish-red stones in the bottom of a running brook.

"My grandsire came from—Derby," he told her, and somehow she was convinced he did not tell the truth.

"It's no matter," she said earnestly, "except that I find it hard to place your speech."

"Sorry, miss," he said with a return to the sullen remoteness he had exhibited for the most part since their first meeting. "I'll be ready in the morning. Early."

He saluted, rough forefinger to what he must think was his forelock, and left her. She was vaguely disappointed. She could not think why.

Lady Sanford's party trundled away from the embassy in good time that morning. When Lady Sanford made up her mind that Paris was not the glittering, glamorous round of gaiety that she had expected, she was quite willing to see that her duty lay with the delivery of the mysterious parcel.

To give her credit, she would likely have understood the importance of the parcel, even if Paris streets had rung with music and song, but she would have left the city much more reluctantly.

"I cannot fathom the cause of such gross dullness!" she exclaimed before they were out of sight of the embassy.

"Perhaps the Princess still feels the loss of her parents," suggested Nell. "It cannot be easily forgotten when one's entire family has been executed in such a spectacular way."

"I do not mean the Princess," corrected Lady Sanford. "With that very dull husband of hers—Angoulême, a sniveling weakling, from what Lord Westford says—how could she help but be wretched? I doubt I could summon up sufficient presence even to be civil in such an instance."

Nell smiled. "I cannot imagine you marrying him in the first place."

"I mean the ambassador's wife. One might certainly expect to find some grace in the wife of an ambassador to France, after all. I wonder that Lord Chawton isn't given the post."

"Is that possible?"

"Of course. I should think that Penelope would make her father an excellent hostess."

Conversation languished. Nell was cast down by the reminder that Penelope Freeland was in a good position to influence Rowland. She wished he had not been quite so correct in his offer—or rather his failure to offer. While he had made sufficient promises to hold Nell in thrall, yet the fact was that the betrothal was not yet *official*.

But it would not do for Nell to be dreary all the days ahead over Rowland. She smiled now at her aunt. "By the way, that is a very fetching outfit you are wearing. Have I seen it before?"

"Of course. Henriette made it for me. I shall be glad when this mad infatuation for green fades away. One could have a wardrobe entirely of Pomona-green, almond-green, dark green, water-green, sage-green. One looks like a cucumber when one is à la mode."

"You look well in green, Aunt."

"At least better than the Duchess of Netwick! That woman!" Lady Sanford gave a refined snort of contempt. "I vow she sees the world through green—the green of that vulgar emerald."

"Shall we see her in Vienna, do you think?"

"I had heard that she intends to spend the winter there. I wonder if Providence could find a way to immure her in a snowbound pass in the Alps?"

"No matter," said Nell, "for you know no one will even look her way if you are there."

"Nell, you are a dear child."

"Besides, we've made good progress since we left Paris. We may easily arrive in Vienna before the duchess."

"I have the oddest feeling, Nell, that I have lost my grasp on this expedition. My coachman is back in that dreadful town on the coast with one of my footmen to keep him company. My new coachman is a man I do not entirely trust, and I do not have a clear view of the way we are to go on."

Flushing slightly, Nell protested. "But you have given your consent to all that has been done!"

"Yes, but I should like to interview my coachman." She gave a light laugh. "An entirely futile undertaking, for of course I could not dismiss him in the middle of a field in a foreign country. Best let it go. Then perhaps you can inform me? Are we going to travel through the mountains?"

"Reeves says not."

"Then let us pray for a heavy snow just ahead of the duchess." There had been an odd note in Nell's voice when she spoke the coachman's name that caused her aunt to glance sharply at her. "Reeves, then, is guiding us as well as driving?"

"He says," Nell told her reluctantly, "that he knows the way to avoid the mountains. He says this is the road the Crusaders took, centuries ago. On their way to Jerusalem, you know."

"I am not entirely ignorant," Phrynie pointed out. "I have heard of the Crusaders. What I do not understand, quite, is how an untutored coachman is so well informed, both on the roads and in obscure historical events."

Nell felt her cheeks warm. "He does seem to be somewhat unusual."

Phrynie all but commented, "And you seem to have spent an unusual amount of time with him since we left Calais." But she kept silent.

Phrynie was reasonably content with her lot at this time. She adored traveling and was always eager to gain what amusement she could from wherever she was placed. She was slightly disturbed over the nonappearance of her nephew, but she accepted the fact that the parcel, whatever it was, must get to Vienna, since Nell had undertaken the task. An obligation once incurred must be carried out. She hoped that her own credit—coupled with a few judicious alterations of plain truth, and a bold facing down of the malicious Duchess of Netwick—would serve to make their arrival in Vienna *tout à fait convenable*.

Phrynie had been prepared to give up her intense longing to be at the scene of the congress in Vienna, for there was bound to be a plethora of parties, balls, and enormous fun in London. Now, thanks to a discreet lack of curiosity in London as to Nell's motives, she was well on her way.

"I must confess," said Phrynie after a long silence, "that I am delighted to leave Paris behind. Even the unknown trials ahead will be more amusing than the embassy."

Idly Nell inquired, "Did you ask whether your friend Bolesley was in town?"

"Yes," said Phrynie stiffly, "he was, and his wife as well. But that, no matter what you think, is not the reason I was happy to leave. It was that vinegar-faced Westford woman!"

Nell did not suspect the real moving force behind her aunt's compliance with her urgent need to travel on. Phrynie was a woman who knew her duty, and at present the safe delivery of the parcel was uppermost in her thoughts. However, Phrynie, while comfort loving as a rule, welcomed the unexpected as much as her niece did. Phrynie was gratified now to feel that youth and adventure had not passed beyond her reach.

Now she glanced at Nell. When she caught her niece's eye, she grinned mischievously. There was no need for words to pass between them. They understood each other.

By this time, the equipage had trundled out of Paris and was, so Nell told her, on the road toward Champagne.

"Champagne," Phrynie mused. "What do you remember about this region? A town called Epernay, of course, but also—Haut something."

Nell said, "We'll ask Reeves when we halt to rest the horses."

"I am sure," said Phrynie drily, "he will know. He seems, does he not, to be omniscient?"

"Not at all," said Nell stiffly. "I did not say he would know, Aunt. I simply said we will ask him."

Phrynie looked at her thoughtfully, but said nothing. She did promise herself, however, to keep a watchful eye on her niece. She laid her head back against the small satin pillows that Mullins had placed for her comfort and closed her eyes. No need to worry, she told herself before she slipped into a doze. Nell is head over heels in love with Foxhall.

Nell had not shared with her aunt certain unsettling remarks that Reeves had made. She had spoken to him before their departure to make sure that he knew the route they were to take. She had found him in the paved courtyard of the embassy, making sure that the four horses were properly harnessed.

The conversation was now as clear in her mind as at the moment it took place.

"Reeves?"

"Yes, miss."

"Is all in readiness for departure?"

"Yes, miss."

She looked at the baggage-laden coach, frowning. It seemed a frail vehicle to carry them all such a long way. She had no clear understanding of the magnitude of the journey ahead, but she was beginning to suspect that it would prove longer and more trying than she knew. Her doubts must have been reflected in her expression.

Reeves, in a voice different from his usual mixture of gruffness and upper-servant remoteness, said, "Best take it a day at a time. We'll get through, don't fret."

She managed a brave smile. "Thank you, Reeves." With a rush, she said, "I truly do not know how we would have gone on without you."

"Coachman's accident," he said, "was my good fortune."

He held her eyes with his steady gaze. She felt his confidence flowing to her, and she was suddenly short of breath. She turned away first. "Do you know the road we should take?"

"Yes, miss."

Curiosity inspired her to ask, "How do you know, Reeves? Surely you have not traveled in France at all? You *are* English, are you not?"

"Yes, miss."

She needed to break down that barrier that he erected between them, quite properly. But she was never one to deny her own impulses. "Then I should like to make sure," she said coolly, "that we may safely entrust ourselves to your guidance."

He looked straight at her, and the spark in his hazel eyes was far from formal. The light was gone in an instant, and she believed she must have imagined it. When he spoke, he was once again the perfect servant. "I have made inquiries, miss. I am informed that it is unsafe to travel through the mountains at this time of year, particularly with such a small party."

"Unsafe? Then, how—"

"We shall travel by the road that the old armies took to the Holy Land. Mebbe take longer, but we'll get there." After a moment, he added as an afterthought, "With your permission, miss."

There was nothing for her to do but to give it. He had taken thought on their best route, and she had not. "Do as you think best, Reeves," she told him.

Her cheeks burned even yet as she remembered that curious moment when their eyes locked, a moment of what might be called, for want of a better word, friendliness.

She had intended at that time to consult her aunt, for after all the entire equipage and staff belonged to Lady Sanford. But the ambassador was bidding her farewell, and there was no time for consultation. Lord Westford was, in his pontifical way, sending them out into the perils of the road.

"For you must know there is still much anti-English sentiment in the countryside," he told them. "That pipsqueak Emperor has stirred them all up for years to come."

"But surely nobody will harm us," said Lady Sanford airily. "After all, we can pay our way, and the landlady at the Blue Dolphin was most kind."

"Besides," added Nell, pointing out an obvious fact, "the Emperor has been exiled."

"But all his friends," said the ambassador, "have not."

Nell remembered her fears, the first night in the embassy, that someone had stolen the parcel. She was prepared to take on the possible dangers attendant upon the possession of the parcel. But how futile it would be to come to a particularly nasty end simply because she was English.

But Reeves had said they would get through, and his confidence wrapped her like a warm blanket.

These thoughts occupied Nell for some time. At length, the coach slowed and came to a stop at the side of the road. Full of the fears that the ambassador had instilled in her, she leaned out of the window and called to the coachman. "What is the trouble?"

"No trouble, miss," said Potter, dropping off the box to speak to the ladies. "Coachman says time to rest the horses. Not traveling post, you know." Suddenly aware of his presumption, he added quickly, with a jerk of his head toward the front of the coach, "*He* says, miss."

"I see." Visited by a wish to uncramp her legs, she opened the door and stepped down to the road. She shivered in the sudden chill after the warmth of the coach interior and drew her furs close. Reeves was at the horses' heads and she joined him. "Reeves, is all in good order?"

"Yes, miss."

Was that all the man could say? she thought in sudden pique. She decided she would force him to answer more fully. It was not that she wished to hear his voice, she told herself firmly, even though it was unusually deep and musical. "My aunt wishes to know," she said, "whether a town called Haut something is on this road. I told her I expected that you would know."

"Yes, miss."

When he did not continue, she prodded him. "Well, Reeves, do you know?"

"Yes, miss."

She glanced sharply at him. Could it be that he was laughing at her? She blamed herself for that moment in the yard of the embassy when she had not, as would have been proper, put him in his place. It had been most satisfactory, then, to feel that she had an ally on whom she could lean in a figurative way. But he clearly believed that he had been given leave to further intimacy. She opened her lips to give him a thorough set-down, but instead, to her astonishment, she heard strong amusement in her own voice as she said, "Then, pray tell me, Reeves, if it is not too much trouble?"

He erected the barrier again. "Yes, miss, the town is called Hautvillers, and it is beyond Epernay on the road we are traveling. Is that all, miss?"

"No, Reeves," she said, allowing an edge to appear in her voice. "How far is the town—Hautvillers?—from here?"

"We may reach it by nightfall, miss."

"And," pursued Nell, "is there an inn there?"

"Yes, miss. At least, I am informed there is one nearby."

Nell's temper was not improved by her conversation with him, however enlightening. "And, Reeves, pray tell me, is it an inn suitable for my aunt's patronage?"

"So I am told, miss."

In spite of his wooden demeanor, she was as convinced of his inner amusement as though he lay on the ground before her, rolling in hilarious guffaws. But there was nothing overt in his manner that she could disapprove. Besides, the fact was clear—they were dependent on Reeves. Where in this bleak November countryside could they find another coachman?

She hesitated, indecisive, wondering just how she could properly end this too-prolonged conversation. Suddenly, as though losing interest in his joke, he said, "I did make inquiries at the embassy, miss."

Gratefully accepting the small olive twig, she said, "Of course, Reeves. I understand." She did not in the least understand, but it was of no account, after all, how Reeves got his information. Nor why he chose to laugh at her. He was no ordinary coachman.

The man was impudent, no question about it. But perhaps he had earned the right to be independent—he had been, apparently, a sailor at one time, and a fisherman, judging from his appearance at Calais. She wondered then whether he had sailed with the fiercely provincial Norman fishermen. If he had, it would explain his fluency in French, including a certain low jargon that she had seen commanding respect from ostlers from Calais to Paris.

It was likely, too, that he had seen service in the peninsular armies, as had many thousands of Englishmen. If he were accustomed to violence, then, it could only redound to their benefit. As he had said, they were a small party indeed.

They were soon under way again. The road out of Paris had been bleak and uninteresting. Now the character of the landscape altered. The road itself was well marked, consisting of great frozen ruts made in all likelihood by the broad wooden wheels of farm wagons bringing in the *vendange* from the wine country to market in Paris.

The road ahead now stretched straight and broad into the horizon. Thin trees had been planted on both sides of the track, providing in some future time a pleasant green wall enclosing the road. Farmland stretched away on both sides of the road, and the land here seemed more prosperous than that nearer the capital.

The next time they stopped to rest the cattle, Nell was determined to avoid the coachman. She walked briskly back in the direction they had come until the coach was a small object in the distance, a dark splotch on the pale frosted ruts.

She breathed deeply of the chilly air, feeling the cold sharp in her lungs. She must make sure she had sufficient exercise on the journey, for the stuffiness of the coach interior had brought on a headache. She wandered slowly a little farther away from the coach.

She did not hear Reeves approaching. When he spoke, she quivered. "You startled me!" One might suspect, she thought crossly, that he was practicing to be a successful footpad.

"I'm sorry, miss. I came to warn you—best not to stroll too far alone. It is not safe."

She looked around her. The scene was peaceful, bucolic, uninhabited by pedestrians. The only living objects she could see were a small herd of black and white cows, beset by curiosity as to the strange two-legged creatures on the road.

"They do not seem unduly belligerent."

He seemed about to throw up his hands in exasperation. He said forcefully, "Beats me how a lady dare not walk down Oxford Street in broad day without a maid and a footman to protect her and then believes that all the rest of the world is filled with kindness!"

She was startled. "Reeves, who are you?"

"Lady Sanford's coachman, miss. John Reeves by name."

Dissatisfied, but not knowing just how to wrest the truth from him, she turned again to the bovine spectators. "I cannot think they are in the least ferocious. Indeed, I understand them, I believe, better than you do. For you must know that I am accustomed to being around the stock on our own farms."

"No doubt." As an afterthought, he added, "Miss."

He made to turn away, but she was reluctant to let him go. Nodding her head toward the cows in question, she asked, "Do you truly think they would attack me?"

"Not them," said Reeves. "But you know this is war's old invasion route. The way the armies have always come to Paris."

Perversely, scornfully, Nell said, "I don't see any armies."

"Where armies go, stragglers remain behind. No armies now, perhaps, but the inhabitants are not likely to mind a robbery—or worse."

Without further protest, she turned and walked quickly back, Reeves beside her, to the coach and mounted into it. She realized how foolish she and her aunt were, driving through an alien landscape as though they were simply tooling up from London to Essex carrying jewels and fine gowns, as well as their own vulnerable persons.

Not until they were under way again did she remember—all traces of subservience on the part of Reeves had vanished, at least for the moment. She withdrew into puzzled thought. Reeves was not what he seemed. But if he were not, why did he choose to take employment as Lady Sanford's coachman? There was no way, she decided, that he could know about the precious parcel. At least . . .

No, she reflected, she had covered her tracks carefully. Reeves could not know about Mr. Haveney's visit, for he was in France at the time, unemployed on the waterfront at Calais where she had found him.

But all the same, she would see to it that night that she removed the parcel from her jewel case and found a safer place to hide it.

Chapter Thirteen

They came in early afternoon to a town called—so Reeves informed them—Dormans. Here the road crossed a bridge over the Marne River to the north bank, and for a while the traveling was less difficult.

Epernay was far behind them, and they had reached a point beyond Cumières when they halted again to rest the horses. On this occasion Lady Sanford descended from the coach as well as Nell, and in spite of the brisk wind gusting up the slope from the river valley below marched ahead to speak to Reeves.

"Reeves, where are we?

"I dunno what your ladyship means."

"Perhaps I can be more explicit. I am assuming you know the names of the villages, if that is what they are called, through which we have passed?"

"Yes, my lady. If you were wishing to know, that last 'un was called Cumières."

"And the next one?"

"Hautvillers."

"Your French accent is excessively good, Reeves. You have lived in France, I surmise?"

"No, my lady. Only passed through, as you might say."

"Well, you have done well then. I vow you speak as well as though you had been tutored in it since your childhood."

He said only, "Your ladyship is kind. Was you wishing to stop for the night?"

"Yes, Reeves, I should. I do not know precisely our direction, but I am told the château is near Hautvillers."

"There is an inn farther on at Champillon, called the

Royal Champagne, my lady. Very comfortable, I am informed."

"However, Reeves, I wish to halt at the Château Pernoud, near Hautvillers. Pray secure directions to the château when we near the town."

An odd expression flitted across the coachman's rough features. For a moment, he seemed ready to object to Lady Sanford's plan, but instead he touched his hat and went to his horses.

Nell noticed without favor that there was no amusement in the man when he addressed Lady Sanford. He apparently found all the entertainment he needed in Nell. She resented his impertinence more than she could ever say. She would find a way to put him in his place, indeed she would!

The Château Pernoud, where they arrived in the late afternoon, stood, as suited its age, on a defensible promontory overlooking the valley of the Marne. The coach lumbered down a winding drive through a heavy forest lying between the road and the gaunt arrangement of old stone that was the castle.

Nell gazed at the crenellated turrets, the slits of windows wide enough for a flaming arrow to be shot from the interior while protecting the castle defenders, the ivy-blanketed walls of gray rock.

"Just like *The Mysteries of Udolpho*," she breathed. "I wonder whether Mrs. Radcliffe has seen this place?"

"More like *Romance of the Forest*, it seems to me," said her aunt. "You won't remember that one, but it was popular when I was a girl."

"How do you know about this place?" marveled Nell.

"Well," said Phrynie, complacently, "I have never seen it, of course. But I was invited once, long ago, by the Comte de Pernoud, who I sincerely trust still owns it."

"You know the count?"

"He visited in England at one time. After the Revolution, of course, when aristocratic *émigrés* swarmed across the Channel. My dear husband was much taken with him and insisted that he spend a month with us at Sanford Hall. Now, my dear, you are speculating—I can see suspicion springing to life in your eyes—and I must inform you that you are quite incorrect. I should never have dishonored my husband, you know."

"Of course not."

"The count was most understanding when I met him later in London, after I was widowed. I was still in half mourning then."

Their acquaintance might have flourished long ago, but the count's memory was green as springtime. Professing himself delighted at the advent of unexpected guests, he proclaimed himself enchanted beyond measure at the sight of his old acquaintance, Lady Sanford.

"Acquaintance, Count?" asked Phrynie in a gentle voice.

"Dear lady," responded her host, "a bit more than acquaintance."

Belatedly Lady Sanford remembered the pristine presence of her niece. "Friend, let us say," she said firmly.

When Nell could examine the château more at her leisure, she could see that the entrance tower was as forbidding in aspect as the Tower of London. But the wings, even though of the same gray stone, added on either side spoke more of Louis XIV than they did of Rollo the Viking. The windows of the east wing were of the casement variety, opening pleasantly to the outside in clement weather. The west wing, as Nell faced the entrance, was older, judging from its more austere facade.

The suite upstairs that was put at their disposal was impeccable if, thought Nell ungratefully, you like ancient towers and antique furnishings. There was, however, a fine Chinese rug on the floor and a bright fire in the grate, evidence of excellently trained servants. She had instructed Reeves to hold the baggage, all but the small jewel cases and bandboxes, with the carriage.

"Yes, miss," he had said. Something in his manner held her. "You are not entirely happy that we are staying here, are you?"

"It's not for me to say, miss, but it looks chancy to me. The château, if that's what it's called, looks like it might have a dungeon underground."

She turned to look thoughtfully at the stone building. "I wouldn't be greatly surprised. But it's only for tonight, Reeves, and surely not much can happen in a few hours."

"If you need me, miss, I think they put us over beyond the cobbled yard. Where the stable is. I'll keep my peepers open on the horses, too."

"Peepers? Oh, a night watch? Why ever for? The count is a friend of aunt's."

"Aye," said Reeves, "but I should judge his servants are not?"

"You are right," she conceded handsomely, "as always."

Reeves's expression turned wooden. "Yes, miss."

Nell dressed in the lilac crape that she had worn to dinner in the embassy. She had packed other gowns, in anticipation of events to be attended in Vienna, but they were all in the baggage now watched over by Reeves. He had not intended to alarm her, she was sure, but all the same she felt a frisson of uneasiness as she draped a shawl of deep lavender trimmed with silver thread lace around her shoulders.

She followed her aunt down the winding stairway, not hopeful about the quality of dinner. "Probably a haunch of venison," she suggested to her aunt, "smoked on a spit in that great hearth in the foyer."

"I do not doubt," Phrynie pointed out, "that there is sufficient game in these woods to provide for an army of knights. One can only be thankful that one lives in the modern day, Nell, for I cannot conceive that a roomful of metal-clad gentlemen would be in the least restful."

"My idea of that time, on the contrary, is one of windows open to the balmy breeze, while gentlemen strum their lutes and sing plaintive love songs."

Phrynie gazed at her, enthralled. "In their *armor*?"

"Truly I think not, Aunt. Besides, this air is far from temperate. Perhaps I am thinking of the south of France."

Phrynie's education had not been broad. Because Nell had shared her brother's tutors, she was better informed than the ordinary young lady of breeding. Now Phrynie brushed the troubadours aside with an airy gesture. "How dull to listen to love songs all the day long. But as long as the champagne is adequate, I believe we shall survive our one night here."

"Isn't this the region where that wine comes from?"

"Oh, yes. But so often one cannot count on logic in these matters. The shoemaker's children, you know."

Nell was pleased to see that the château was not ancient in its entirety. As she had guessed, the wings had been added at some time in the past century in a successful attempt to improve the Pernoud style of living. Since the ancient rock structure was impervious not only to siege but also to alterations, the additions were attached to the original fortresstower at right angles. The original castle looked out over the valley, as Nell had seen. The wings formed two sides of a small cobbled court. At a short distance the stables and other domestic offices formed the other two sides of the square.

The present count clearly preferred the modern rooms. One door cut in the two-foot thick walls of the round tower stood ajar. Beyond it could be seen a library of the kind frequently found in gentlemen's houses in England, containing a massive table, fitted in all likelihood with several shallow drawers, and rows of leather-bound books on shelves. A flickering light indicated that a fire burned in the grate.

Another door on the same foyer wall led into a spacious salon, with windows providing another view of the river valley. This room was illuminated by wax candles in plentiful supply. There were chairs with elegantly curved legs, a pair of settees that might well have been at home in Marie Antoinette's salon at Le Petite Trianon. The unkind thought came to Nell that perhaps these were the identical items of furniture that the lamented queen had possessed. Nell believed she had heard that many of the luxurious appointments of the royal family had vanished. If so, why not to this out-of-the-way place?

The salon in Château Pernoud stretched the entire length of this wing, judging from the several windows at the opposite end of the room. A door close on Nell's right hand provided access to the library, and another door farther along the same wall led, as she later learned, into the dining room.

Phrynie's eyes sparkled as brilliantly as the diamonds she wore around her throat. Trust her aunt, thought Nell darkly, to be dressed appropriately for a gala, even living out of a bandbox.

Nell's thoughts moved smoothly from her aunt's diamonds to her own jewel case, holding mere amethysts, a string of small pearls left her by her mother as well as the garnet earrings. And, of course, the parcel.

She swallowed too fast, and choked. She waved the count's concern aside. "I'm quite all right, thank you. The salad is delicious." She had intended to move the parcel from her jewel case to secrete it in her bandbox, in case the count's servants were curious or light-fingered—or both—but Phrynie had been impatient to descend to dinner.

Upon further consideration, she concluded that if the count's staff were indeed prone to pilferage, her aunt's sapphires would be the first items to disappear. Besides, there was nothing to worry about, for Mullins was to stay in their rooms. Her supper was to be brought up to her on the pretext that she was overly weary from the long carriage ride. Clearly Lady Sanford too was uneasy over their night's lodgings. She had not sufficiently accepted Reeves's caution. She would rectify her lapse later, before she retired for the night.

She allowed her mind to drift, as it seemed often to do, toward Reeves. If Stuston were still with them, even though he would have mistrusted every Frenchman on sight, she would not have been so convinced of the worst as she was by the simple fact that Reeves expected to stand guard that night.

He would not, she was certain, take such precautions without reason. But why was he so apprehensive in a private residence? Nell herself would expect to be safer here than on the road, where only cows placidly chewed their cuds and the landscape was empty.

Just now, Phrynie was entertaining the count. "How delighted you must be that the Bourbons have been restored, and you are back in your ancestral home."

The count hesitated only a second. "Of course it is good to be home again. My servants, even though I had to be away for years, were nonetheless loyal to me, and I found my affairs in good condition when I returned."

"I wonder that you did not stay on in England. So many émigrés found London a delight."

"So they did," said the count. "I myself found refuge—elsewhere."

"Oh?" said Phrynie, inviting him to continue. When he seemed not to wish to relive painful memories, Phrynie, with the tact that was such a large part of her charm, turned the subject deftly. "We were just now in Paris, you know. So many new buildings. I had not seen Paris since I was a very young child, as you know, but my mother spoke of it so many times that I do believe I could have found my way around the city blindfolded. I particularly admired the Rue de Rivoli. The colonnade is so unusual."

"Those are the things the Emperor did for their spectacular value, for display, so to speak. You did not see the covered food markets? Nor realize that the city's water supply is now adequate?"

"No, I confess we were not shown those amenities. We were there for only a day, however, and I am sure that Lady Westford would have instructed us eventually."

Amusement gleamed in their host's pale blue eyes. "Ah, yes, the Lady Westford. One cannot ignore her, however much one might desire to."

Springing reluctantly to the defense of her countrywoman, Phrynie said, "She was kind enough to take us to the Tuileries. But the court seems very quiet."

"I imagine," said the count drily, "that the Princess has much the same sentiments as I. My father as well as hers was caressed by Madame la Guillotine."

At that moment Nell happened to glance in his direction. She was startled by the fire she glimpsed in his eyes. The count might appear old, and his father's execution must have been at least twenty years before, but whatever emotion the recollection engendered was far from dead, or even breathing its last.

She sighed in relief. The count was one of them, with every hatred of Napoleon and the mobs that ensued upon his father's death, and every reason to keep France in Bourbon hands. He could have no reason to abduct the mysterious parcel, whose only value was to secure a just peace at Vienna.

It was much later when Phrynie and Nell mounted the winding stone steps, hollowed by generations of feet, to their rooms. Nell was aware of an overwhelming desire for her bed. The day's travel had been long and wearying, and she remembered that from the outset of the journey her sleep had been troubled.

Such a responsibility to carry the parcel across the entire western world—almost!—was worrying, and in one of her rare fits of exasperation, she wished for a few short but telling words with her brother.

Phrynie followed Nell into her bedroom. "Now then, isn't this a lark?" she crowed. "I had not expected to enjoy this trip, but I must confess I am, even before we arrive in Vienna."

"I am delighted," said Nell. "I was a bit apprehensive over stopping here, I admit, particularly when I first met your count. He is like a dried apple, isn't he?"

"Not dried," retorted her aunt. "He has sufficient spirit remaining."

"I did not notice. But I assume you were informed of his spirit when he took you into the library? I had not realized you were so fond of books."

"Don't be impertinent. I suppose you will wish to be off at an early hour? In that case, I shall retire at once."

Mullins was yawning in a chair before the hearth in Lady Sanford's room, waiting for her mistress to return. Nell yawned too. "Too much fresh air, I fear. I am unaccustomed to it. The crab bisque was delicious, but much too filling."

"If I ate that much every night," agreed her aunt, "I should soon sink into a stupor."

Nell agreed wholeheartedly. She yawned again, and slipped through the connecting dressing room to her own room. She removed her gown and folded it, ready to be packed in her bandbox in the morning. She remembered then that she had meant to move the parcel from the jewel case to the bandbox before they went down to dinner. She would do it at once.

She unclasped her amethyst necklace, curled it up in her hand, and went to place it in her jewel case.

She opened the case. She stood immobile, not even breathing, her desire for sleep vanished.

The parcel was gone!

It could not be gone, for Mullins had been here all the evening. Probably, as had happened before, she had automatically moved it from jewel case to bandbox, and in her haste the deed had slipped from her mind.

She fairly threw her garments out of her bandbox. No parcel. She upended the bag over the bed. There was simply no parcel!

She rushed wildly around the room. She looked in pockets, she shook out her nightdress and robe, she flung the bolsters from the bed and threw back the covers, she fell to her knees and looked under the bed.

She sank into her chair, the contents of the bandbox strewn around her on the floor. Her head in her hands, she heard someone moaning, a pitiful little sound. She knew that someone was herself, but she could not stop.

She was undone!

In a moment, Phrynie stood before her. "My dear child, whatever is the matter? I heard you—Nell darling, what is it?"

"The parcel. Gone."

"Gone? It can't be!"

"It is not in the room. Gone. Stolen." Her voice rose to a wail. "I shall quite simply kill myself."

Chapter Fourteen

"Then it *was* valuable."

Nell looked up at her aunt. "Did I not tell you so?"

"Of course you told me—that the Haveney man called it important, and that invisible duke thought so. But that did not convince me that the parcel contained anything but musty documents. I've seen plenty of them, you know, in Mr. Hastings' office. He's such a fuddy old thing. But honest, of course, or my husband would not have trusted him with his legal affairs."

"Aunt, how can you think about some lawyer when I am quite *undone*."

Phrynie bit her lip. She recognized now, perhaps even better than Nell, the importance of the parcel. From the moment that Nell told her she had usurped her brother's business, Phrynie had tried to convince herself that Tom would come along and relieve them of the burden. A burden, moreover, that Phrynie did not consider to be more than an excuse Nell was using to get them to Vienna.

Phrynie knew she was no better than Nell when it came to casting discretion to the winds in favor of a strong desire to be in Vienna. But now, knowing that the Duke of Whern's man had in truth entrusted them with vital information that must get to Castlereagh, she knew well that they stood on the brink, as it were, of disaster.

"Now, Nell. Get your wits together. We must *think*!"

"The parcel is gone," repeated Nell sturdily. "And it's my fault. I should never have accepted it in the first instance."

"Nell, pray do not repeat yourself in that idiotic fashion. The parcel is gone, I concede, but it is no more your fault than mine." She reflected, and added in an altered tone, "Perhaps not as much."

Suddenly she was struck by an idea. "What am I thinking of? Where was Mullins? She was here all the time. Nobody could have stolen anything!"

"But they did!"

"Nonsense. If the parcel were not stolen, then it is still here and we shall find it." She stepped to the connecting door and summoned her maid. Mullins, wearing to the knowledgeable eye of her mistress a guilty face, appeared in the doorway.

"Mullins, where were you all evening?"

"H-here, my lady."

Phrynia regarded her with justified suspicion. "I have little patience, I assure you. The truth, if you please."

Mullins was a pitiable creature. "I was here all the time, my lady. Except for when I had my supper."

"Supper! I made arrangements for your supper to be brought up to you. I confess I was not too well pleased with the count's staff—the ones that I saw—and I did not wish my jewels to be unprotected."

"But the housekeeper came up, my lady, and said the food would be much hotter if I cum down to eat in the kitchen, like. And it didn't seem to be any harm to it. Was they?"

When faced with a real crisis, Phrynie did not lose her head. It was obvious that there had been opportunity for the parcel to be removed from their rooms, and it was more than likely that the housekeeper had been sent to entice Mullins away.

"Let me think. You saw the parcel last, Nell, before dinner? Or last night in the embassy?"

"Tonight," Nell said dully. "When I took my amethysts out of my jewel case."

"You're sure."

"I'm not sure of anything. But I did see it in my jewel case."

"Was it locked?"

"No need. I left the key right there beside it."

Phrynie shook her head. "My dear, aside from the parcel, it is beyond all foolishness to leave one's jewels in such an exposed position."

"In your friend's home?"

"He is not that close a friend. In fact, I remember hearing some gossip about him, but I can't remember just what it was."

"Perhaps he is a famous jewel thief?"

"Don't be sarcastic, Nell. It doesn't suit you. Besides, your jewels were not taken."

Mullins spoke up. "Her ladyship's jewels, I just looked. The blue ones is still there. But the diamonds is gone!"

"Fool!" said Lady Sanford, really exasperated. "I'm wearing them! Now let us think, Nell—"

"Perhaps Mullins might find some task to perform?"

"Mullins, leave us." When the maid had scurried away, Phrynie closed the dressing-room door behind her. "Quite right. The less she knows the better, since she cannot follow a simple direction. I fear I must replace her when we return to England." She paused, and added wistfully, "But she does have a marvelous hand with hair."

"Hair, Aunt?" said Nell, as though returning from a far distance. "But what will I ever do?"

"As I was saying, let us think for a moment. We must be sure the parcel is not here, fallen behind a chair, for example."

Their search proved, as Nell expected, futile. Phrynie frowned. Reasoning as she went, she said, "If the parcel was there in your jewel case—now, Nell, I believe you—then someone came into this room while Mullins was disgracefully eating her food and took it. It could not have been the count, for I was with him every moment."

Nell put her finger on the weak link in her aunt's discourse. "But who knew anything about the parcel in the first instance? It was inside the leather case, and the case itself was closed. I am sure it was not obvious to anyone who happened to look through the door. And look—the bed has not been turned down yet."

"But a curious maid—"

"Would have taken the jewels, if she were merely looking for valuables."

"And left the beds as they were, to conceal her presence. Nell, how very clever!"

Nell repeated, "Who knew the parcel was valuable?"

She eyed her aunt steadily, watching her relive the evening, trying to recall any clue that might lead them to the truth.

She knew her aunt well. "What have you thought of, Aunt? Your expression gives you away. Come, pray tell me." She paused, as an unwelcome thought came to her. "Aunt, you didn't mention the parcel, did you? You did!"

"Nell!" Phrynie's voice rose in indignation.

"How could you!" Nell wailed. "You told the count!"

"Very well. But I didn't tell him what it was."

"When?"

Making a virtue of her full confession, Phrynie explained. "He asked me to step into the library, you remember. And we sat down before the fire—most uncomfortable chairs, I must say. And then he asked me—in the kindest way— whether or not we were in trouble."

"Trouble?" echoed Nell.

"Traveling alone, you know, the two of us. And you will remember, Nell, I told you at the start that a journey like this was not in the least ordinary. I did think that it was most discreet of him to inquire in such a fashion. Do you know, Nell, he even asked if there were bailiffs on our track! He said if we needed horses, or footmen, or even if there were some way he could make our way smooth ahead, he would bend every effort on our behalf." She paused to reflect, and added in some disgust, "Had I known at that time what a cake Mullins would make of it, I should have requested a replacement for her."

"I see now how it was. To reassure the count, who means nothing to us, you told him about the parcel."

"Well, it did seem so common to let him think that two ladies of quality were traveling without escort to Vienna. Certainly he would have questions about such a havey-cavey arrangement."

"And," said Nell ominously, "you simply told him that we were carrying valuable government documents to the congress."

"Not at all," said Phrynie loftily, "I simply hinted, you know, in the most delicate fashion, that there was a reason for us to travel in this unobtrusive fashion and I could not reveal it even to him." Phrynie was not a fool. "I think it must have been after that that Mullins was decoyed downstairs. And I must say that the count, for all his distinguished titles and his ancient lineage, is no gentleman!"

Together they went over every moment of the evening, every nuance of the count's conversation, every movement that they knew of the servants. "For let us face it, Aunt, the count himself did not mount those ancient steps to this room and go through my possessions."

"Quite right. He did, I now remember, stop to speak to that factotum of his. I should not like to show any prejudice, but I cannot like a servant with a squint."

"Do you think the count," asked Nell, going directly to the point, "gave him instructions then to search our rooms?"

Phrynie considered. "It could well be. I recall that that was after we came out of the library. I noticed particularly because I thought—"

Nell recalled that as her aunt and the count had emerged from their "visit" to the library her aunt had appeared oddly flushed, and one jeweled hand had gone up to smooth her hair.

"Did you see the servant again?"

"N-no. At least, I don't remember. We remained in the salon, you know, until we came upstairs."

Nell remembered. "I did hear a door close nearby. Before we came upstairs. Did you?"

Phrynie shook her head. "No, I didn't."

"Suppose that were so—the door closing, I mean. That could have been the time that the servant put the parcel—"

"In the library!" Phrynie finished. "Could it be?"

"Well," said Nell, now practical once more, "it's our only hope. I shall have to go and see."

"Go and see" meant at first to Nell that she would slip easily down the stairs, cross the foyer and, making sure first that the count had retired to his bedroom, see whether the parcel had been taken to the library.

"Where does the count sleep?" Nell inquired, her mind on the logistics of the problem.

"How would I know a thing like that, Nell?" her aunt said with some resentment, and added, "Upstairs in the wing over the salon and the library. You must make sure that he does not hear you."

Nell suspected that the count might well be waiting, wide-awake, for a clandestine visit from Lady Sanford.

"Well, I shall be no braver in ten minutes than I am now," said Nell.

"Nell, shouldn't I go?"

"No, Aunt. If the count found you downstairs after he thought you were already retired, he might mistake your intentions."

"To think the day would come when my niece instructed me on morals!"

"Dear Aunt, wish me luck!"

"I hate to have you serve as cat's paw for me."

"Don't worry, Aunt. I'll be back with the parcel in no time, if it's there."

She was back almost as quickly as she had prophesied, but she was empty-handed. Her expression spoke a volume.

"He's down there in the hall," she said grimly. "The servant who has the squint. He also has a chair, and is clearly expecting to spend the night in front of the library door."

"Then it's true," cried Phrynie. "The servant would not be on guard unless the count ordered him. Therefore, the count is at the bottom of this. Oh, Nell, how guilty I am!"

"Aunt, you cannot shoulder the blame for the count's crime!" Suddenly it was Nell who was in charge, and Phrynie who had crumpled under the weight of their disaster.

"I wish," she said wistfully, "that I could remember what it was I heard about him."

Nell's wish, unspoken, was that they had gone on to the Royal Champagne inn. Surely the comfort of this private residence was not superior to a well-managed *auberge*. And the count then could not have put their entire journey, to say nothing of their reputations, in jeopardy.

Nell sank into a chair. "Well, one thing we can be sure of. The parcel is in the library. The count would not carry it with him to secrete it in some other place and leave the servant to guard the empty library."

Phrynie sat up. "Nell, there's only one servant. Could we—do you think we could—*overpower him*?"

Aghast, Nell stared at her aunt. She was momentarily captivated by a vision of two ladies of quality stealing down a winding medieval staircase and attacking by brute force a large and formidable man.

"Regretfully, Aunt, I must say I do not think so. Besides, the struggle would rouse the castle."

But the idea of stealing down the stairs brought an alternative to her mind. "Weren't there a pair of doors farther along the corridor? I wonder where they lead?"

Their rooms were situated in the ancient tower. But there had to be access to the wings on either side, Nell reasoned.

"Mullins can show me." Nell and the tearfully repentant maid went down the few steps from Nell's door to the end of the hall.

"The housekeeper, I think she was, had me come down this way, miss," said Mullins, pointing to the left-hand door. "The back stairs, like. That door there," she added, indicating that one opposite, "is supposed to go on to the count's rooms. He don't like anybody coming in on him, so they said, and the door is bolted. But this one here isn't, I don't think."

Mullins took hold of the latch. It moved beneath her hand and the door swung open, soundlessly to Nell's relief. Together they peered down into darkness. "You're sure the stairs go all the way down?" whispered Nell.

Mullins nodded vigorously. "Steep they be too."

They returned to Phrynie. "Mullins showed me a door at the end of the hall, with stairs that lead down. She says they give upon the kitchen and I can believe it, for there is a strong smell of cabbage. I'm going to see what I can do."

Phrynie cried in distress, "Nell, you simply cannot travel around an old castle on your own, like a Minerva Press heroine. I'm going with you."

With difficulty, Nell dissuaded her aunt from accompanying her on what was, in the least objectionable terms, an illegal sortie to steal back the parcel. The final convincing argument mounted by Nell was surprisingly effective.

"Suppose the count comes here to you, on some pretext," she suggested. "Of course, I know you don't expect him, but he might wish to continue—conversation, shall we say?"

Phrynie frowned. "I do not expect him."

"Of course not. But he may come to see why his tacit invitation has not been accepted."

"Nonsense!"

"On the contrary, Mullins showed me a door at the end of the hall which leads directly to his quarters. It's bolted, she says, but not on our side."

"The count does not expect me to pay an immoral visit to him, Nell!" exclaimed Phrynie in outrage. "How can you think it?"

"Aunt, I apologize. I do not in the least think it. I merely think it likely that he may wish to know whether we have missed the parcel. Could he possibly come to inquire?"

"I suppose he might. I gave him no encouragement at all, for I do not like his style. But—he was quite forceful, and in truth I do not know what he is capable of doing."

"Dear Aunt, we'll come out all right." Nell wished she were as positive as her words sounded. "Now, let me have your cloak, Mullins."

"Whatever for?" demanded Phrynie.

"I must get into the library. If not by an inside door, then there is no help for it but to try the window."

"Nell, you can't!"

"I do not like the idea above half myself, I assure you. But we must get the parcel back. I shudder to think we might be forced to spend the rest of our lives abroad rather than face the Duke of Whern, whoever he might be." She was aware of her aunt's troubled expression. "If you have a better suggestion, believe me I shall welcome it."

"Were I to go to the count and—beguile him in some fashion?"

Nell objected with vigor. "Not in any fashion! Besides, we might still have the servant to deal with."

"Do you think I could just tell the count we are aware he has removed some of our possessions? No need to make specific mention of the parcel. No, I can see you don't approve. Nor do I, as a matter of fact."

"Mullins, help me with this cloak. I shall endeavor to keep from harming it."

"No matter, miss," said Mullins, with a hearty sniff. "It's all my fault."

"Now, Mullins, you must not blame yourself. Good, it has a hood. I'll just cover my hair, you see, and if need be I'll bring it across my face, so."

"You have a regrettable facility in this kind of intrigue," Phrynie pointed out. "I shall not inquire how you came by such nefarious knowledge."

"Nor," said Nell briskly, "shall I tell you." Pulling the dark cloak close, she whispered, "Wish me luck," and was gone.

Chapter Fifteen

Mullins, anxious to make amends for her dereliction, accompanied Nell as far as the door at the end of the hall. "Watch the steps, miss. I think the hall at the bottom goes straight to the outside."

"Will the outer door be barred?"

"I dunno, miss."

There was, if it could be seen in the faint light, an odd emotion on the maid's face. All this skulking around in the night ought by rights to be left to her betters. Such havey-cavey goings-on were entirely beneath her dignity. Mullins had worked her way from parlor maid up to the infinitely satisfying and undemanding position of personal maid to Lady Sanford. She shrank from revealing any knowledge of the workings of lower levels of domestic service.

But, aside from her wounded dignity, she was out of her element, in an alien land, beset in all likelihood by cutthroats and outlaws, and far too many Frenchmen to suit her taste. She longed with all her heart to be back in Mount Street, all the tools of her trade at hand, enjoying the gratifying deference to her position of the lesser servants.

"Mullins!" whispered Nell urgently, "you're not coming down the steps with me?"

"No, miss, begging your pardon, that I'm not. I may be to blame for this hullaballoo, but I'm not about to wait down there in the dark for who knows what kind of monster. You can smell the damp and the mold all the way up here. No, miss. Not if you was to fire me this minute!"

"We would in that case have to leave you behind when we depart."

The maid gasped, but no amount of persuasion on the part

of Nell, sadly hampered by the vital need for silence, would serve.

"Well, if you can't, I suppose I should be grateful that I won't find you slumped in a swoon when I return. Do you think, Mullins, that if you put your mind to it you could manage to leave this upper door open, so that I can see my way when I come back?"

The maid agreed, adding a mutter that sounded like "*If you come back, miss.*"

Even Mullins' dubious company would be better than none. But Nell, driven by necessity, stepped with extreme caution down the cement stairs that led from the second floor of the old tower to the ground floor of the west wing. She had no wish to be found at the bottom of the stairs with a broken limb, at least until she had the parcel safe in her possession.

She stumbled at the bottom, expecting another step and meeting the floor. She paused to consider where she was, stretching her hands out to both sides. The corridor was so narrow that her arms were not extended to their full length. In truth, she wondered how the kitchen maids could manage their huge trays in the confined space.

The stone walls were cold to her touch. She shuffled ahead, lest she fall against some obstacle in the dark. Her fingers moved along smooth walls for an interminable time. Then, surprisingly, the wall on her left hand fell away. She held her breath for a moment, until, judging from the intensified aroma of cooked cabbage, she realized that she had reached the kitchen door.

So far, she was encouraged. From what Mullins had told her, the corridor stretched straight on from here to the door opening to the outside. It was entirely possible, it occurred to her for the first time, that the door was bolted from the *outside*. Her inquiry of the maid had been simply to know what to expect when she reached the door in utter darkness.

But suppose that the count's domestic security depended upon locked and barred doors. It was likely that the master of the castle had reason to look to his own safety, judging from his swift and criminal response to her aunt's indiscreet hints.

But then, common sense informed her that safety would depend upon barring the doors from the inside, and this could not be managed by the servants who left for the night. She entertained high hopes that the door would be closed by a simple latch and that it opened from both sides.

She went on, and bumped suddenly against the door at the end of the passage. She fumbled for the latch and felt it give beneath her fingers. How dark it was! She had come far from the dim light provided by the open door at the top of the stairs. If Mullins closed the upper door, as well she might in her muddled way, Nell's return up the entire stairway would be made in stygian darkness.

Even Mrs. Mary Meeke could never have been in such a situation, even though dank stone passageways appeared with monotonous frequency in *Midnight Weddings*.

Hand still on the latch, Nell paused. What would she find outside? She was on the outer wall of the new wing to the west, a duplicate of the extension that held the salon, dining room, and library. Therefore, she must make her way to the left, into the courtyard, and steal unobserved to the library window.

At this moment, there were questions of some importance still unanswered in her mind: Was the parcel indeed secreted in the library, and if so, where? And how would she get into the library when she located it from the courtyard?

Time enough for that, she thought with rosy optimism when she found the pertinent window. Certainly she could not solve either question standing here in blackness, one hand on the latch of the outer door.

Taking a deep breath, she opened the door, carefully lest its hinges squeal, and stepped outside. She must come back this same way, and prudence told her that her return might be accomplished in some haste. Still holding to the door, she felt around on the ground for something to hold the door ajar while she was gone. Her fingers located a stone of some size, and she wedged it in the door opening.

Now she stood on the bare ground and examined her surroundings. She was at the far end of the west wing. She knew that to her right the hill fell away precipitously to the river valley.

Far below she could see the faint glimmer of the moving waters of the Marne. There were small farms along the valley, she knew, because she had seen them in that panoramic view from the salon in the other wing. But not a light was showing now. Everybody in the world, she thought, was in bed as they should be, except for certain wakeful and worried individuals in the building behind her.

It was a clear night. Overhead the stars were as brilliant as spangles on indigo blue gauze. The site of the chateau was clear for the most part of trees, whether by ancient design to provide no shelter for attackers, or simply from the likelihood that, with the heavy forest looming behind, the count had a sufficiency of trees and wished for no more.

At any rate, the lack of cover made it easier to see where she was going. The thought that such lack of protection also made it more likely that she would be discovered was promptly set aside.

Even from this point she could see that her scheme was not as simple as when she had explained it to Phrynie. She had simply intended to tiptoe past the entrance door, discover the window of the library—the first one past the door. she was sure—open it, in a way she had not yet devised, and retrieve her parcel.

The plan in her mind bore little resemblance to the facts.

Ahead and to the left stretched the courtyard. Now she could see that it was not an entirely enclosed space. Rather, the stables and domestic quarters lay at some distance beyond, the buildings standing unattached one to another.

The count's servants kept early hours. There was not a light to be seen in any of the buildings. The only relief in the opaqueness was a splotch of lighter darkness, so to speak, in the center of the courtyard. She stared at it, trying to discover its significance. At last it came to her. The starlight was reflected in a pool of ornamental water she had seen without noticing when they arrived that afternoon, a century ago.

She did not stir for a long time. There was no movement anywhere, and she concluded at last that her presence was so far unnoticed.

There was, she believed, little chance that her movements would be observed, at least from those distant buildings. Nearer at hand, however, was another question. The wing beside her was deserted. At the intersection of this ell with the old fortress was the entrance.

The round tower of the keep stretched to the sky. If Nell were to allow her fancy full rein, she might have imagined herself a medieval damsel, clad in kirtle and wimple, stealing back to the castle after a forbidden escapade. She shivered, not entirely from the cold. The tower was dark, ominous, seemingly ready to sprout armed defenders and flying arrows.

She stood still, trying to get a grip on her rioting visions. To steady herself, she looked along the wing at her left hand. Idly she thought it seemed far too short to contain the endless corridor she had just now traversed. She stepped away from the building. It was then that she saw the light.

The light, from a candle and not the remains of a fire in the grate, streamed out of an uncurtained window beyond the keep. Nell counted—the first window, and therefore the library window. And someone was within!

She considered her next step. Among the alternatives was not a return, her mission not accomplished. Instead, she noted with gratification that there was shelter provided, even though not in abundance.

Along the new extensions shrubbery had been planted and seemed to have thrived. The thick woody branches would provide cover of a sort if she were required to take quick action. She began to make her stealthy way along the kitchen wing. She blessed Mullins' enveloping cloak, for it was of a color to blend in with the shadowy shrubs.

She eventually came to the gravel walk leading to the entrance. A glance around told her she was so far not observed. She crossed the gravel on delicate tiptoe. The library window was a golden-lit rectangle just ahead. Now was the time for finesse. With infinite care, she inserted herself between the stone wall and the thick bushes. She was now certain that no matter who crossed the courtyard on licit or illicit errands, she was all but invisible behind her twiggy screen.

She could hear the ragged echo of her breathing rattling around the square, shouting for notice. It took a strenuous effort of will to understand that the sound was entirely within her head, and the outer world still lay wrapped in slumber. She would be all night at the job at this rate, she told herself firmly. She was as pea-brained as any novel heroine, letting her fancies take such desperate grip on her. She must do what she had come to do and make a speedy retreat. She moved ahead.

She sidled to the side of the window and peered in. The bottom of the window frame came no lower than her waist.

But the curtains were not drawn, and from her vantage point she was able to command an excellent view of the interior.

The sole occupant of the room was the count himself. His back was toward her, and he was near enough that, if the window were open, she could reach in and touch him. All he had to do was to turn his head, at the slightest sound, and see her frightened face framed in the window. Quick as thought she ducked below the sill.

At length, when nothing untoward developed, she rose slowly and peered again through the window. What was he doing? She moved to look from another angle. He seemed to be bending over some object on the large table before him, a magnifying glass in his hand.

Suppose he had unluckily decided to work on his accounts until midnight! It was quite obvious that he was not waiting in his quarters for a nocturnal visit from Lady Sanford. Nell sent a mental apology to her aunt.

The count gave no sign of moving. She took one step beyond the window, leaned her back against the stone wall, and closed her eyes, preparing for a long wait. The damp of frost permeated the thin soles of her evening sandals. But no matter how uncomfortable, how truly miserable she might be, she must stay until the lights went out and she would be able to recover the parcel.

If, in fact, it were in the library!

Breathless, she leaned again to take another look. This time she was rewarded. The parcel sat, in plain view, on the table. It was her parcel, no question about it, and it had been the object of the count's intense scrutiny.

She returned to her post, grateful at least for the knowledge that the parcel was at hand. The only question was how to retrieve it through a closed window in the dead of night, its present possessor not an arm's length away.

Perhaps, too, the squint-eyed servant might later be posted within the library as a guard, leaving his chair in the foyer.

Providence could not be so cruel!

At this moment, she recalled that no more than a sennight since, she had stood in her aunt's sitting room and plotted to get her own way. What she had said to her aunt came back to her now in precise detail: "I should not like to think that Tom's credit would be lost for want of a little exertion on my part."

A little exertion, indeed!

In England, the successful completion of the scheme now in train would have resulted in an invitation to spend a few years in Newgate Prison. But of course this was France—and she would not think about the guillotine. She had a dark suspicion that the count, if he discovered her in her present situation, would not trouble the forces of law in his country, but instead—it did not bear thinking on, for her knees began to tremble.

She could not go through with it!

She even made a move to return the way she had come, but the prospect of returning again empty-handed and facing the collapse perhaps of England's safety was not to be entertained.

But at least dear Rowland was not here to see to what undignified depths she was forced to descend merely in order to see him. Even as strong as was his devotion to her, she had the clear perception that he would not approve. He might even make objections, and she would not be overly surprised were he to forbid her to do aught but return to her bed. But he was not here, and to her surprise she found she was grateful for his absence. Now, setting her fiancé aside, she sent her thoughts in the direction of her next step.

At length—at long length—the light in the library went out. Time must have passed, for when she moved she was stiff from long inaction. Her feet were nigh frozen, and her hands, even though they had been sheltered by the cloak, were cold as well. But the light had gone out, and unless the count were sufficiently eccentric to lie in wait in the dark to protect his booty, the room was now empty.

She forced herself to remain still, giving him time enough to instruct his servant and to find his way to his bedroom. His quarters, from Mullins' information, were on the second floor of this wing, above the salon, the dining room, and even the library. She devoted a moment to the intense hope that his bed was not directly above her. The slightest noise from the library might well alert a man lying awake on the floor above.

She waited. Finally, a light appeared in an upstairs window. She leaned out to observe and saw that only the windows at the far end of the wing were illuminated. The rooms, then, above the library would be unoccupied.

She stepped silent as a shadow to the library window.

The window was of the kind that in England was called casement. It was made in two panels, swinging outward from a joining in the center. The trick, she decided, was to push against one leaf in the hope of springing the lock.

She pushed against the window. It did not move. She pushed harder, and at last she felt it move beneath her palms. It gave slightly, but no more. She ran her hands up and down the center frame as far as she could reach, to find the exact location of the latch that held it, and pushed again, with no more success than before. She felt panic rising in her. She had to get into the library and retrieve the parcel. She had seen it on the desk. Suddenly the unwelcome thought came to her that perhaps the count had carried it with him when he went upstairs. In that case . . .

In that case, she would know soon enough. Just now, she must get into the room. She glanced around once to see if she were still unobserved. It might come to smashing the glass, but that could not be accomplished without a certain regrettable sound in the night and ensuing alarums.

She pushed harder, with diligent concentration, at the window frame.

Her concentration played her false. She did not hear the soft footfall behind her. The first intimation that she was not quite alone came with a hand clamped without ceremony over her mouth and an arm around her waist, pinioning her to the body behind her.

If she had felt vicarious terror on behalf of various Clarissas and Julias and Evelinas, she now passed beyond even the extreme of terror.

Her scream died at birth. The effective gag allowed no sound to escape. She had been too noisy, the squint-eyed man had her in his iron grip, he would march her without ceremony to the count, and it would take more that Phrynie's accomplished persuasion to get them all out of it. . . .

The hand over her mouth smelled of soap, she thought with relief, as she bit hard into the finger that was handiest. At the same time, she kicked backward, wishing she wore her high-heeled slippers. A grunt in her ear told her that her heel had found its mark.

But her efforts were of no avail. The hard-muscled arm

around her waist tightened and lifted her off the ground, so she had no purchase from which to kick again. Her attacker's muffling hand gripped painfully, and she could only shake her head, ineffectually trying to escape from it. The voice in her ear spoke so softly it was hardly more than a breath in the night. But, to her infinite relief, it spoke in English.

"What are you doing, you little fool?"

She turned horrified eyes to him. "Reeves!" She sighed. "Thank heaven it's you!"

He released her so quickly she nearly fell. "Miss Aspinall! But I thought . . ." He stopped short and continued in a calmer vein. "Sorry, I'm sure, miss. But you are wearing the maid's cloak, and I didn't know—didn't recognize you. Miss." Even in such distress of mind, she noticed again that Reeves frequently added the term of respect at the conclusion of whatever he wished to say, as though subservience did not come naturally to him.

He looked around the courtyard, slowly, deliberately. Then he turned to her and placed his lips next to her ear. His voice could not be heard a yard away. "No one's watching us. Now, what are you doing here?"

As though it were the most ordinary thing in the world, she said, "Trying to get through this window."

He blinked. "For what purpose?" he demanded, intensely interested.

"To get back the—at least, to get back an *item*—that is mine."

He did not waste time in futile questions. He said simply, "Stolen?"

When she nodded, he added, "I'm not surprised, the way you two have flitted across the countryside, carefree as birds of the air. I never saw such irresponsible . . ." He stopped short, making an obvious effort to control, if not his disgust, at least his tongue. "Miss," he added woodenly. "Now if you please, step aside."

Chapter Sixteen

Obediently she stepped to one side. Having relinquished with some relief the responsibility for opening the window to the coachman, whose talents seemed to embrace a wide range of activities, she looked carefully around the square. There was as yet no sign of movement. They were still undiscovered.

"Reeves . . ." she breathed.

He jerked his head in a gesture of silence, and she subsided again. He was doing something she could not see to the center joining of the two-leaved window. She would ask him sometime to show her his trick with it, because who knew when she might need to have such knowledge, literally at her fingertips?

Not that she had plans to burgle every residence she came upon, but she seemed to have entered a dreamlike state, standing to one side while Reeves took charge, a state in which all things were not only possible but even likely. She seemed to have taken a giant stride beyond the well-brought-up young lady of quality who properly shunned all knowledge of the ways of the lower classes and occupied herself only with her embroideries and her amusements.

In this altered state of mind, it did not seem in the least out of the ordinary for her and her coachman to be standing outside a nobleman's residence somewhere in France, in the dead of night, attempting to force an illegal entry through a window of her host's house.

Attempting to force the window was no longer true. Under Reeves's deft manipulations, the window sprang open with a sound no louder than a sigh.

Again he bent to her ear and whispered, "It's open. Now how can I serve you next?"

"No need to be sarcastic, Reeves. If the window is open, naturally I should like to get inside the room."

"Can I retrieve your—item, I think you called it—for you?"

Haughtily and entirely illogically, she whispered back, "No, thank you. I must not shirk my responsibility." Then, realizing how ungrateful she must seem, she began to apologize.

He put his hand again over her mouth, this time gently. "Not a word," he told her. "We're not out of this yet."

It seemed to her that his conspiratorial *we* was quite the most comforting sound she could have heard at this point. She could not have borne it had he turned, abandoning both the open window and her, to return to the stables.

He removed his hand. Peering through the window, he said, "Seems to be empty. Where is the item in question?"

"Just there on the table. Let me—"

He glanced swiftly around the courtyard. Satisfied they had not been discovered, he picked her up in his arms and without apparent effort swung her through the window and set her down inside. In a moment, he stood beside her, pulling the windows shut behind him.

"Do these curtains close? Yes, they do. Here's a candle. Shall I light it?"

"The firelight is enough. Truly, Reeves, you did not have to come in too. I'll just get the parcel. . . ." Her voice trembled and died away.

"What is it?"

"It's gone! The parcel was right here on the table."

He eyed her without favor. "It sprouted legs, I must assume, and walked away. Does it have much of a start on us?"

"I'm in no mood for your kind of frivolity, Reeves."

"Frivolity!" He seemed in danger of raising his voice incautiously. With a visible effort, he restrained his censure. "Just tell me, if you please, why the parcel—on which you obviously set store—should be found here on the table, rather than in your quarters upstairs?" His fierce glare was clear to her, even in the faint light from the embers in the grate. He took a deep steadying breath and with an effort added, "Miss."

She was in two minds about the wisdom of confiding in her

aunt's coachman. He was an unknown quantity, and she did not entirely trust a man who alternated oddly between a low dialect and a speech that would have been at home even at Clarence House. On the other hand, she would not now be standing illicitly in the count's library had he not come to her aid.

She opened her lips to make some sort of quick explanation, being sadly hampered by the need to keep her voice all but inaudible, when he gestured sharply. "Someone's coming!" he whispered urgently. "Where does that door lead?"

Without an unnecessary word, she grabbed his wrist and pulled him after her through the door into the empty, dark salon.

"It's the count coming back—"

"Hush!" The admonition was only a hissed breath in her ear, but she was instantly obedient.

Their situation, she realized, was precarious in the extreme. If the sound Reeves had heard was indeed the count returning, he would in all likelihood find the open window and suspect that the intruders were still in the building. He would rouse his staff, they would search the house, and without question would find both Miss Aspinall and the coachman, and . . .

She did not doubt that the count was capable, not only of thievery of small items like the parcel, but also of meting out condign punishment on the spot. Now for the first time, Mr. Haveney's instructions to his young messenger began to ring true. "Grave consequences," he had threatened, would ensue upon disobedience of his orders. But she was certain that the man could not have foreseen these present and very dismaying circumstances.

She must have made a slight unhappy sound, for Reeves, standing beside her in the dark room, put his arm around her and drew her close. She could feel his strength surrounding her, the warmth of him flowing into her. Suddenly she was visited by a wanton feeling—she did not care whether they were caught, as long as Reeves did not leave her.

That betrayal was of only a moment's duration. She stifled such an unworthy thought, but she did not move away from him. What harm could it do to gain the comfort she badly needed—just for a moment?

"It's that servant," Reeves whispered. "With the squint."

"Not the count?"

"See for yourself." He indicated the long line of light that outlined the door to the library, which he had prudently left ajar.

She put her eye to the crack. She could see the servant looking suspiciously around the room. It was obvious that they had made some noise in getting the window open and climbing over the sill. He was just now turning away from the window. There had been nothing for him to see, and his suspicions were allayed.

He did not at once leave the room, however. He bent to stir up the embers of the fire and scatter them safely in the grate. The light in the room faded abruptly, and, satisfied, he went out into the hall, closing the door behind him.

She was impatient to finish her mission. Only Reeves's powerful arm held her immobile for what seemed a long, long time.

"Best be sure," he whispered, "that the fellow hasn't forgotten something."

"But he may come in here!"

"If he does," said Reeves in a matter-of-fact tone, "we will simply step back into the library."

They waited in silence until he deemed it safe to return to the search. This time they moved even more stealthily than before. Even whispers sounded raucous in the quietness.

In the faint light, she could see Reeves's gesture. His lips moved in the unmistakable question, "How big?" His outstretched hands measured an invisible object a yard across. She brought his hands together to approximate the size of the mysterious parcel—that same parcel that, having it to do again, she would not have touched with a bumboat pole.

She pointed to the table, indicating where she had last seen what she had described to Reeves as her item. He moved like a shadow to the side of the table nearest the window. The count, she mimed, had sat in that very chair, when she had first seen him from outside.

Reeves took the count's place and examined the table. To his left and right were shallow drawers. Taking infinite care to avoid any sound, he inched open the drawers. The first was empty, but the second was not. The parcel, no real attempt to conceal it having been made, was there.

She pounced on it. Hiding it in the folds of her cloak, she

stepped to the window. Her sole thought was to run back to her room, secrete the parcel, and stand guard over it until the morning. She had her hand on the sill before she turned back to Reeves with a question in her eyes. She would have spoken, but he signaled her again to silence.

He swept the room with an encompassing glance. He paused for a moment at the table, setting one drawer just slightly open and closing another firmly. Satisfied that all was as it had been, he came to her.

"I'll go first."

On the ground he turned back, picked her up as though she were a fluff of thistledown, and set her beside him on the ground. She watched while he closed the window soundlessly, although of course he could not lock it.

It occurred to her that her aunt's mysterious coachman was far too accomplished in what she could only term questionable skills. He had opened the window easily, had ears like a cat, and displayed a certain skill in concealment. It would be most ungrateful to question him, she decided, for after all, without such Newgate knowledge she would not now have the parcel safely in hand.

She was so relieved at the successful progress of their mission that she was hardly aware that Reeves, holding her elbow, carefully guided her out of the concealing shrubbery and across the graveled walk to the door by which she had come. He grunted with approval when he saw that she had ensured her return by placing the rock in the doorway.

"Thank you, Reeves," she said, turning to him at the door. "I do not know quite what I would have done without your help." It occurred to her that she had said much the same thing to him once before, when Stuston was hurt.

"You're not safely in yet." He seemed by this time to have forgotten any expression proper from servant to mistress. He took her arm and drew her inside the narrow passageway. It was much darker than before, she thought, and realized that the stars had furnished ample light for her adventure.

Reeves pulled the door close behind him. "Wait till your eyes get accustomed to the darkness." He was standing very close to her in the hallway. She could feel his breath warm on her cheek.

The clean lavender scent of his soap seemed heady in the confined space. Somewhere before she had breathed in the spicy aroma of a man's shaving soap and thought it an Elysian scent. She could not now remember whose person had carried that fragrance. She was aware now only of the vibrant masculinity of the man who had come out of the darkness to rescue her.

Stirred by an emotion she did not understand, she faltered. "I should . . ."

Whatever she would have said was lost forever. The coachman placed his hands unerringly on her shoulders and pulled her to him. One hand cupped her chin and lifted it. She felt, in the most reproachable and delightful way, his lips moving gently on hers. She told herself that to permit such conduct from a coachman was scandalous, yet . . .

For one breath, she felt in him a gathering together, and with quivering curiosity she waited for what must come next. But, to her regret, he let her go.

"Now I must get you upstairs. Careful, don't stumble, or we'll make a great racket and set the household about our ears."

His arm around her waist, they reached the top of the stairs without incident. The door Mullins had closed—a lifetime earlier this evening—opened easily onto the hallway, dimly lit by a wall torch halfway along its length.

"Reeves?"

"Don't worry." He smiled down at her. "I am no gossip."

"I didn't think so. But—"

"Don't worry," he repeated. "I shall not care to tell the count to his face that he is a thief. But I do think it appropriate to make an early start in the morning. Perhaps even before the count arrives at his desk?"

"Oh, yes."

He touched her cheek with one finger. His voice was tender, as he said softly, "Good night. Sleep well."

She turned and took one step toward her room, where Phrynie waited. She heard behind her one last word from her coachman, uttered in a tone that quivered with quiet amusement. "Miss."

Chapter Seventeen

Nell hastened down the short corridor, her mind riotous. She needed to put her thoughts in some kind of order. There was certainly no dearth of subjects to consider. Some were things she could tell her aunt, others she would die rather than have reach Phrynie's disapproving ears. But she did not expect to explain Reeves's assistance. It would not do to narrate in detail the coachman's use of his unexpected talents, for Lady Sanford might well decide to dismiss him at the next town.

Better the doubts we have than those unknown. At least, Reeves seemed to be on their side, and a more useful partisan would be hard to find. She must at once allay Phrynie's present anxiety, rejoice in the recovery of the parcel, and devote time to the consideration of a new and more secret place to hide it for the future.

Phrynie, clearly on the watch for her, opened the door before she reached it. "Nell, at last! You've been gone ages. Do you have it? Are you all right? Come in here by the fire, your hands are like ice!"

At least for the moment, Reeves must be placed on the shelf. It was incongruous—she smiled secretly at the thought —even to attempt to put that forceful individual aside like a useless satchel, but it must be done. She dared not reveal his part in tonight's events.

"Tell me," demanded Phrynie. "You succeeded, I can see that. Are you all right? You appear very odd to me."

"The parcel," began Nell, sinking into a chair beside her aunt's hearth. "Here it is. Mullins, your cloak. It was just the thing."

At Phrynie's direction, the maid stirred up the fire and departed. "Now then, my dear child, what happened? I shall wish to hear it all. Pull your chair closer to the fire."

"Do you think, Aunt," asked Nell inconsequentially, "that ladies ever kept warm by these fires? What an insignificant blaze!"

Phrynie retorted, "Forget the fire. Besides, your cheeks look warm to me." She looked carefully at her niece. It was clearly a time for setting the evening in order. She would get nothing from Nell in her present witless state. To give the girl credit, she had every right to tremble, and even to give way to hysterics. The only way to satisfy Phrynie's quivering curiosity and at the same time to relieve Nell's overset nerves was to exercise firmness. "Nell, where did you go when you left me?"

"Down the stairs."

"To the outside? And then what did you do?"

Little by little she extracted the tale from her niece. The child must have been too long chilled, she thought, for her wits had surely scattered. "And the count is the thief?"

"I saw him through the window, Aunt. The parcel was on his writing desk in plain sight. He had to be the one too to put the parcel out of sight in his table drawer. I cannot understand, Aunt. I should think if he were without money he would have taken our jewels. Surely yours are worth a fortune."

"I should not have brought them if we were not expecting to be entertained in Vienna." Phrynie lapsed into thought for some moments. "I wonder, do you not, what is in that package? It does not look in the least official, you know, for the government seems to lavish red tape and sealing wax even on a directive to a scrubwoman. Why would the count feel it was worth stealing? And what would he do when he got it into his hands?"

"One might suspect that he was not a royalist after all. But how could a nobleman be other than a Bourbon partisan?"

Phrynie wore an arrested look. "That's it. I remember now what I heard about him. He joined the Emperor. That's it!"

"But his father was executed, along with the King!"

"Ah, but he hated his father! Now I recall. It was quite a bit of scandal at the time. The only way he could keep his estate from being confiscated was to turn his coat and join the rebels."

"And you didn't remember that?" marveled Nell.

"That was years ago, you know. Besides, I pay no heed to politics—they're so dreary." She paused, summoning up memory. "He joined the émigrés in London for a bit, but he did not seem to be one of them, if you understand me."

"We should not have stopped here," said Nell, more to herself than to her aunt.

"I know. But it did seem rude to pass on by without making a call. Nell, I cannot apologize sufficiently for my indiscretion. Can you forgive me?"

Nell rose to enfold her aunt in a warm hug and kiss her soft cheek. "Of course, Aunt. I should not ever mind what you do. At least—I have never burgled a house before. Perhaps the experience will be useful one day."

Surprisingly Phrynie giggled. "If that is the worst activity you find to do, I shall be content."

At length, Nell was alone. There was time now to take out the matter of the coachman and consider it thoughtfully. How little she knew of him! He was an excellent coachman, and an experienced housebreaker. She was required only to contemplate the competence and speed with which he opened a locked window to admire his proficiency in illegal pursuits. He was properly deferential, even wooden, in his attitude. "Yes, miss" and "Yes, my lady." She felt her cheeks blazing. Deferential indeed, and far from wooden! Indeed Lord Foxhall with every right in the world would not be so impudent!

How could she travel on in Reeves's company, knowing that delicious moment in the darkness lay between them, more like an abyss than a bridge? While Nell was not entirely unsophisticated, the question of how to deal with an impertinent servant had never come her way before. She could give a Tulip a set-down or airily dismiss a dandy so that he did not trouble her again—or even deal kindly but firmly with Nigel Whitley's offer so that he went away without encouragement but with a sense of gratitude for her kindness. But Reeves was a hard nut to crack. He slid away from any attempts to place him in the proper slot like a salmon escaping from the net.

She was thankful now that she had not explained Reeves's share in the events of the evening just past. She was positive that Lady Sanford, in an excess of zeal fueled by her own guilt, would take a disapproving view of both the coachman's intervention and Nell's easy acceptance of it. Her aunt would peremptorily dismiss him from her service at the first opportunity. Nell must not allow such an event to transpire.

She could take the reins herself, thought Nell, if it came to that. Her father's coachman had taught her well. She could manage four horses for a short time, but it would be impossible for many reasons to drive the chariot into Vienna, herself on the box with whip in hand.

He should not have taken such liberties, she thought, climbing wearily into bed. But while her ingrained decorum shouted aloud at the infamous arrogance of the man, she was honest enough to recall that she had not found his kiss repellent. In fact, and she would have died rather than reveal this to anything more animate than her pillow, she had wished he had not drawn away.

She would be very very cold to him on the morrow. He would not dare to approach her again in such a fashion. And, she told herself, that was no reason to feel so unaccountably low in spirits.

A curious thing came into her mind. He had not seemed in the least curious about the odd parcel, or why it had been stolen by the count. From what he said, he expected the stolen article to be an earring or perhaps another piece of jewelry. When he caught sight of the plainly wrapped parcel in the table drawer, he was not, as far as she could discern, surprised. But equally astonishing, he asked no question about it. Could it be that he already knew what it was?

Nonsense! There was no possible way he could know about Mr. Haveney's parcel. Reeves had been in Calais for days before the duke's man had called in Mount Street, hadn't he? No, she decided, he had something else on his mind. And that something else she would never think of again!

She lay in bed a long time before she felt sleep approaching. Her last thought was, better the rogue she knew than a rogue she did not.

Morning arrived all too soon for Nell, in one way, for she had too little sleep. But in another way, she was more than anxious to put the Château Pernoud behind her forever. Her aunt had recalled that the count was a turncoat, a traitor to his family, and therefore capable of any depravity. Nell could regret that her aunt's memory had been tardy, for had they spent the night in the *auberge* in Hautvillers she would not now be suffering from a throbbing head and a throat made sore by her chilly vigil in the night.

Phrynie swept into Nell's room, already dressed. "Come, Nell, wake up! I do not wish to stay in this dismal spot a moment longer than necessary." Her voice dropped. "Do you think the count will—do anything to us?"

Nell opened her eyes. Her aunt was leaning over her, and she could see a spark of apprehension leap in the sapphire-blue eyes. "Do anything?" She threw back the covers. "Has something else happened?"

"Not that I know of. I sent Mullins to rouse Reeves and Potter at once. I should not like to stay even for a cup of coffee."

But her wishes were not fulfilled. Even though the count himself was barely out of his bed and sleep still blurred his perceptions, he insisted upon providing at least coffee. Before they had finished the light repast, he told them, "I have arranged for a picnic luncheon to be placed in your coach, Lady Sanford." Over her protests, he added, "Here comes Emile now to tell us that it is done."

Emile proved to be the servant with the repellent squint. He mumbled a word or two to his master and then retreated a short distance.

"I am sure," said the count, "that you will find no inn along your road suitable for a nuncheon. That is, if you continue on the road to Saarbrücken?"

Phrynie cast a glance of inquiry at Nell. Receiving no answer, she said, airily, "I must confess that I do not pay much heed to the way we are to go. I have every confidence in my coachman."

To Nell's suspicious eye, the count appeared nettled, as though he had not received the information he wished. But Reeves was suddenly beside them, and Lady Sanford was quickly installed in the coach.

As he handed Nell into the carriage after her aunt he murmured, in a conspiratorial fashion, "We must hurry before all is discovered." She refused to meet his eyes, contenting herself with a short nod of agreement.

It was clear that Reeves followed his own advice, for although the chariot left the drive before the entrance in a leisurely fashion, the horses at a decorous walk, by the time they rounded a curve and were hidden from the chateau by the forest, the team had been put into a fast trot.

The rhythmic rocking of the vehicle combined with her unaccustomed exertions the night before to put Nell into a drowsy mood, and before long she was entirely asleep. As she half awakened when the carriage slowed she realized that she was wrapped in a feeling of certainty that she was safe while Reeves was at hand. With a start she understood that she did not confine that feeling only to the occasions when he held the reins in his hands.

Even their own coachman, now at home on the Aspinall estate, had not instilled in her such a feeling.

The question, triggered by the thought of the old family servant, followed at once: where in the world was Tom?

Reeves did not pull the team up until they were far along the road, and the weak sun was nearly at its zenith. He sent Potter to inquire of Lady Sanford whether he should look for a posting house for the ladies' nuncheon.

"A nuncheon? No need, Potter, for the count has provided us a picnic, you know. I am sure there is plenty for us all."

Nell broke in. "Aunt, I should much rather," she said with a significant glance, "stop at an inn. It is hardly the weather for an outing, you know."

Phrynie understood her. After giving instructions, and after the coach was under way for the town that lay in sight on the horizon, she murmured, "Quite right. He may have dropped some toxiferous substance in the wine."

"I should detest thinking so, as an ordinary thing, you know," said Nell, "but only a hen-witted idiot would not see that it would be quite to his advantage if we were unable to inform anyone of his crime."

Phrynie managed a laugh. "I wonder what he will do when he finds the parcel gone?"

"Let us hope that he does not send after it."

By this time, Nell had in hand sufficient questions to hold Reeves in conversation for a fortnight. She had little hope of receiving satisfactory answers, but certainly she must make the effort.

At the posting house, she ate little, scheming to find Reeves alone. The opportunity did not present itself until they had stopped for the night. Reeves had sent the coach on to the stables, promising to follow at once to see to the cattle. He watched the huge vehicle trundle away and turned to find Nell standing beside him.

"Sorry, miss," he said. "Were you wishing to have your luggage brought into the inn?"

"Will it be safer?"

Reeves permitted a wintry smile to cross his features. "All depends on where your—your valuables, I should say—are located." His lips tightened. "Miss."

"I am keeping an eye on them myself," she retorted. "I did not tell you that Mullins was instructed to guard our jewels last night, and the count's cook apparently lured her away."

He nodded. "I suspected something of the sort."

She was reluctant to leave him. "Do you think, Reeves," she said slowly, "that we have done with the count? By now he must have found out that the—the parcel—is not in his table drawer. Will he know we have it back?"

Reeves gave himself over to grave thought. "I do not know. But it would be well to take no chances."

"I wish—" she began wistfully, then broke off. "No matter."

"That you had never left London?" he suggested.

He had the unsettling ability to read her mind. "Surely you cannot think I am enjoying this—this reckless jaunt?"

"Perhaps you may find some compensation for your trials." She glared at him. With a bland expression, he continued, "When you arrive in Vienna. Miss."

His impertinence struck her. He made her feel a fool, teasing her to make her remember his overtures and then pretending all the time that he had meant something entirely different. Suddenly his remark, along with the smile that hinted of conspiracies past and to come, recalled her to the impropriety of standing in the open with her coachman, gossiping with him as though he were an old friend.

She drew herself up to her full height. "Perhaps I neglected to fully express my gratitude for your intervention last evening. If so, I must apologize."

A wicked gleam came into the coachman's hazel eyes. "Nay, miss," he said in his broadest country speech, "I'd say you did, all right and tight."

She stamped her foot angrily. "I must say . . ." Her voice died away. He stood waiting for her instructions, but she made an impatient gesture and hurried across the stable yard, burningly aware of his gaze following her.

After the ill-cooked dinner, Phrynie acknowledged that she was exhausted and soon went up to bed. Nell lingered in the sitting room that had been put at their disposal until the fire died down and the room chilled. She was overwhelmed by a desolate feeling of loneliness. Restless, recalling only too well the latter part of the evening before, she could even fancy that her shoulders still burned where Reeves had—in the most outrageous fashion—placed his hands and pulled her close to his hard body. She rubbed her lips now with the back of her hand, as though to erase the memory of his insolent kiss.

Impertinence! Outrage! Despicable advances!

The words came to her tongue, but she recognized them as completely without validity. It was not Reeves who was to be condemned, but Nell herself. Nell, who never deceived herself for long, knew that the weakness, the license, was in herself.

She was not sure how the impulse—nay, the *need*—to respond to him had arisen in her, where the urge that had driven her had been hidden all these years. She only knew that when he had touched her, he had called forth a part of herself that she did not know existed. She had wanted Reeves to press her more closely to him, to keep on kissing her. . . .

Deliberately she wrenched her thoughts away from her disgraceful behavior and forcibly brought Rowland's classic features to mind.

She consoled herself to a degree by remembering that dear Rowland had not touched her. He—the Paragon—had spoken of respect and trust and control—and if he had behaved as Reeves had, her response to him would have been the same as to the coachman. It was a comforting thought—or would have been if she believed it.

How handsome Rowland was; his nose was straight, his features classic though manly. His stature was above the average, his limbs in splendid proportion. Not in the least stocky.

She had lost her sense of humor, she realized. How idiotic she was to compare a coachman with peerless Rowland! A world apart. But as she climbed the narrow stairs to the bedroom she was required to share with her aunt and Mullins, she managed a smile, picturing Rowland's expression were she to ask him to help her break into the library of a nobleman of France!

She fell asleep at once. It was past midnight when she awakened. At first she did not know where she was. The darkness overhead bore no resemblance to her airy room at home, and it took a few moments for her to realize that she was in a room in an obscure inn. She sat up in bed, listening.

Some sound had awakened her, a sound now lost. She strained her ears, expecting it to come again. It did.

The sound was very close, nearly beside her. Someone was lifting the latch to the door leading from the hall, very slowly, very cautiously, obviously up to no good.

She had awakened in time, for the intruder was still outside the room. Her bed was nearest the door. It was clear that she alone was awake. Mullins was snoring vigorously, and Phrynie's lips made delicate and regular popping sounds.

Stealthily Nell threw her covers back, and swung her bare feet to the floor. Very slowly, expecting the bed to squeak in protest at her movement, she stood up. If she could just reach the space behind the door before the intruder came fully inside, she would surprise him!

Arming herself with materials at hand, she picked up the boot she had been wearing in the carriage. It was made of velvet and fur, but fortunately the high heel had a satisfyingly sharp point. Not now weaponless, she slipped carefully across the bare floor.

The noise at the latch ceased. She realized she was no longer frightened. She wished the invader to succeed, to enter the room, giving her the chance to dispatch him. Then, she would scream the house down.

Her wish, to begin with, was granted. Her eyes were more accustomed now to the dark, and she could distinguish objects. Now she fancied she could see the iron of the latch outlined against the lighter wood of the door. The latch lifted and the door moved inward, the opening revealed by the appearance of a darker blackness outside. Nell raised her hand, boot heel at the ready. Just another step inside . . .

Mullins gurgled and her snores stopped. The intruder froze where he stood, waiting for the maid to fall asleep again. She didn't. Instead, she opened her eyes and saw the door was slightly open. Without the slightest warning, she emitted a piercing scream.

The scream startled Nell, and she dropped her boot with a clatter on the floor. The intruder cursed in French and turned to flee. From beyond him came a faint but growing light.

Someone was coming up the stairs, carrying a lantern.. A fellow thief? Nell picked up the boot. When the intruder hesitated on the stair landing, the light from below caught his features. Even though they were distorted by the angle of the light, she gasped in recognition.

"You!" she breathed, but she was sure he did not hear her. He was sensibly intent upon flight.

Phrynie struggled muzzily from deep slumber and cried out, "What is it, Mullins? For heaven's sake stop that racket or I'll send you home at once!"

Careless of danger, Nell hurried around the door to peer out into the hall, with some vague thought of capturing the intruder. She heard booted footsteps pounding down the stairs, and a confused melee of masculine outcries and thuds at the bottom, where the intruder must have impinged with some force upon the man with the lantern. The thief was out of sight, gone without trace, except for the sour unwashed smell he left behind him, but the lantern holder was racing up the steps to her.

"Oh, Reeves!" she cried out, recognizing him with relief.

"What happened?" he demanded. "Did you see anything? Did he get—whatever he came for?"

"No," she said quickly. "I woke up and he was just opening the door. He—" She stopped short. Was the intruder after the jewels they carried? Surely anyone could have seen Phrynie and her carrying the small cases into the inn and guessed what they held.

But there was, after all, the attraction the parcel had had for the count. Suddenly she thought she must have imagined the squint-eyed face she thought she recognized. Surely the count's servant could not have followed them solely for the purpose of stealing the mysterious parcel back.

And no one here at the inn knew of the parcel. She must be mistaken. The man's features had been twisted by the flickering light from below, and she had the count's *ménage* too recently on her mind. The intruder was—must have been—simply a common thief after their valuables.

"Of course there was an intruder, Aunt," said Nell, nettled. "I should hardly have gotten out of bed and stood here in the dark ready to hit him with my boot heel, had there been no reason. Mullins saw him. At least, she saw something."

"Mullins?"

"Aye, my lady, I seen him. A big hairy monster he was, with claws on his fingers!"

"Nonsense, Mullins. Pray be silent, before we have him breathing fire. Reeves, you have not answered me. How came you so swiftly?"

"I be too wakeful, my lady," said Reeves in his broadest dialect. "So I cum over to get a bit of beer to settle me innards, like."

Nell was exasperated. What humbug! It was much more likely that the coachman was watchful for their safety. Why could he not say so?

One reason struck her like a blow. He had eyes now only for her, eyes that held a devilish gleam as well as the baldest admiration. Confusion enveloped her. She had not troubled, feeling haste and silence were imperative, to find her robe. She stood revealed in the lantern light in her gauzy pink night-shift, her hair covered by a fetching cap with pink ribbons. Her aunt's coachman was clearly riveted to the floor by the sight.

"Oh!" she gasped, and leaped for the shelter of her bed.

"I will deal with you, Reeves, in the morning!" said Phrynie icily. "You may leave us now."

"Very good, my lady." His tone was wooden but he cast a wicked glance toward Nell, cowering under her blankets, and closed the door softly behind him.

She listened carefully. She did not hear his steps retreating down the stairs. He was still near, she thought, and with a sigh of contentment closed her eyes and slept.

By the time they were ready to leave in the morning, the dangers of the night just past had faded from her mind. Reeves had come to her rescue once more. Deliberately putting him in his proper place, she told herself, I must remember to ask Rowland to give him some kind of reward.

But she knew she never would, for Reeves was not the sort of man to whom one tossed a few coins.

The small town where they had spent the night was soon

behind them. She had essayed a small smile at the coachman, but he failed to return it. Lines appeared on his face that had not been there yesterday. She was positive now that he had stayed awake on the landing after their alarum for the rest of the night.

She had managed to speak to him for a few moments before their departure. "Did you manage to sleep at all, Reeves?"

"Enough, miss."

"I trust there was no further disturbance? I did not hear any."

"Quite right, miss. There was none."

"I wonder, Reeves—did you recognize the man?"

He looked sharply at her. Instead of answering, he countered, "Did you?"

Her voice was level. "I thought I did. But I could not make sure. He was gone so quickly."

Reeves rubbed his shoulder. "Aye. I was a bit in his way."

"I must think he was not after our jewels."

He stood, not moving. The parcel lay almost tangibly between them. "Not the jewels," he agreed.

She glanced behind her to where her aunt was engaged with Mullins and her bandboxes. "We have only Potter and you for protection, Reeves. Perhaps I should have brought a pistol."

"Good God!" breathed Reeves.

"I am a very good shot, you know. But I left it at home, at Aspinall Hall. But I really cannot be to blame, for who would have imagined that I would find a use for it?"

"Who, indeed?" agreed Reeves. Then, as usual much too late, he added, "Miss."

Recognizing that she would get no more conversation from him at least at this time, she picked up her skirts and joined her aunt in the carriage.

Phrynie, her sleep broken for two nights in a row, was captious. "What was that man doing last night?"

"I suppose he was after our valuables, Aunt."

"I do not refer to him. It was clear enough what he wanted. I mean that coachman you hired."

"Reeves?" Nell asked innocently.

"Of course, if that is his real name. Which, I should like to point out, I doubt. The man is an enigma. He's no coachman."

"He handles the cattle excessively well."

"And so do some of our notable whips," Phrynie pointed out with acerbity. "He doesn't act like a coachman."

Nell, caught up in rosy recollection, agreed. He surely didn't!

"I do not trust him," pronounced Lady Sanford. "I cannot think what you were about in hiring him."

The time Nell had dreaded had clearly arrived. She knew she could keep the events of the night at Château Pernoud secret no longer. With one exception, of course! "Aunt, I must tell you—"

Phrynie listened with all the attention Nell could wish for. She reminded her aunt of the tale she had told about the recovery of the parcel. Getting through the window, retrieving the parcel from the drawer, and hurrying back through the night and up the dark stairs . . .

"I've heard this, Nell. And I must say I find my credulity strained at the seams to think that you managed all this entirely by yourself."

"You did not tell me you didn't believe me."

"Was I justified?"

"I fear you were. But I shall tell you all."

"Pray do."

"When I was trying to open the window, you know, I did not hear him coming and—" The person of Reeves now entered the narrative. Nell left out nothing—except for keeping private the memory of the scalding incident on the stairs. She included the alarum when the servant Emile entered the library and closed the window, and the inestimable help that the coachman had provided.

At the end of the narrative, Nell waited for the explosion she considered inevitable. When it did not come, she ventured to glance at her aunt. To her great surprise, Phrynie was overcome with silent laughter.

"Aunt! Then—you're not angry?"

"Yes, indeed I am," insisted Phrynie between fits of laughter. "I vastly wish to have been with you. It sounds like quite the most entertaining event since—well, since Darnford and I had to—" She stopped short. "Never mind what Darnford and I had to do, Nell. But I should be much more in charity with you had you invited me along. Of course, I do not blame you. Indeed, I vow I did not think you had it in you!"

In great good humor with each other, they traveled on. Phrynie speculated about Reeves's antecedents, and Nell pointed out that no matter who his parents could have been, he was certainly on their side as far as this expedition went.

"But now he knows about the parcel, Aunt, and that is why he kept watch last night."

"His father was undoubtedly a familiar at Newgate," suggested Phrynie, "but I think it exceedingly tactless to mention it."

Nell remembered later that she had not mentioned the fact that she had recognized the intruder in the night. If Emile had come this far after them, it was most likely that they would hear again from the count's emissary. Next time he might not be so easily routed.

Chapter Eighteen

They traveled for days. It seemed to Nell that the road was endless, but paradoxically she was loath to arrive at their destination.

She had discovered it was less trying to consider that the journey was a venture unto itself, without beginning and without end. Indeed, she had no need to deceive herself, for the start back in London, the parcel in her jewel case, and the expectation of Tom's following upon their heels seemed so long ago as to have taken place in another century.

Equally remote in time was their journey's end. She thought about Vienna, when she considered it at all, as though in a dream. Nothing existed but the jolting of the carriage, the rhythmic sound of the horses steadily covering leagues, and a succession of inns hardly worthy of the name. Her world narrowed to her aunt and Mullins, Potter the footman—and Reeves.

She dared not think of how Reeves marked her days. She exchanged a few innocent words with him in the mornings, just before they took to the road, and a few more of similar inconsequence in the evenings.

She did not even know whether he continued to keep watch nearby at night. He had become remote and noncommunicative again, and she felt keenly the loss of his amused glances and dry comments. But they had covered a surprising distance. Leaving France behind, they had moved into an area of Germany where the people and even the landscape seemed hostile and unforgiving.

"This is interesting country, is it not, Nell?" said Phrynie after one of her infrequent glances through the chariot window. "I do not say attractive in the least, but one does not expect the entire world to be as comfortable as one's own country. However, one advantage to traveling particularly in such uncivilized regions exists. I believe I have lost at least a stone in weight. I vow even my slippers no longer fit well."

"You may indulge without guilt, then, in the whipped cream and chocolate you expect in Vienna.

"I had thought of that," responded Phrynie drily. "I shall never in my entire life eat *pompernickel* again."

The road narrowed, and now they were traversing a forest road so straitened that from time to time they could hear the tree branches brushing the sides of the vehicle.

Nell peered out. "Do you think there are wolves in these woods?"

"Without doubt. We shall trust that we can outrun them. I confess I shall resist strongly any attempt to persuade me to take this road again."

"How will you return to England then?"

"As yet I am not thoroughly conversant with alternate routes, you know, but that is a lack easily mended."

"Perhaps," ventured Nell, moved by some obscure reason, "we might even stay in Vienna."

Her aunt was startled. Then, easily, she suggested, "I suppose that if Foxhall were assigned to the embassy there, you might as well marry at once."

"Oh," said Nell, as though the thought had not occurred to her, "of course. Dear Rowland." She fell silent again.

Phrynie realized that she was much troubled about her niece. In London, Nell's bubbling conversation had centered obsessively on the great love of her life. There was hardly a sentence that she uttered that did not include an allusion to dear Rowland, his sayings, his manly beauty, his impeccable manners.

To give Nell credit, she had not mentioned his title, his expectation of inheriting an earldom, nor his substantial income. But for the last few days, "dear Rowland" had unaccountably vanished from her conversation, and Phrynie longed to know what subject had routed from Nell's thoughts the constant paean directed toward Foxhall. She would never learn from Nell, she was sure, for the girl had withdrawn into long periods of silence.

But Phrynie recognized a duty when she saw it, and she

turned her full attention to her niece. "Nell, have you noticed how free we have been of intruders in the night?"

"I do not regret such a lack, believe me."

"Why do you think that creature tried to enter our room, Nell?"

"Your jewels would be sufficient attraction, I should think."

Phrynie was silent for a few moments. Mullins had been most obliging to those who wished to carry on private conversation, falling heavily asleep as soon as the carriage left the inn yard and only rousing sufficiently to eat, perform a few simple duties, and fall asleep at night, no matter how uncomfortable her cot.

Phrynie looked at her maid without favor. "I shall have to consider what to do with—that." She nodded toward the sleeping woman. "She has been of absolutely no help to me at all."

"In addition," Nell pointed out, "she obliges us with unearthly screams at the most inopportune moments."

Phrynie made up her mind to speak directly about a vague uneasiness she had entertained for some time. "Nell, did you recognize that man the other night?"

Nell smiled. "You mean the hairy monster with long claws?"

"That woman!" When Nell did not answer the question at once, her aunt insisted. "Did you?"

Nell had learned at least one lesson along the way. It was not the thing to try to deceive her aunt, at least in some things. Full confession was much easier on the mind, for one did not have to guard one's tongue against an inadvertent slip. However, she did not intend to tell her aunt quite everything.

"I—I'm not sure, Aunt."

"Aha! I thought you did." Phrynie swooped directly to the point. "Was it someone from the count?"

"I thought it was Emile."

"Emile? Oh, yes, Squint-Eye. But—" Phrynie's speculations held her silent for a moment. She lowered her voice, even though Mullins had begun to snore. "Nell, what is in that package?"

Nell felt near tears. "I don't know, Aunt. Truly, I don't. You mentioned love letters, but I cannot think that is right. Whose letters would be worth stealing?"

"Only an idiot writes that kind of letter," pronounced Phrynie. "Without a doubt, there is something more. It's not heavy. Ah well, I suppose we shall never know its contents."

"Nor do I want to," insisted Nell.

"I do suppose, my dear, that we still have it safe?"

"Yes, for now at least. But one cannot but expect some further incident."

"I expect no such thing, Nell. It's been days, and we are half a continent away from the count. If he needed the parcel, for whatever purpose one cannot conceive, he would have appeared long since."

Nell did not speak for some time. When she did, she had not moved far away from the subject. "One might think," she said without logic, "that if the parcel were indeed as valuable as Mr. Haveney seemed to think, he would have arranged for better safeguards for it."

"Such as your brother? Who has not yet, I hesitate to point out, appeared." Phrynie's voice reflected skepticism.

"At least, Tom wouldn't have traveled weaponless."

Phrynie conceded the point. "Nor would he have spent the night at the Chateau Pernoud."

Or hinted so broadly at secrets, Nell thought, but being essentially kind, she refrained from saying so.

"Well," she said finally, "with Reeves to protect us, we will be safe enough from thieves in the night, or even footpads on the road."

She spoke too soon.

The coach began to slow, and came to a halt. They had now left the forest behind and emerged upon what seemed to be a vast field without more than a cart track to serve as road.

"I can't see why we have stopped, Aunt. I did think that the forest furnished a prime opportunity for ambush, but that's all behind us."

That something was amiss was certain. Shouts came from the front, and Nell could discern Potter's shrill protests. "No! I won't do it. I'm always doing your dirty work! You do it!"

"All right," came the coachman's deep rumble. "It's naught but a bush the wind's brought. Here, hold the reins. Think you can do that much?"

Potter's remark was lost to the passengers in the coach.

"Only a bush in the road," Nell relayed the information to her aunt.

Phrynie frowned. "Bush, in this wide expanse, caught in the ruts? And the wind blowing up to a gale?"

They looked at each other in surmise. "I don't believe it either," said Nell at last.

They could hear Reeve's voice speaking reassuringly to the team. As long as the horses knew he was at hand, they would not bolt in spite of the quivering hands holding their reins. Suddenly, something went wrong. Reeves's voice rose in sharp protest. There were other voices, unrecognizable.

"I'm going to see what's going on."

"Nell!"

"Do you stay here, Aunt. It's safer!"

"With Potter on the box? Don't be a fool!"

Nell dropped to the ground beside the coach. She knew that Phrynie was right behind her, but she could not waste time in protest. The scene before her was, to say the least, heart-stopping. It took a moment to assimilate the details.

A knot of men gathered in the middle of the road, the man in the middle of the knot struggling in a melee of arms and legs and shouts and curses. Reeves, suddenly, fell to his knees under the battering blows.

Reeves! Nell thought she screamed, but if she did, it had no effect on the struggle ahead. She did not stop to think. As from a distance, she heard Phrynie exclaim in an agonized whisper, "An ambush! Nell, they're going to kill us!"

Nell's whirling thoughts settled on the instant. With grim determination, she said, "I have no intention of dying in a Bavarian ditch! There's a gun in the pouch on the box."

"Nell, you can't! Leave it to Potter!"

"I am more apt to shoot him," said Nell fiercely. "He's no use at all!"

Nell seemed to be thinking with uncanny speed. It was as though she were guided by a force outside herself. She took note of the struggle on the road, the horses beginning to plunge, frightened by the uproar, and Potter, useless on the box, the reins slack in his fingers.

She climbed to the box. "Give over, Potter. If you can't help, at least get out of the way." Her push was not gentle. She rummaged in the box and found the gun. So automatically that later she did not remember doing it, she checked the load and aimed at the villains.

There were three of them. Two were holding the fallen coachman by the arms, and the third was methodically slamming his fists into the victim's face. Even from here she could hear the sickening thumping sounds.

"Stop that!" she screeched. At the same moment, Mullins unfortunately awakened and thrust her head out of the open carriage door. Her screams could have been heard in the next province. As one, the three attackers turned in their direction. They saw a determined young lady climbing down from the box, holding an enormous weapon in her hands.

They dropped Reeves. His head struck on the frozen ground, and he lost interest in the proceedings for a moment. He did not see the young lady taking careful aim and, as coolly as though she were aiming at targets on the range at Aspinall Hall, pulling the trigger.

The resulting thunderclap provided sufficient incentive to the attackers to increase their speed by half. She had no wish to kill anything, even such brutes as these. But she was satisfied that they would not return in the immediate future and ran to Reeves, kneeling beside him in the road. She beseeched him to open his eyes, and he obeyed. What he saw stirred him to groan desperately, "Good God, woman, don't shoot me!"

She realized then that she still held the gun, a tendril of smoke rising from the muzzle. Hastily she thrust it behind her.

"You don't sound hurt at all. I'll get Potter."

"Let him—see to the horses." He closed his eyes.

She realized that he had taken real punishment in the few moments before she had come to his rescue. Those fists smashing into his face had meted out damage that would in the morning make his face one mass of swollen purple. She remembered an occasion when Tom had run afoul of the Bully at the fairgrounds—a round cheese the prize for whoever could down the Bully! Tom won no cheese that day.

And where was Tom when she needed him so desperately?

Reeves had gone ashen beneath his bronzed complexion. She could almost feel the lump on his left temple swell under her fingertips.

"Reeves, don't faint on me! We'll get you into the coach!"

A moan was his only response. She looked back at the carriage, desperate for help. Phrynie, to her great relief, had taken Potter in hand, judging from his thoroughly cowed expression. Phrynie herself stood at the heads of the lead pair of horses, and while they were still far from tranquil, they seemed well on their way to being so. There was no end to Phrynie's talents.

Nell turned back to the fallen coachman. His eyes were open now and he struggled to speak. She bent down to hear. "Listen to me," he said fiercely. "I've not much time. Take the carriage and your aunt to the next town, where you'll be safe."

"Not without you!"

"Don't argue. Just do it." She tugged at his arm, trying impossibly to lift him. "Parcel—safe," he breathed. "They won't come back if—you've—gone."

"Oh, Reeves, you're hurt! I can't leave you here!"

His eyes opened again, and anger flared in them. "God! Do what I tell you! Why are women so damnably stupid!"

She felt a pang of regret that she was not holding his head. Dropping it would not have been a salutary experience for him, but it would certainly have relieved her own feelings.

She stood up and glared down at him. "Stupid? I am not quite so stupid that I did not manage to rout your attackers. I wish you will not regret your words, but I sadly fear you will."

Her retort fell on unconscious ears.

She hurried to her aunt. "We've been ordered to go to safety in the next town," she said briskly. "I think we must hurry. Already I see that the brutes are hovering—just out of pistol range."

"How shall we accomplish this flight?" said her aunt drily. "Walk? In these boots? It may have escaped your notice that our coachman is unable to drive."

"Serves him right," said Nell with spirit. "I shall drive. I've driven a team many times."

"I devoutly hope," said Phrynie piously, "that you drive better than your father."

With a wisp of humor, Nell assured her, "Oh, yes, I do. Our old coachman taught me." She glanced over her shoulder. "Hurry, Aunt. We've got to get that—that *thing*—to a safe place. They won't hurt Reeves anymore, I think, as long as he doesn't have the parcel."

She would have left Potter to stay with the supine victim, but she could not order him to risk his life. She gathered up the reins, saw that Phrynie had bundled Mullins and herself with scant ceremony into the coach, and—trying to remember all that old Haines, the Aspinall coachman, had taught her—whipped up the team.

The chariot, containing the parcel and leaving the man behind, moved swiftly down the road.

Chapter Nineteen

The next town was only a short distance down the track. The inn appeared, Phrynie was relieved to note, to be better than average. Nell drove the coach through the gates into the cobbled yard, to the amazement of the two ostlers who came running from the stables.

Nell's German was rudimentary, but she was able to understand the constant repetition of *Fräulein* and *Pferd*, and knew that her arrival on the box of an English traveling chariot would be an event soon entering legend.

Phrynie emerged from the interior of the coach. "Nell, a superb job. Now perhaps you will explain to me how it came about that we left my servant lying badly injured on the road while we ourselves fled to safety?"

"Aunt, I must go back. They may have killed him."

"Don't fly up into the boughs, Nell. Of course you must return to rescue him. Why we did not see to that small task while we were on the spot eludes my understanding. But of course I am sure you will make all clear. After we eat."

"Aunt, I cannot take time to eat. I couldn't swallow a morsel."

Phrynie turned to the landlord, suddenly standing at her elbow. "You understand English? Good. I shall require two of your best bedrooms, a private sitting room, and a hot nuncheon served at once."

"*Verständlich, gnädige fräu.*"

"And brandy, at once."

"Aunt—I wish a cart, and horses. I must go back without a moment's delay."

"First the brandy," Phrynie ordered, "and then the cart."

Phrynie was quite properly anxious that Nell be restored in

spirit before setting out to rescue the coachman. However, she realized, after Nell had unthinkingly gulped down the fiery liquor, that a restoration in spirit was not necessarily identical with the imbibing of *spirits*.

Nell drank the small glass of *Branntwein* in two swallows and said, with a suddenly expansive wave of the hand, "Now the cart. And horses, of course, and where is Potter?"

"Nell, do you think . . . ?" ventured Phrynie.

"Of course, I do. Nearly every day. And now I think I must go get Reeves. Dear Reeves."

"Good God, child, you're drunk!"

"Don't believe it for a minute. I feel just fine. I want my cart, that is all. Pray, Aunt, do you obtain my cart for me. I shall need straw in it, for dear Reeves may be badly injured."

Or dead, more likely, thought Phrynie, guilt like a pall weighing her down. "I shall get Potter."

Nell had lost her sense of time. Indeed, she was almost euphoric as reality tilted and slid away from her. Phrynie was in two minds. Reeves must be rescued, there was no question about that. And since, as they had left the scene in what was no less than a mad rout, Nell had mentioned the urgent need to safeguard the parcel, someone must stay here in the inn for the same purpose.

And Nell, in her present condition, might easily give away diamonds, sapphires, and the future well-being of the British government.

Mullins, of course, was worse than useless.

"Out of doors with you, Nell. I can't think why I was such a fool to give you brandy."

The fresh air did wonders for Nell. There was a nasty moment when the world danced dizzily around her and her stomach suffered a mighty quake, but she weathered the crisis. She turned, somewhat chastened, to her aunt and said, "I really must go back."

Phrynie agreed. "But Potter will go with you. And an ostler from the inn also, for if you have to lift—" She almost had said *dead body* but altered her words. "Lift dead weight, you will need two men."

Nell, after what seemed an eternity, whipped up the cart horses and maneuvered the vehicle out of the gates and turned it in the direction from which they had arrived. The cart was small, but the straw that bottomed it was fresh. The landlord had offered the loan of two blankets and the ostler, Hans. Potter, torn between the shame of his cowardice and his wish to render Miss Nell whatever service she needed, slumped beside her on the hard wooden seat.

The brandy had, in the way of strong spirits, lifted her for the moment and then fled, leaving her in a condition lower than even that moment when she saw Reeves slump to his knees, held up by two of the band that had ambushed them.

The horses she drove now were the sorriest nags she had seen. Even the Aspinall farm animals were of better quality. She plied the whip she had borrowed from the Sanford chariot but to no avail. She must simply hold her impatience in check, for the horses could not even break into a trot. She dared not think of what they would find ahead of them. Reeves dead, Reeves dragged away and thrown into the ditch, Reeves carried off never to be seen again . . .

This line of speculation she could not abide. Instead, she turned her thoughts to the half hour just past. She had left Reeves as angry as she had been since Tom locked her in her room so she would not follow him to an exhibition of fisti-cuffs at Halstead. She had at that time an intense longing to see a pair called Gully and the Chicken, expecting to see a monstrous example of poultry.

Reeves had called her stupid. All women are stupid; there was no mistaking the burden of that explosive cry. She did not believe his harsh words were the product of pain and in-jury. After all, he had kept his head enough to order the par-cel to safety.

Stupid, was she? Not quite too hen-witted to manage the four restless horses and drive the chariot to the nearest town! Not so unintelligent that she could not mount this rescue op-eration! She meditated for a few pleasurable moments, form-ing scalding phrases that she would pour down on the hapless head of the coachman—and gasped with fear that he was mortally injured. Fearing only that she would never, in that case, be able to point out to him his manifold mistakes.

That way, too, was not to be thought of.

Instead, she checked over the arrangements she had made. Once again she had borrowed Mullins' cloak. In place of her own ornate bonnet of burgundy velvet, with ruching in a paler shade lining the brim, she pulled up the hood of the rough woolen garment and hid her curls. Her disguise was eminently suitable for the occasion. It would be witless to appear in her proper person, for the villains would rob her, hold her for ransom, or simply use her and toss her broken body in the ditch.

Her only hope, as she saw it, of finding Reeves and bringing him back in the cart was to appear as innocuous as possible. She would approach the site as a simple farm girl. Only when faced with actual peril would she flourish the pistol, now secured in her belt beneath the enveloping brown cloak.

Reeves had insulted her marksmanship, which, she thought more than likely, was as good as his. She had practiced many hours under her father's tutelage as well as old Crouch's, the Aspinall game warden. She could shoot a playing card out of a man's hand at fifty paces. And Reeves had shouted, "Don't shoot me!" Some day she would pay him off for that. And the next moment her anger dissolved, to be replaced by the desperate hope that he would survive long enough to suffer her revenge.

She nursed her grudge as they retraced their journey. If she did not remain angry with him, she would be cast into a blue-deviled mood that would do neither of them any good. She would need all her wits about her. First, she planned to rescue him. And then she would explain to him precisely how abhorrently arrogant and wrong-minded he was.

The horses, meanwhile, could not be persuaded to more than a sedate walk. The journey in the chariot had taken no more than ten minutes, but the return covered more than half an hour. They moved along in silence. Potter was awed by the events just past, and by Miss Nell's clear contempt for him. Wrapped in misery, there was no way he could explain what had happened to his courage, for he did not himself know. It was only that everything was so strange, even the words folk said, and he longed with all his heart to be back in London, where he knew what was what.

Everything here was topsy-turvy. *Bitte*, for instance, sounded ominous in his ears, and yet it was a kindly word in meaning. How could you get along, Potter demanded of himself, when nothing was what you'd expect?

Now, Nell pulled the horses to a slower pace. The road held a slight curve here, and just beyond was the place of the ambush. Along the inner edge of the curve stood a small coppice of spindly trees, growing in a low place that Potter would have bet gold would be flooded in the spring. At least at home it would, but who knew even how spring rains behaved in this forsaken land?

Nell peered through the leafless branches of the saplings, examining the road beyond the curve. "Best not to come full tilt on the place," she murmured to Potter, "as though we could with this pair. We must not let the thieves have the advantage."

Potter breathed more easily at his mistress's mild tone. She was not angry with him. His courage came rampaging back.

Nell saw, then, a shapeless darkness on the road ahead. There he was. She did not know she had held her breath until it came out in a gust of relief. He had not been removed, dead or not. *There he was!*

But he was not as he was. There were other men, moving in inexplicable ways around him. "Potter," she said tightly, "what are they doing?"

Potter peered in his turn through the obstructing branches. "Dunno, miss, but it don't look good."

She turned her horses to the right, off the road. "Do you come with me, Potter. I may need you."

Eagerly he jumped down from the wooden seat. He was brave as a lion, he again told himself, as he wound the reins around a sprig of a bush at the side of the road and followed Nell.

Nell was in the van. The sight that met her eyes chilled her down to the bone. Reeves seemed to dangle between two men. They too had a wagon, for it stood beyond them a short distance. There were saddled horses too, which indicated that she could not hope to outrun them in her farm cart, even supposing she had enough foresight to turn the cart before they left it. She paused long enough to perceive details. Each of the two men held an arm of the coachman, trying to get him on his feet. He slumped limply between them, his head lolling on his chest.

Her way was clear before her. The time for action had come. She took her pistol from her belt, and with a word to Potter, ran forward.

Potter, formerly brave as a lion, now realized he was a very small lion. Although his spirit charged ahead with Miss Nell, his feet were unalterably slow to follow.

Nell drove ahead to the attack. "What are you doing?" she screeched. "Let him go! I'll shoot the first man——"

She stopped and steadied the gun with both hands. Whether she would indeed have shot either of them was never to be decided. The two men, clearly members of the local peasantry, were startled out of their wits by the sight of the young Amazon aiming a large weapon with a muzzle like a cannon. They did not make the mistake that Reeves had made. They recognized from Nell's firm stance, the gun steady in her hands, the ferocious competence in her eyes, that this was not the first time she had held a pistol. They dropped Reeves out of hand and backed away, their hands in the air.

"Bitte!"

"Go on!" she cried, gesturing with the gun. "Get right away!" She believed they did not understand her and searched her wits for an appropriate German word. None occurred to her.

She stepped toward the fallen coachman, her eyes still warningly on his assailants. "Leave him alone! You've killed him!"

She did not hear Potter's strangled cry of warning behind her. It would have done no good, had she heard, for there was no time to act.

She realized, too late, that the two who had been manhandling Reeves were not alone and was deftly caught from behind. Her assailant's free hand snaked down her arm to catch her wrist, pointing the gun harmlessly toward the open fields beyond. She managed an abortive kick backward before she was lifted off the ground.

The pressure tightened on her wrist, and she dropped the gun. The villain's hand then clamped roughly over her mouth. The sudden silence told her she had been screaming the heavens down. Without so much as thinking, she promptly sank her teeth into the fingers muffling her screams. That will show him!

The sudden pain caused the unknown man to relax his hold on her waist, and she felt the hard ground beneath her feet. Instantly she kicked backward. The sharp heel of her carriage boot caught him hard on the shin. Gratified by his grunt of pain, she kicked him again.

She writhed in her captor's arms. He held her painfully

tight, and she redoubled her efforts to escape. She bit his finger again, hard, and this time he tore his hand away. She would be free in a moment. . . .

He gave vent to an out-and-out curse—and she gasped in disbelief.

The curse, surprisingly, was in English. But the voice! That voice she knew, the voice that was the last she had expected to hear, especially here, and particularly now.

Chapter Twenty

"Tom Aspinall, what are you doing here?" she shrieked. "Where have you been?"

By this time, he had recovered both from the pain of his tooth-lacerated fingers and the shock of recognizing his young sister. His indignation was quite equal to hers. "What in blue blazes are you doing here? Dressed up to the mark, I don't think. Whose cast-off rags are those you're wearing? I can't believe that our aunt would allow you to parade around in that rig!" His thoughts took a new and unwelcome turn. "I suppose Aunt Phrynie is somewhere nearby? Or are you—pray do not tell me you are—traveling unchaperoned in this vile country?"

Inured to her brother's strictures, which were reminiscent of her father when he pretended to be displeased with her, she countered, "You are certainly well overdue, Tom. I cannot think that your injury was severe. You are not even limping."

"I am, you bad-mannered infant! Those boots have a wicked point to them. I wonder I am not lamed for life!"

"If Charlie Puckett's cast-off mount couldn't do it, then my poor velvet boots wouldn't have a chance. You've made me worry and go through all kinds of danger and peril, and I don't know where we are or how long it will be till we're in Vienna and rid of that . . . And now I find you trying to kill our coachman!"

"Coachman!" retorted Tom, rubbing his damaged shin. The strained emotion in his voice threatened to overset him. He pointed a finger at Reeves. "Him?"

His gesture brought Nell back to the purpose for which she

had come. "Reeves!" she wailed. "Oh, Reeves! How bad is it?"

Tom was not so deeply affected. "If you will notice, my dear sister, your—you did say coachman, did you not?—is recovering. Rapidly."

So he was. His eyes were open, and the glint of amusement in them, while indicative of his probable survival, was none-theless excessively provoking to her. "Reeves . . ."

Tom interrupted. "Where is Stuston?"

"In bed where he belongs," she said shortly. "At that inn."

Tom gazed in exasperation at his sister. "I think," he said firmly, "I should like a more detailed explanation."

"Why?" retorted Nell, battered beyond civility by anxiety over Reeves and irritation with her brother. "He is not your coachman, since our aunt employed him. And if you had our safety and comfort at heart, Tom, you would have been there at the time, and all this wouldn't have happened!"

Stung by the vague accusations, especially since they were unjust, he retorted in kind. "How was I to know you'd all lose your heads and take to the road like a Romany caravan? I vow I thought Aunt Phrynie had more sense, even if you don't!"

A voice, faint yet full of authority, broke in on them. "Children," reproved Reeves. "Do stop behaving as though you were still in the nursery. I assume that those fellows of yours, Tom, were to take me somewhere?"

"You're not a grandfather yourself, you know." It was the last arrow in his quiver. "I hired them," he continued, "when I came upon your lifeless body. Is it possible you are recovered sufficiently to stand?"

At his gesture, the two countrymen chased by Nell's threats to a short distance away returned to the scene. Under Tom's efficient direction—he was surprisingly competent, Nell thought, beginning to realize she was not sufficiently acquaint-ed with her nearest relative—Nell's wagon was turned to face back toward town and Reeves was carefully lifted and placed in the straw and covered with the blankets. The local helpers were paid off.

The saddled horses were brought forward by Aston, Tom's man, who touched his forehead to Nell and kept all emotion from his features.

Tom slid onto the cart seat beside her, and took the reins.

"You have not yet informed me," he said after a minute, "how you came here. I agree that you are well armed and well able to disable anyone so misguided as to attack you. But traveling in this cart? With these cattle fit only for the abattoir? And in those monstrously unbecoming garments?"

"I do hope I have sufficient decorum," she informed him frostily, "not to behave in such a harum-scarum fashion. You did not truly think so?"

In a kinder tone, he told her, "No, of course not. But you must admit your appearance out of nowhere, brandishing that cannon and calling for vengeance, is a bit dramatic. Can you indeed explain it?"

"I have no need to explain myself to you, Tom. You are never at hand when I need you. And Aunt Phrynie is—" Her voice broke. "Oh, Tom!"

Reeves was behind her in the straw, alive, and while far from well, not mortally wounded. And Tom, her dear brother, had come at last, and she could turn over the parcel to him and travel to Vienna with a light heart.

The pathetic little cry moved him deeply. He transferred the reins to one hand and put his arm around Nell, drawing her close. "Go on, Nell, use my shoulder. Cry all you want. It's not the first time, is it?"

Her answer was strangled, but her tears were fresh and real—and abundant, as well they might be, having been held back since she had seen Stuston lying injured on the cobblestones at Calais.

"It's my fault," she sobbed incoherently, "first Stuston and now Reeves. If I only—"

Her brother interrupted. "The world is full of *ifs*," he said stoutly. "If I hadn't fallen into Charlie Puckett's trap and bought that hardmouthed hack, for one thing. If I'd been on hand in London—Nell, you haven't yet told me what you are doing here?"

But he was not destined to receive an answer to that question immediately. Nell was too overwrought to make sense, he considered—all he could decipher from her broken and strangled phrases was something about burglaries and deformed monsters in the night. Nothing to worry about, he thought, for the dear child had quite plainly garbled some nightmare ramblings and offered them up to him in lieu of excuses. He had really too long ignored his sister. He must make it up to her—but not right away.

"Your coachman will be all right, I think," he said seriously. "This one, that is. But what of Stuston? Why is he not driving you? You said he was in bed in the inn? What inn? And surely you are not wandering across the Continent in this farm cart? Truly, Nell . . ." He was edging closer to a state of complete exasperation, judging from the tone of his voice.

Nell had caught hold of the comfort offered in Tom's assessment of Reeves's injuries. "Are you sure?"

"I suppose you mean—that fellow in the straw behind us?" He looked over his shoulder at the unconscious figure of the coachman. "He'll not put his spoon in the wall, if that's what's bothering you." Relenting, he added, "You did say something about breaking into some place—but you don't need to accuse yourself of murder as well!"

"You don't believe me," she said in a forlorn voice.

"I tell you it's hard to keep a straight face when one's sister speaks of felonies in such offhand ways! I hardly thought you would know the first way to go about it!"

She sat thinking, chin in hand. If Reeves was not dying, then it would be only logical to think of the next step. Tom was here, ready to take over the parcel that Mr. Haveney intended in the first place to consign into his hands. But without the parcel, she would arrive in Vienna without any excuse except the indecorous one of following dear Rowland.

She would have to think about that.

The cart moved at a rate something less than a snail's pace. The horses, far from being anxious to return to their barn, were more than resentful of the weight added by the victim and the new driver. There was plenty of time to make at least a start at explanations, and she could feel Tom's growing impatience with the entire situation he had come upon.

"Well, first I must tell you about Stuston," she began.

He broke in. "Admirable as that incident might appear as a beginning, my dear sister, I profess an anxiety to know exactly how this lunatic jaunt began. I wheedled Whitcomb until he told me his last sight of you—my aunt's traveling chariot, coachman, groom, footman, maid, and my two nearest relations setting off down Mount Street." He slapped the reins smartly on the haunches of the pair pulling the cart, entirely without result. "Am I correct thus far?"

"Yes."

"And now I find you alone but for a trembling groom, yourself dressed in what I consider to be mere rags, and journeying in a farm cart loaded with straw."

"I can quite see, Tom, that you are puzzled."

"Puzzled! My dear child, that is only the first step in the matter of how I feel!"

"I'll tell you about it."

"Without doubt you will," said Tom heavily, "for I shall not submit to any degree of fobbing off, you know."

"No need to be insulting, Tom."

He had, he felt, every need to be insulting. But he was no fool, and he knew that to allow his feelings full vocal rein would not elicit satisfactory responses. He had been told certain things by Arthur Haveney, foremost among which was that the precious parcel destined to reach Castlereagh at the earliest possible moment had been placed by that fool of a messenger into the hands of a delicately nurtured female, far too bent on having her own way. There was much in all this that Tom did not understand. He found Nell's explanations to be, as usual, a tangle of half-recognized phrases, all as though seen through a heavy fog. Nell was logical in her actions. It was only in her explanations, swooping and elliptical, that a masculine mind bogged down.

He had recourse now to the only method of eliciting any kind of sense from her. "Nell, is the chariot lost?"

"Of course not."

"Then why are we not riding in it? Wait—I lost my head just then. Pray don't answer that. I do not think I want to know why, just yet. Instead, tell me—Stuston. What happened to him?"

She made a commendable effort to put the experiences of recent days into some kind of form that even her exasperating brother could understand. "He fell on the pavement at Calais. He is now, so I believe, recovering from his broken bones in an inn. The inn is called," she said with scrupulous attention to detail, "the Blue Dolphin. Aunt Phrynie left the footman Samuel to tend him."

"That accounts for two of your party," said Tom. "How does this man behind us fit in?"

"He helped me get Stuston back to the inn. My aunt needed a temporary coachman, and Reeves offered. How fortunate it was that he was in Calais just then and without employment!"

In an odd tone, Tom said, "Fortunate, indeed!" He threaded his way carefully. He had more than a suspicion that when his young sister had mentioned burglary in an off-hand manner she was dealing with no more than the truth. He suppressed a shudder. "All right, Nell. Now I must assume that—you call him Reeves?—drove you to Paris. After Paris? And I must assume as well that our aunt is still with you?"

"Of course? You surely don't think I'm capable of continuing this long way without her? *Unchaperoned*? Tom, you cannot!"

Capable of anything, he thought, but did not say. The understanding of his sister's adventures that was beginning to come to Tom was cut short. The village at last loomed ahead of them, and the horses at last trusted in their instinct for shelter and provender and picked up their pace.

Nell, relieved that she was not for the moment required to continue her narrative of perils overcome and felonies committed, thought it well to attack in her turn. "If you had been in London, Tom, when you should have been, all this would not have happened."

"I can see that you need some kind of tight rein," he countered. "One might have thought that our aunt—"

"Not that, Tom. What I wished you to come to London for in the first place was to speak to dear Rowland."

"Rowland? Good God, I hope you are not referring to that idiot Foxhall?"

"Idiot?" she screamed. "You haven't the slightest sensibility if you think that, Tom, and I'm sorry you came along now, however late."

"Don't ruffle your feathers, chick. Since we are agreed that we are not speaking of Rowland Fiennes, we can take up the subject of your Rowland, whoever he might be, at our leisure. I believe this is the proper inn, especially since it seems to be the only inn, and we shall see to our friend the coachman."

Nell subsided. Tom had mistaken her meaning just now. But dear Rowland must be put on the shelf for the moment. She was most anxious that Reeves be tended to at once. Tom, the harum-scarum brother she had romped with—although not, as Reeves had suggested, in the nursery, since he was five years older—was proving to be other than her recollection told her he was.

For one thing, his German, though hardly fluent, was sufficient to accomplish his wishes at once. Reeves was placed gently in an airy bedroom and a surgeon summoned. Tom received the doctor's conclusions with a grave expression and arranged for a nurse who met his standards.

Nell went to her aunt in the sitting room. "You'll never guess, Aunt, what happened."

"You were gone so long," said Phrynie, waspish with worry, "I feared you had been carried off to some count's *schloss*."

"Aunt," Nell cried sincerely, "never, if he could but see you!"

"Well, I must assume no count. But I have the gravest suspicion that I have just seen Tom go past the door. I could not be right, of course, for he would have stopped to speak to me."

"Oh, Aunt, that's just it! I must tell you—" She proceeded to relate the events of the hours just past. She had barely finished when her brother joined them. She half rose from her chair. "How is—"

"Fine," reported Tom with relief. "Only two or three days in bed will be required before he can resume his duties with you. Aston is staying with him now." He turned to Phrynie. "Aunt! I am delighted to see you. Has my sister imposed so much upon you that you left that delightful house in Mount Street for a pleasure jaunt?"

"Coxcomb! I do not know where you learned such very *nice* manners, but they do not suit you."

"Very well, Aunt. I was hoping, you know, to win your approval, which I prize most highly."

"My approval would have been given gladly," she told him, "had you made yourself available in London a fortnight since."

"I do not quite understand, Aunt? I know that Arthur Haveney wanted me, and indeed that is why I did not listen to Whitcomb. Can you believe he told me at first that you had gone into Essex for the holidays?"

"He was to tell anyone so who inquired. I did expect him to have sufficient wit to know you were to hear the truth."

"At any rate," he said genially, "I am here now. What did you need me for? I am persuaded that you are far better able to deal socially with the *ton* than ever I could."

"Nell did not tell you?"

"She did say something about an offer, but I could not make sense of it."

"Pray do not speak of me as though I were not here," Nell interrupted with spirit. "I have indeed had an offer. The gentleman in question was forced to leave London—don't raise your eyebrow, Tom. He left on *business*."

"A Cit? I cannot credit this!"

She went on as though he had not spoken. "If you had been where you were supposed to be, he would have gained your permission, and our betrothal would by now have been reported in the *Gazette*. But no—you had to buy a horse from Charlie Puckett—" She broke off. She heard her voice echoing in her ears and realized how right Reeves had been— they were indeed squabbling like children in the nursery. She sank back in her chair and swallowed. It was never easy for her to admit she was wrong. Nonetheless, when such apology was required, she managed handsomely. "I'm sorry, Tom. I had no right to ring a peal over you."

"Yes, you did," retorted Phrynie, in her forthright manner. "If you have lost him because of Tom's dereliction, I shall never forgive him." She reflected a moment. "Forgive Tom, that is."

"Lost him? What kind of buffoon would not come up to the mark simply because I was out of town? Nell, who is this idiot?"

Chapter Twenty-One

She favored her brother with a glance of dark warning. "Promise me you will not speak with foolish impulse, and call him an idiot."

"Very well, I promise. But that will not signify, if he really is an idiot."

"He is not. He is the most handsome man on earth, and he is so civil, so graceful, so devoted to his government duty—"

Tom gave vent to a smothered oath. "I was right! I cannot believe I am right. Nell, you couldn't—you're speaking of Foxhall! Is she, Aunt? Could she possibly be attracted to *him*? A posturing nonentity?"

He found his answer in Lady Sanford's expression. "I was right. He is an—I promised, however, didn't I? And that word, so apt in description, shall not pass my lips. Nell, I cannot agree that you and Foxhall would suit."

"Your sister," Phrynie pointed out, "has a strong affection for him. And she could do worse, you know."

Tom had leaped to his feet and begun to pace the small sitting room. "Of course she could," he agreed handsomely, but loudly. "If she looked hard enough for a witless wonder, perhaps, like Abercrombie, or fortune hunter like Soames!"

"If you did not trust me, Tom, I wonder you did not come yourself to Town and winnow out all those undesirables," suggested Phrynie acidly.

Nell rose from her chair. Had she come this far on the pretext of the parcel, to be with dear Rowland—had she been by mischance forced to burgle a nobleman's residence, threatened to shoot any manner of villains, disguised herself and hired a wagon and horses, been attacked even by her own brother, only to have him tell her he would not approve

166

her betrothal? Not Nell Aspinall, she thought, and advanced on her brother.

"Tom, give me one good reason . . ."

Lady Sanford abstracted herself from what bade fair to develop into a pointless but noisy argy-bargy and gave herself over to reflection. She had noted before, without real alarm, that Nell's constant preoccupation with Foxhall seemed to have waned. She believed now that Nell's indignation with her brother was due at least in part to her failure to get her own way.

But it was, of course, entirely possible that Foxhall still held undisputed sway in the girl's affections, and in the most practical aspect, Nell could do much worse than to wed the handsome and wealthy Lord Foxhall. Phrynie's lips twisted wryly. Not every marriage was happy, and not every match was impeccable. Nell's choice seemed at least well above the average.

An exclamation from Nell brought Phrynie abruptly back to the present. "Dear Rowland will insist upon your approval!"

"And rightly so," countered Tom. "But you seem to have all but given him your answer without my permission. What if I had not appeared now?"

"I would have thought of something!"

"One might think you would already have thought of something better than Foxhall!"

"I am devoted to him," Nell told him loftily.

Phrynie watched the exchange closely. It would not be the first time she was called on to play referee.

"I have not kept close enough watch on you," confessed Tom.

"What good would that have done? Do you have another suitor in mind? One of Rowland's position, perhaps, or a more prestigious title, a greater income? I think not."

He stared at her until she looked away, flushing. "I did not know these mattered to you."

"Of course they matter," Nell flung at him. "Do you think I would be happy to cast off all my friends? Would I be content to live in a two-room cottage in a village, the wife of a blacksmith perhaps? No need then for me to cut my former acquaintance, for they would be the first to ignore my existence. Is that what you wish for me?"

Suddenly Nell noticed that both her near relations were

staring at her in some surprise. She knew she was protesting too much, was too eloquent on a question which was—which had to be—purely fanciful. Indeed, she did not know quite where her protests had come from. She had no intention whatever of marrying a blacksmith. But she was certainly not going to give up Foxhall.

Phrynie took a hand in the discussion. "We have three days, so you informed me, before Reeves can travel. I am sure we may have a much more fruitful discussion of this subject at a more appropriate hour. Tom will give his approval, I am sure."

She cast a speaking glance at her nephew.

"All I want, Nell, is for you to be happy," he mumbled.

"I know, Tom," said Nell, subdued and truthful. But she was much distressed in her mind on more than one head.

"Nell, you are exhausted, and it is hours since you ate," Phrynie continued. "Tom, I do not know your circumstances, but I should like to think you have traveled hard to overtake us and would be glad of a rest. Not another word until at least we have had dinner. I am heartily weary of the subject of Foxhall."

She sent Nell up to dress for dinner. Receiving a significant glance from his aunt, Tom lingered. "Do you really disapprove of Foxhall?"

"He's all right, I suppose, if you want a statue of a Greek god to stand in the foyer. I cannot see him making Nell happy."

"In truth," said Phrynie, reluctantly, "nor can I. But she may well be happy as most women."

"I want more than that for her," said Tom simply.

"Then what will you do?"

For perhaps the first time in his life, Tom stunned his aunt with his capacity for shrewd perception. "Nothing," he said. "If I disapproved, she'd be all the more determined to carry him off to the Austrian counterpart of Gretna Green. She has to be handled very carefully, anchored down to keep her from haring off with unknown parcels, to say nothing of some very strange incidents she mentioned and which I don't want to credit. And quite simply, I don't believe Foxhall has the wit to manage her."

"And I suppose you know someone who can?"

He looked levelly at her. "Yes," he told her, "I do."

Her thoughts flew as fast as his. But she refused to believe her own perceptions. He could not mean—and even if he did, she would fight such a result with all her formidable wits.

She smoothed out the wrinkles on her forehead, lest they become permanent. How very tumultuous she was finding life with the younger generation!

Relations between Nell and her brother were far from cordial for the rest of the day. But Nell's affection for him was strongly engaged, and it was not long before she regarded him again with fondness.

So rapt had she been by the need to obtain Tom's permission to marry dear Rowland that she had all but forgotten the parcel in the heat of argument. She must give it to Tom at once.

Unfortunately, to place the parcel in the hands it was originally destined for had disadvantages. She was beginning to realize that her brother was possessed of an inconvenient curiosity, in addition to an uncomfortable clarity of vision when it came to her. She had no choice. She must turn the parcel over to Tom and sustain his close questioning.

Ever the practical planner, she decided to make a virtue of what she could not avoid. If there were to be condemnations, then it was better to have them done with in a hostelry somewhere in the uncharted wilderness called Germany.

For a moment she envied Lady Hester Stanhope, last heard from in early October heading an expedition to Baalbec, far away from family censure.

Alone with him in their private sitting room, she unburdened herself. Tom listened with gratifyingly rapt interest.

"I wondered, you know," he said at last. "You were most open about your journey as far as Paris. I expected a romp, of course, for you cannot behave well for more than a fortnight."

"Tom! That's not true! And even if it is, you must agree that I could do nothing else. And I have not enjoyed this— this expedition in the least."

"Now there, dear Nell, you are bamming me. You have enjoyed every moment."

She chuckled. "I will admit it was not something I had a great deal of experience in, you know." It occured to her that

Tom was not as surprised at her narration as she expected. "He told you!"

"He?"

"Reeves, of course. Tom, I shall be really provoked if you turn him in. It was my fault, you know. Reeves only helped me." In a burst of honesty, she added, "But I did wonder how he had learned such deftness in criminal matters."

Tom was amused. "Tell me, Nell," he said eventually, "why did you take the parcel in the first place? It couldn't have been—no, pray don't tell me that you had in mind a journey to Vienna for the sole purpose of joining that—" Remindful of his promise, he substituted, "that impressive diplomatist?"

Nell had endured enough. She had held up admirably throughout this entire anxious time. She had stooped to criminality, had sustained frights, alarms, and a good deal of physical hardship. And nothing was turning out as she expected!

She put her hands to her face, and began to weep. Tom was deeply moved. "Come on, Nell, don't turn into a watering pot," he said crossly. "I'm not going to ring a peal over you. What's done is done. I merely asked why."

Muffled words reached him. "You know wh-why."

"You have told me about Foxhall, I admit that. But still the why of it escapes me. Lord knows I can't see the fellow, but if he can make you happy, he'll have my blessing." If he had mental reservations, like those he had indeed expressed to Lady Sanford, no one could have discerned the fact. "But if he is entirely devoted to you, can you not trust him?"

"Trust him!" Nell turned watery eyes to her brother. "Of course I trust him." She sniffed. "But Aunt Phrynie said that Miss Freeland will be in Vienna, and you know she has expected him to offer for her this long time, and I just—thought—"

Tom took pity on her, and finished her sentence. "You thought the parcel would be an excuse to get to Vienna. I am persuaded that Aunt Phrynie would not take you to Vienna simply to be at Foxhall's side."

"Oh, no, Tom, she wouldn't. Nor did I really expect her to do so. But I do love him." She considered for a moment. Deciding that perhaps the tone of her voice was a bit flat to convey her emotional message, she added, "Overwhelmingly."

Clearly Tom still had misgivings. "Do you?" he said skeptically. "And what do you think he will say when you arrive in Vienna?"

She looked at him in surprise. "Why, he'll say—"

"Will he be pleased that you cannot live without him?"

"I am sure he will not," she said sadly. "He must be so very proper, you know, for Lord Castlereagh is exessively strict." She sighed. "Tom, I have made such a coil of it all!"

He agreed entirely. He regarded his sister, though, with a tenderness that surprised him. He had taken her far too much for granted, he realized, and while he had not been watching, she had grown into a very appealing young woman. Suddenly, with great fierceness, he was determined that no harm should come to her. If her happiness lay with Foxhall, even though he had doubts on more than one front, he would do his best to help her achieve it.

But, having made that resolve, he immediately took exception to it. After all, the primary word was *if*—as in *if* her happiness lay with Foxhall.

"So you have the parcel to give him the reason for your arrival in Vienna. Just how will you explain the existence of this parcel which is to be delivered in the greatest secrecy?"

Her expression informed him fully. She had not in the slightest degree thought of such a barrier. Of course she could not arrive in Vienna, parading the parcel through the streets. Unwittingly she had come to the same conclusion as the Duke of Whern some time back: "Might as well send it across Europe announced by silver trumpets and a detachment of Household Guards."

"Oh—!"

"You see, Nell," he said gently, "there is still something to be considered. If I arrive with you and Aunt Phrynie in Vienna, no matter how proper our little entourage is, it could be viewed in an unfavorable light."

"How can it be? My brother and my aunt—surely we have the privilege of traveling where we will?"

He waited. Nell's wits were sharp enough to show her the interpretation that could be placed on her action. It took very little time, before she exclaimed, as a thought hitherto absent thrust itself on her, "Will he think I have brought you to him simply to receive his offer for me?"

Tom appeared to give the suggestion some consideration.

"I do not know him quite well enough. But, Nell, will he not believe you if you tell him that our meeting was more or less by chance? Tell him the truth?"

Her silence told him more than he wished to know. If Foxhall dared to disbelieve his sister, he himself would ram the truth down that gentleman's handsome throat.

She turned suddenly practical. "He might believe me, and in truth I think he will. But we may trust Miss Freeland to suggest the unthinkable!"

"Unthinkable?" Tom laughed.

"Well," she said, reluctantly smiling, "at least one hopes it is unthinkable to dear Rowland that I would hare after him."

They talked a little longer. Nell worried that the parcel might not arrive in time. "For we have been delayed a bit, in Calais and Paris, and now here. And of course, I think Reeves is not convinced that all danger is past. You know when that—that attack on the road happened, he insisted I take the parcel to safety. But," she finished blithely, "with you and Aston to add to our protection, we will be safe enough."

"Don't worry," he told her gently. "Trust me."

She thanked him, and rose on tiptoe to kiss his cheek. Tom would indeed take care of it, as he always had—except for the occasions when he was not to be found.

He knew of her love for Rowland, and he had assured her that her happiness was paramount with him. Trust him, he had urged her. She did not know exactly how he would manage, but in the morning, she was enlightened, and not with pleasure.

Tom was gone.

Chapter Twenty-Two

Tom gone! And Aston with him!

It was outside of enough. Nell had enjoyed just hours ago that intimate conversation with him, curious because it was perhaps the first time in their lives that the brother and sister had talked like adults—even like reasoning adults—without acrimony and without squabbling.

But even as gratifying as their closeness had been, he had not confided in her his intention to leave the little group behind. In fact, she had plainly indicated her expectation that he and his man Aston would join their party, thus decreasing its vulnerability to attack. And the wretch had said nothing about abandoning them to their fate!

What of the parcel?

He must have informed his aunt of his intentions. Nell swept into her aunt's sitting room, her indignation apparent even in the swirl of her skirt. "Aunt, why did Tom leave? And without telling me?"

The room was small. In fact, Phrynie thought as she looked up from her book—*Waverly, or 'Tis Sixty Years Since*, by an unknown author—the room was too circumscribed to contain the vigorous young lady who glared at her and demanded information.

"Did he not tell you?" said Phrynie. "No need to fly up into the boughs, my dear. He told me nothing. I wonder . . ." She pondered a moment. "He did come upstairs to see me last evening, before you came up. He was excessively restless, even for a man like him who has no fixed purpose in life. I should not have been surprised had he called for his horse on the instant. Like young Lochinvar, you know, riding out of the west."

"What has *Marmion* to do with anything?" cried Nell, exasperated.

"I really don't know," mused Phrynie. "Only this new book by that mystery man—*Waverly*—and I was able to find a copy just before we left, for it is in great demand, and for some reason my mind runs along Scott's long ballads. All right, I know that Tom is worrying you."

"Doesn't his unconscionable departure distress you in the least?"

"I think not," mused Phrynie. "For you must know, I expected nothing from him in the first instance."

"I did. I expected him to travel with us, as he intended from the beginning." Phrynie laughed, and Nell, calmer now, had to smile. "I know—it was I who intended, not Tom."

"From the beginning, Tom's company was the vital part of your plan, you know, and I went along with the notion, even though of all persons I have ever been acquainted with, Tom is perhaps the least to be relied up. Unless, of course, one considers his father, but I admit I am prone to bias on that account."

Nell, seized with fresh insight, could have told Phrynie why she had allowed herself to throw common sense out of the window and be persuaded to embark on this journey. Phrynie went along for the simple reason that she too found London dull and the prospect of the holidays in Essex quite without appeal. She longed for bright lights and music and dancing, and at this time only Vienna could provide such pleasures. She refrained from saying so.

"Well"—Phrynie sighed—"it's not to be helped, I suppose. If Tom has gone, that is one more instance of his complete disregard for his family. I shall be relieved, Nell, when you are safely wed—and creditably too—and away from your brother's authority. Although, to tell the truth, I never thought he had much."

"You did not see him dealing with the innkeeper, arranging for Reeves's care. I would not have believed his competence myself, had I not seen it. He was quite a different person."

"Unfortunately," said her aunt, "his alteration did not survive long."

Nell was desolate. "I did not think my own brother would abandon me."

"One might think anyone out of their wits to stay in this inn," Phrynie pointed out, "and I cannot fault Tom for departing. But I do feel he is much to be blamed for leaving us behind. When do you think we may ourselves leave?"

"I could drive the coach myself, if it were needed."

"No, thank you, my dear," said Phrynie firmly. "I do not choose to place my life and limbs at the mercy of a driving pupil of your father's."

"Our old coachman taught me!"

"Ah, yes, I recall you informed me so. And you did well in the emergency, I give you that. But nonetheless, child, I have the liveliest sense of what our friends in Vienna might say, were you to arrive in sole charge of a four-in-hand. It would take more than even my *cachet* to deliver us from such a *contretemps*."

Nell relented. "He says he will be quite restored by tomorrow."

Phrynie raised an eyebrow. She was troubled and did not quite understand the cause. Nell had subsided on the subject of Foxhall, and, equally, gave evidence of more time spent with their equivocal coachman than was seemly.

But soon they would arrive in Vienna, she thought with relief, and "dear Rowland" would bring Nell to her senses. She understood Nell better than the child thought. Phrynie recalled with some nostalgia, even from this distance in years, a certain groom who had been told to accompany her when she rode out in the moorings, even before her first Season in London. She could even yet bring to mind his chestnut hair, his tufty eyebrows, and those speaking brown eyes—much like, she mused, a crafty fox. Enough of memories!

"I shall visit Reeves myself," said Phrynie. "There are a few questions I should like to ask him."

Lady Sanford, with only a token rap on the door, swept into Reeves's room. "Reeves, I hope I see you better?"

He was dressed and sitting in a chair. His pallor was pronounced, but his eyes were steady and without fever glaze. His glance slid past Lady Sanford, to find, with obvious satisfaction, the figure of Nell behind her.

He made a movement to rise, but Phrynie forestalled him with a gesture. "I am tolerably improved," he said carefully. It occurred to Nell again that he walked a narrow line between broad country and butler, so to speak. His dilemma served him right—he gained much amusement from Nell, she knew, but her aunt was a different matter entirely, formidable and shrewd. Let him wriggle on that hook!

"Enough to take again to the road tomorrow?" He nodded. "Very well. Now, Reeves, I shall wish to know the full extent of your knowledge of the road ahead to Vienna."

Reeves frowned. "Your ladyship is not pleased with our progress?"

"I have had the strongest suspicion, Reeves, that you do not know at any moment precisely where we are. We have fallen into low, despicable posting houses and eaten such dreadful meals. I am persuaded that you have for the most part been wandering at random, taking any track that appealed to you. Am I correct?"

Suddenly Reeves seemed transformed. It was clear that he recognized his employer's right to be informed. His attitude now was that of one expert discussing a slightly knotty problem with another.

"Very good, my lady," he said, pulling himself erect in the chair. "I believe—in fact I know—we have now joined a main road from the north. This village is at the crossroads. The route will cross the Danube River downstream into Austria. However, I believe the crossing is at least two days' journey from here."

Where was the "thankee kindly" of yore? wondered Nell.

"Then," said Phrynie, "our journey should be much more comfortable henceforth."

"Comfortable?"

"Now that we are on a main road."

"Begging your pardon, my lady, but we shall not travel on the main road. I merely answered your inquiry as to where we are at the moment."

A dangerous light flared in Lady Sanford's eyes. Stuston would have driven the coach over the tops of the Alps had Lady Sanford instructed him to do so. Here was a mere temporary coachman, of whose virtues she was not convinced, telling her how she was to go on. It was not to be borne!

"And," she said in a soft but minatory tone, "why not?"

He answered, apparently at a tangent. "This land we are crossing is cut up into small countries, provinces, some not so large as the holdings of some English landowners. I myself—" He stopped short, as though he had caught himself on the verge of making a bad mistake.

"So," urged Phrynie, "what of these provinces?"

"Well, my lady, each of them thinks it is a sovereign nation, so to speak, with its own government, and particularly its own customs."

"Customs? Nonsense. We are merely passing through. What do the customs of the country have to do with us?"

"Not that kind of customs, my lady. These customs levy duties, *douanes, geld*—whatever you wish to call them."

"I shall call them outrageous!"

"But I did not think," continued Reeves, as though she had not spoken, "that it would be agreeable to two ladies of such quality to see their—pray forgive me—intimate apparel in the rough hands of rude customs officers."

"I should say not," agreed Lady Sanford, faintly.

"To say nothing of your ladyship's jewels," Reeves went on inexorably. "And many items, like gems or fine fabrics, are confiscated out of hand."

"I should speak in very strong terms to my ambassador!"

"My lady, there is no English ambassador in these tiny countries. And traveling is excessively expensive as it is. I do not wish to hire additional cattle, for if I did, your ladyship would have to pay excessive *postgeld*, or horse hire. There would be *Schossegeld* to pay were we to travel on turnpikes, or *Schwagergeld* to pay the postilions. As it is, you have paid *Schmiergeld* for the greasing of the coach wheels at every inn stop. And *Trinkgeld* for the ostler to wet his throat . . ."

Lady Sanford was appalled. "I did not know this, Reeves. But let me understand this. You have taken us across roads that were no more than cart tracks, through forests full of wolves, installed us in hovels disguised as hostelries—I vow I have lost a stone on this journey—all to avoid customs?"

He bowed his head in agreement. At least, thought Nell, no customs men had opened their baggage, and the parcel, as well as the jewels, was still safe.

"You know suitable byways, then, to serve us the rest of the journey?"

"I shall do my best," said Reeves.

Lady Sanford left then, presumably to return to Waverley, the Laird of Balmawhapple, and Bailie Macwheeble. Nell was thankful that the unknown author could spin a tale fit to beguile her aunt. The journey would have been unendurable for Phrynie otherwise, and she might well have passed her irritation on not only to Mullins but to Nell.

Nell recollected her aunt's conversation at breakfast that very morning.

"I do not scruple to tell you, Nell," her aunt had informed her, "that I shall endeavor never to embark on such another miserable, wretched journey for the remainder of my life!"

"Aunt! I was persuaded you were enjoying this gypsy life."

"You thought no such thing," retorted Phrynie. She lapsed into a reminiscing mood. "I admit there have been several points of some interest!" Suddenly she smiled mischievously. "Nell, to be honest, I wouldn't have missed this for a good deal. We may be killed on the road, or—or savagely attacked by wild men or wolves—but at least it's better than moldering away by the chimney nook."

Diverted, Nell had asked with genuine interest, "Do you know what a chimney nook is?"

"Of course I do. Many of Sanford's tenants, when they were old and their teeth were gone, mumbled all the day in the chimney nook of their cottages. Dreadful! I often thought I should quite probably leap off Westminster Bridge before I arrived at that condition."

Nell reached to touch her aunt's hand. "You'll always be a great beauty," Nell told her. "Something about the bones of your face, I believe."

"Don't flatter me," said Phrynie, insincerely.

Now, Nell lingered in Reeves's small room, loath to leave. "What will you do when we reach Vienna?" she asked.

"Would you be wanting a coachman on your return?"

"I do not know my aunt's plan," said Nell. Suddenly amused, she told him, "After we landed in Calais, from the ferry, you know, she said she would never again set out to sea. We may in that case never leave Vienna!"

"Would you like that?"

She hardly knew how to answer him. She had recognized along the way that given a preference, she would be content to abjure urban life forever. She liked, as did her aunt, amusement and music and the stimulation of witty companions—but in the long run, she knew they would pall. Someone like the Comte de Pernoud, for example, would repel her even in the short run.

She took so long to answer Reeves that he was moved to speech. "It did seem to me," he ventured, "that you are more than ordinarily familiar with country ways. Miss."

She nodded slowly. She recognized that this was a special moment—that Reeves was demanding that she look at herself more discerningly than she ever had. And for reasons that did not appear clear, she knew that she wanted—even needed—to be honest with him.

"I miss the country, you know. I never spent much time in London, until this last Season. My mother had enjoyed her Seasons, but when she married my father, she settled into his ways."

"Was she happy?"

"I never thought much about it," Nell confessed. "But she must have been, for my father would have taken her to London if she had wished."

They had come a far distance in a short time, she realized, and she did not of necessity refer only to the leagues covered from Calais. The journey she was making now was without landmarks, without marked roads, just as Reeves had guided them across the wintry wastes of Germany's small countries.

She clung desperately to what she knew. "I suppose my aunt will wish to linger in Vienna for some time," she told Reeves.

"And of course," he said, suddenly gentle, "you will meet your fiancé there. Will you be married at once?"

"I—I don't know." Not only did she not know how soon she would be wed, but she was also apprehensive about Rowland's welcome. Phrynie's warnings that he might not be pleased to see her under the apparent circumstances of her running after him—like a camp follower!—had left their mark.

"Tell me about him," suggested Reeves.

She did, slowly and not entirely coherently. "He is so handsome," she began, trying to bring his admirable person to life in her mind. She was hindered in her intent because odd little pictures, entirely imaginary, crept in to blur her vision.

Could she see Rowland outside the library window at the Chateau Pernoud, asking no questions but simply bending every effort to help her gain her objective, without one word of censure?

The answer was in all likelihood in the negative.

"He is so elegant in his ways, and you will agree that such beautiful manners reflect a noble mind."

Reeves did not in fact agree, but she hardly noticed. Her speculations moved on to summon up a picture of Rowland watching all night on the stair landing, lest she come to harm. The picture was not clear.

"But of course," she explained, more to herself than to Reeves, "his reputation is spotless. One does not progress far in his chosen field without an impeccable *cachet*."

She lifted her speaking gray eyes to meet his gaze. There was a light in his eyes that took her breath away. For a long moment she could not think. She was positive that whatever she thought, she would regret.

The smile that touched the coachman's lips was odd, as though he had come to certain conclusions that were significant. She longed to know what he was thinking.

But more than ever, she was afraid to ask.

Chapter Twenty-Three

The silence that fell between them was comfortable but not long.

Nell's unquiet thoughts swirled around in stormy chaos. It came to her that if she could sweep aside the obscuring clouds, she would come to a kernel of truth, one that would set her, after she understood it, on a far shore. She would never be the same again, nor, she suspected, would she want to be.

Whatever Reeves was thinking was not reflected on his features. With an effort he steeled himself in his impersonal demeanor. Only his hazel eyes, warm as summer sun on the golden flowers of the Cumbrian tormentil, rested on her until she grew conscious of his gaze.

He opened his lips to speak. But whatever he would have said was lost, for unexpectedly as spring thunder a crashing tumult arose in the stable yard beneath the window.

"What in the world?" she breathed, and ran to the window. Reeves was behind her at once.

The sight that met their eyes was one to astound the most world-weary of spectators. Napoleon Bonaparte himself could not have arrived in greater state.

The carriage that now filled the courtyard, seemingly from the brick wall of the inn to the far fence, would have put any lesser vehicle than Lady Sanford's own traveling chariot to shame. Indeed, from the window, Nell could see nothing but the new arrival, which blotted out all else.

It was a great state coach, an enormous, boxy object painted in the gaudiest of colors.

"Surely not red and gold?" murmured Nell.

"When the mud is removed," suggested Reeves, "it will outshine the sun."

"Who do you think it can be? The Emperor himself? Or maybe Tsar Alexander? I am acquainted with him."

"Then," said Reeves grimly, "let us hope it is not the Russian. He would complicate matters inordinately."

She was tinglingly aware of his warm breath in her ear when he spoke. Again the scent of his shaving soap, the clean smell of him, and the warmth of his hand sent her trembling as he took her elbow without apology and moved her aside so he could gain a better view of the scene below.

It occurred to her that they were both aware of the existence of the parcel, and the necessity to deliver it swiftly to its destination. Not only did Reeves consider himself her ally in the matter—it was as though he had taken over the chief responsibility for its safety. She had only to recall how he had adroitly avoided all customs inspections, how he had brought them by devious ways doubtless to throw off all pursuit, to realize he was a fellow conspirator without parallel.

Reeves was intent on the events unfolding below him. "Only one carriage, I thought, but look yonder," he said in a low voice. "Another, and still another. Good God, it looks like the entire court of the Emperor!"

"Postilions," she murmured, "and the grooms, and that next coach surely has servants in it for it is not half so grand."

Reeves's features fell into grim lines. With such a conclave in the stable yard he would be hard put to leave as he had hoped in the morning. It was even doubtful that Lady Sanford's blue chariot could be brought out from the shed.

"The door is opening," announced Nell. "Here come the passengers."

There was only one, in the event. The mysterious aristocrat demanded a high standard of service from his staff. Two footmen leaped from the box at the back and ran around to open the door and assist the passenger to alight.

"Probably an invalid," suggested Nell.

"I hope not," said Reeves. "The inn is too small for this kind of invasion."

Nell watched, enthralled. The occupant of the carriage at last came into view, one well-shod foot at a time. The gentleman appeared to be possessed of health and all his faculties. A lordly creature indeed, she marveled. The Tulips of fashion in London weren't in it!

"Who can he be?" Even from the upper window, Nell

could discern the elegance of his linen, his white gloves, and the grace of his figure. "He is a Nonpareil!"

"What is he doing here?" muttered Reeves.

"You said this village was on the main road, did you not? He is most likely traveling to Vienna, as we are."

The gentleman below looked around him, and even from here Nell fancied she could see his lip curl in disdain. Surely he was not accustomed to patronizing an inn of such lowly pretensions.

"I should perhaps go down and support my aunt," said Nell. "I fear he may impose on her . . ."

Reeves laughed aloud. "Lady Sanford will manage," he said. "In truth, I should not wonder if the gentleman chose to travel on rather than admit defeat."

Suddenly convention, as though it were a vinegar-faced Mrs. Grundy, dropped like a wall between them. She had stayed far too long in his room for a visit to a sick servant. And surely he had dropped the servile touching-of-the-forehead manner that ill fit him.

She wished she could demand answers of him. She felt excessively comfortable with him, and since that night on the darkened staircase he had not made any overt advances. But yet, he was a coachman and an enigma. And when they got to Vienna in a few days, he would doubtless disappear on his own pursuits.

She did not wish to think of that. "Are you certain you are well enough to go on?"

"Yes, miss, I am. Only a bump on the head, after all."

"I wish Tom had stayed," she said. "Or at least left Aston with us. I am persuaded you should rest another day."

"I think not, miss, if you will pardon me."

"The parcel, of course," said Nell. "I cannot see that another day's delay is vitally important."

"Perhaps not in itself," said Reeves. "But if it is taken from us, the postponement may be more than one day."

"Do you think—Reeves, did you recognize those men who beat you?"

"I was not quite sure. But it will not hurt to move on quickly, I judge."

"Very well. My aunt will be ready. Unless, of course, our newcomer persuades her otherwise."

Reeves said simply, "I trust not."

Phrynie had grown weary of the Scottish gentleman called Waverly. Setting it aside, she picked up a piece of embroidery she always kept with her. It was limp from long handling, and some of the silks had knotted together. She was not an adept needlewoman, but she believed that if she continued to make an effort, in some miraculous way she would master the art.

Since she had held this conviction since she was eight years old, without visible result, her diligence was commendable.

It was with a good deal of relief, then, that she heard the sound of carriage wheels in the courtyard. Tossing her needlework aside without regret, she hurried to the window. She was in time to see the lumbering gilded coach trundle through the gateway from the street, its roof barely clearing the beam spanning the entrance.

Accustomed to the pinnacle of elegance in her own world, she now realized she was agape at the spectacle before her. Luxury she might have expected—but what she saw now was gaudy to the point of vulgarity. A red and gold coach, indeed! Baroque in style, outsized in proportions, with gilt touches wherever trimming was indicated, and in many places better left untouched.

Postilions accompanied the vehicle, as Nell had seen from an upstairs window, and were now trotting their horses toward the stables. An inordinate number of grooms and footmen appeared, scurrying around like ants streaming out of a disturbed hill. A gaggle of outriders, clearly armed, cast wary glances around the stableyard. The black horses, to Phrynie's knowledgeable eye, were a superbly matched six.

So un-English! It was like Cinderella's coach come to life! In truth, those armed guards had a distinct resemblance to rats, wary and alert. Surely, thought Phrynie with anticipation, whoever traveled in such style should be a prime candidate to relieve her boredom. Even a withered spinster of narrow mind would be welcome. Unaware of Nell and Reeves watching breathless from a window above, Phrynie was enthralled by the possibilities she envisioned. Even her grandest imaginings, however, did not come up to the reality.

The elegant gentleman, nominally assisted by two footmen, placed his well-shod feet on the ground, and Phrynie breathed a sigh. No withered spinster he, but a gentleman of obviously lordly habits. How delightful! Not ordinarily a pessimist, Phrynie yet watched now to see whether or not a dumpling wife and half a dozen plump progeny might emerge from the interior of the coach. There was surely sufficient room in the vehicle for so many.

The gentleman was traveling alone.

Waving aside an attendant who had the appearance of a valet, he moved toward the door of the inn. Phrynie left the window. With an anticipatory smile on her face, she placed herself in a position to overhear the colloquy taking place in the outer room. Although she could not distinguish individual words, the tenor of the voices was unmistakable.

There was the effusive welcome by the landlady, the request for accommodations, the assurance that there were rooms available. All the normal counterpoint of arrival went smoothly. But suddenly the even stream of the dialogue was dammed. The newcomer's light baritone voice was raised. It was, she found, a carrying voice. She now, regrettably, could hear every clearly enunciated syllable. Her governess had taught her well, and she understood German with ease.

The newcomer's objection, as voiced firmly to the landlady, was simple. He wished a private sitting room placed at his disposal, at once.

"But, Excellency, I have only the one."

"I shall take it."

"But it is already occupied."

"Then remove the occupants."

"But, Excellency, I cannot."

The voice of the unseen traveler altered in an unmistakable direction. He was, quite clearly, furious. "Cannot? It is a word I do not wish to hear. Remove the occupants at once."

"But they are ladies, Excellency—English ladies."

"Nonsense," said the newcomer. "No English ladies would be here in such an inn! I myself would not have stopped save for an accident to my coach wheel. Pray do as I say, and let me hear no more about English ladies!"

Phrynie took exception immediately to the high-handed ways of the new arrival. She threw open the door of the disputed sitting room. She had not the least fear of being evicted from a room she had paid for, but she felt impelled to instruct the owner of that baroque monstrosity in the stableyard on the subject of manners. He had much to learn, she considered.

She stood in the doorway, fixing the newcomer with a glare in which contempt was strong. "I fear you are mistaken, sir," she told him in excellent German, "for indeed English ladies do travel abroad, wherever they wish." She favored him with a brittle smile. "Although I shall take care not to submit myself to the rigors of traffic with such a benighted population again, I assure you."

The newcomer stood as though nailed to the floor. He stared at her with surprise, which was very soon transmuted into stunned admiration. It was an alteration to which Phrynie had long been accustomed. On her part, she saw a middle-aged gentleman of ordinary height, smooth-shaven, with eyes of a penetrating blue. His features were on the unremarkable side, but there was an indefinable aura of power, of authority, even of arrogance, which accompanied his every gesture.

Far better than a wizened spinster, thought Phrynie, to beguile her enforced tedium here! A mild *amour* would keep her in practice for the glittering evenings she anticipated in Vienna, but she resolved to keep her manner quite remote and cool. This man would not be snared by an overt flirtation, for he was doubtless a veteran of such encounters.

Of course, it was not in the least desirable that she ensnare a man—remember, she told herself, the abominable taste apparent in that coach—except for a few hours this evening.

Only to beguile the tedium, and only to avoid the petty unpleasantness over the possession of the one sitting room—so she believed. But there was something about the man, some presence, so to speak, that had its own appeal.

"But," she heard herself say, not in the least remotely, "I should be pleased were you to share my sitting room."

A sense of attraction to the other was not entirely Phrynie's. The newcomer found himself, entirely contrary to his previous attitude, answering the fair-haired vision, "Madame, I shall be delighted to share—your sitting room."

For the first time in a decade, Phrynie blushed. Here was an opponent worthy of her finest steel. She opened the door wider, in silent invitation, and the gentleman, without even a glance at the landlady, passed within.

Chapter Twenty-Four

When Nell descended to the first floor, to quiz her aunt on the subject of the flamboyant new arrival, she found Phrynie not alone in their sitting room.

With her was the Tulip of fashion whom Nell had last seen descending from that fairy-tale coach. Her aunt and the gentleman held glasses in their hands and seemed in great charity with each other. Trust Lady Sanford!

"Nell, my dear," her aunt greeted her, "I should like to present to you Archduke Josef Salvator."

Merely an archduke? Nell thought at least an archangel! Or the Emperor himself.

"He has, like us, been forced to find refuge here."

The archduke rose, clicked his heels in an excessively military fashion, and bowed low over Nell's hand. "Exquisite," he murmured, "such a lovely child." Diplomatically, however, lest the aunt be irritated, he chose to temper his praise. "She has promise indeed. Perhaps one day she may be as lovely as you, madame."

Phrynie all but purred. "The archduke tells me that a storm is rising. Perhaps that may keep us here another day."

Only hours ago, she had demanded in great irritation that they move on at once. Now, she gave Nell the impression that a week spent here would suit her well.

Tactfully, Nell agreed. "Certainly our coachman would benefit from another day of rest, for I am persuaded he is not yet well enough to go on. I have sent Potter to him, and I should truly welcome another visit from the surgeon, Aunt."

"Of course. Reeves must recover."

The archduke required to be put into possession of the pertinent facts. At the conclusion of Nell's carefully edited ac-

187

count of the accident on the road, he nodded in comprehension. "I shall send my man to him. Fulke is quite knowledgeable in these matters. He is newly returned to me from the allied armies, where I suspect he was engaged in activities that I would not wish to know."

"You mean a *spy*?" breathed Phrynie, her eyes wide.

"Perhaps," the archduke agreed. "But I assure you he has done with such childish pursuits."

Nell glanced at her aunt. Spies were all well and good if they no longer spied, so to speak, but Pernoud's lackey of the squint eyes was all she wished to deal with on that head.

"Have your footman seek out my man—after he has attended to getting my bedroom in order, of course—and lead him to your invalid. I daresay he will set all to rights, and you will be on your way shortly." He produced an engaging smile. "Not, however, dear lady, before I myself am ready to depart."

Nell expected her aunt, noted for a certain independence of mind, to say with gentle firmness that she would leave when she was ready to leave.

To her great surprise, Phrynie murmured only, "So very kind, Excellency." Virtuously she added, "I should not wish to send my devoted coachman into such a storm as you anticipate." She bent to refill their glasses. It was significant that she did not call for a third glass. Instead, she said, "Nell, I am sure you wish to set the archduke's beneficent offer in train. At once."

The message was clear. Phrynie was enjoying herself once again. She had countered the archduke's selfish demands, taming him like a kitten. And she seemed well on her way to a state of enthrallment with Josef Salvator's person. Nell feared that her aunt might well forget the need to deliver the parcel, still in Nell's bandbox. Tom had not even suggested that he carry it on to Castlereagh to spare them any further danger. Indeed, she did not even know that Tom had gone on to Vienna. He could well have returned to England, for all she knew.

Nell felt abandoned by everyone. Tom first, and now Phrynie, who clearly would be more pleased by her absence than her company. And Reeves—he had so far abandoned his guise as coachman to consider her an equal. The coach-

man had better be put in his place, at once. If only she knew
what his place was . . . !

At the sitting room door she looked back and caught sight
of her aunt. Phrynie was turned slightly away from her new
friend. Out of his view, she winked broadly at Nell, while she
spoke to him.

Vastly relieved, Nell closed the door behind her. Her aunt
had not deserted her, after all.

Nell had never seen her aunt in the throes of a flirtation. It
would have been an education had she been allowed to stay.
But what would she ever need to know of the movements of
man and woman, deftly advancing, strategically and invit-
ingly retreating? She had dear Rowland, and flirtation was
quite out of the question with him.

Fulke accompanied her to Reeves' bedroom where she left
him. She waited in the hall until he could report to her.
While she waited, she could hear the men's voices within, engaged in what must be an absorbing conversation. For a long
time, during which Nell's fancies held her fast—was Reeves
much worse?—the door remained closed. When at last Fulke
emerged, he was startled to see her still close by.

"Is he all right?"

"Oh, yes, miss. He—that is—he will be fine."

He was not entirely truthful, she believed. But she knew
well enough that servants often formed alliances against their
employers, and at those times it was useless to attempt to ex-
tract information they did not wish to give. Not for the first
time, she wished with all her heart that she had not embarked
on this hazardous journey. She should have simply told Mr.
Haveney the truth. And she would never have encountered
the villainous Comte de Pernoud, or the rogues on the road—
or Reeves.

But she had, and she could not return to her life only a
month ago, when she was as innocent as a babe in leading
strings.

The archduke had arrived almost in the guise of a fairy
godfather. Nell could indeed have believed that the red and
gold traveling coach had, not long since, been an orange
pumpkin. Even with Lady Sanford's prestige, the landlady's
meals had been, to give them their highest credit, palatable.

But the feast that the archduke—"pray call me Josef, madame"—provided that evening, was of a class often called Lucullan.

Hampers were carried in from the third carriage—the second one having transported footmen and an odd groom or two, as well as an ostler and Fulke and a courier who was so far invisible. Fulke included a flair for French cooking among his many agreeable qualities. He concocted a meal for his master and the two English ladies that would even have outshone the best efforts of Lord Atterbury's chef.

Over a very fine apricot liqueur at the conclusion of the meal, Josef leaned back and smiled. "I am delighted, madame, that I thought better of securing this parlor for my sole enjoyment."

"My dear Josef," said Phrynie gently, "there was never a question of your securing this parlor for yourself." She smiled at him. "I must admit that this supper was of a kind to make me remember the civilized world, which I vow I had almost forgotten."

The archduke shot a quick glance at her. If he recognized the indomitable quality of this English lady, he chose not to mention it. "So be it," he said cryptically, and raised his glass. "To—what shall we drink to?"

Nell, captious over her failure an hour before in her room to resurrect Rowland to life in her mind, said, "To a speedy arrival in Vienna!"

"Nell," said Phrynie, lifting an eyebrow.

"A good idea," interposed Josef. "We must hasten by all means to the capital. I have sent word ahead, naturally, to have my palace opened for me. I wish to entertain of course. So many foreign visitors coming for this treaty making. I should not have expected ever to feel any gratitude for that little French Emperor, but I admit that without his villainies I would not have had the opportunity of making your acquaintance, Euphrynia."

Nell blinked. She had not heard her aunt called by her full Christian name ever before. This twosome—Josef and Euphrynia—was traveling apace!

"I shall wish at once to give a ball," he continued, "to honor my—new acquaintance."

Nell was suddenly aware of currents flowing beneath the surface of this pleasant dinner *à trois*—and strong currents at that. She set her glass firmly on the table. "I must thank you for an unusually delicious supper, Excellency," she told him, "but I must beg to be excused now. I must . . ." She cast wildly about for some believable reason. Neither was listening, so she simply left.

The remainder of the evening limped along. Nell finally went to bed, for lack of anything else to do.

Her aunt came up much later and stumbled to her bed. The archduke's store of beverages, in addition to being potent, must have been in good supply. It was a very short time before Phrynie was breathing heavily in deep slumber.

Nell's thoughts would not subside sufficiently to allow her to sleep. She had lain awake far too many nights recently, and tonight would be such another. She tried again to materialize Rowland's features against the darkness. Stubbornly they refused to appear. It was in all probability not his fault, for a different, far less handsome set of features insisted upon intruding. How could she concentrate on a classically handsome face, the face of a veritable Apollo, when a somewhat crooked nose, heavy brows, and a penetrating and lively pair of hazel eyes clamored for attention?

She sat up in bed. It was pointless to try to sleep, but she was reluctant to waste the night in mere aimless tossing about. She set her mind to deal now, once and for all, with Reeves the coachman.

If, indeed, he were a coachman by trade.

She might as well use this opportunity to attempt to set her thoughts logically in order. On one side, she considered Reeves's behavior as a coachman. He knew horses, indubitably. But so did nearly every Englishman of her acquaintance. He was competent and loyal. He instructed poor Potter, who rarely came up to the mark. He served as guide, finding the safest routes and the ways least apt to come upon customs barriers, for their safety and comfort. He saw to the carriage and the baggage.

All this was more than Stuston would have done. Her aunt's old servant had earned, he believed, the right to sit back and direct others. Reeves, on the contrary, had taken over the entire management of the journey from Calais to Vienna.

Quite simply they could not have managed without him.

But on the other hand, she considered, as she had all too often previously, his uncoachmanlike behavior.

Who was he? His speech, as she had often thought, was a bewildering variety of countryman—"Thankee kindly, miss, Ah just cum all over faintlike" indeed!—and of mock butler. And when he was not careful, when his thoughts ran ahead of him, he spoke like an educated gentleman.

He *was* educated. She had not seen him at a loss as to language. French had not baffled him, nor had German except in the villages where odd dialects prevailed. He was learned in history and letters—*vide* his referring to the Crusaders' routes as well as, once, to Dr. Charles Burney's miserable travels in Germany.

The conclusion was obvious—Reeves was no coachman!

But he was equally clearly no gentleman of reputation either. Else why would he have been standing near at hand on the waterfront of Calais, dressed in rumpled fisherman's clothing?

If he were gentleman born, then somewhere along his way he must have badly blotted his copybook. It was the only explanation she considered possible. Misbehaved so badly, she told herself, that he could not show his face to his peers but must skulk forever on the outer fringes of society, earning his living where he could, no matter how rough.

Such a waste! She wondered sentimentally if a woman were at the core of it.

Deliberately now, she set him beyond the pale in her thoughts. Her own breeding could not allow her to contemplate any further acquaintance with society's castoff. She refused to recall his tender kiss on the chateau stairs, the amusement that often lurked in his eyes. She would not remember his brief glances that hinted that he could, if he chose, sweep her willingly off her feet. She had helped him to that belief, she knew, for she had not drawn away on the stairs. She had even, her cheeks now burning with shame, responded to him.

She would now remove him from her mind, put him forever on a shelf and forget him. To assist her in this endeavor, she threw back the covers and tiptoed to the window. If she became chilled through, she might, upon returning to her warm bed, fall asleep at once.

The stable yard below the window had fallen into night

silence. Somewhere there would be horses, asleep on all fours. Postilions must be housed in the wing that stretched back at the rear of the inn itself. Tucked away in the small corners of the building must be the grooms, footmen, the courier, and outriders, all belonging to Phrynie's archduke. Potter was doubtless sleeping on a cot in Reeves' sickroom.

Already the storm that the archduke had predicted was sending its vanguard of snow slanting across the yard, melting and turning the cobblestones dark in the torchlight from the entrance. A movement below caught her eye, and she leaned forward to get a better view. The bulk of the vehicles—Phrynie's as well as the archduke's—loomed all along the outer fence of the stable yard. The shadows surrounding them were profound.

The movement she had seen was not in that vicinity. It had come from directly below her. She could see, if she moved to one side, the step before the front entrance of the inn. The movement had come from there, and it now came again. Now she could discern the man.

He detached himself from the shadow of the building and moved out across the cobbles. She could hear no sound of boots. He must be wearing soft leather shoes. Reeves had such a pair. The figure below moved across to the deep shadows beside the coaches, aligned in a regular row, their shafts before them like slender paws stretching into the vacant area of the yard.

Something about the stealthy movement of the man gave her a frisson of fear. He was up to no good. Her thoughts flew to Reeves. He would investigate at once. . . .

But Reeves was in his sickbed, and she dared not disturb him.

The man below had reached the shadows beyond and disappeared somewhere along the serried row of vehicles. His direction was no more than ordinarily erratic, indicating only someone whose purpose was not quite clear. As she watched, the figure took on a semblance of familiarity.

Recognition struck her. There was no need to disturb Reeves with her discovery of a man, illicitly abroad in the night.

For Reeves himself was already abroad—the very man she had seen, walking just a moment ago with healthy stride toward the shadows!

Chapter Twenty-Five

Reeves, she thought resentfully, could march around all night in the stable yard if he wished, and she would not care. What matter if he had been so ill that afternoon—pale of face, weak of limb?

She had made up her mind that she must forget everything that had to do with Reeves. She was affianced, almost, and besides, the coachman-cum-gentleman represented all that she had been taught to abhor. To make a good marriage, to take her place in the level of society to which she had been born, was what was expected of her.

She lingered, however, at the window, waiting to see Reeves emerge from the deep shadows of the coaches.

She must consider the alternatives—to marry where she wished, to dear Rowland, or admit that she found Reeves far too attractive to suit. She did not think she was a snob. But to throw her cap over the windmill was not to be thought of.

Reeves was still hidden in the shadows below. It would do no harm to be sure he had not collapsed in weakness. Besides, she was caught up in curiosity over what his purpose was in this stealthy expedition in the dark.

She thought back over the afternoon's events. The only untoward incident that could have a bearing on Reeve's actions was the arrival of the archduke. He had sent his man up to see Reeves, to ascertain the state of his health. And that was all.

Nell was now chilled sufficiently to turn back to her warm bed and fall asleep at once. But she was too wide-awake to consider sleep. What was Reeves doing? She was quite sure he would not welcome her intervention, even if she could find him in the shadows.

She was almost ready to give up the question and go to bed. But just before she turned away from the window, she thought she saw movement on the front step again. Reeves must have doubled back out of her sight. She would just wait to see him inside the inn and then go to bed.

She heard a door shut quietly below. But the figure below was still on the step, apparently just now emerging from the building. At this rate, the stable yard would soon be more densely populated than the inn itself.

The man below, unaware of the watchful eyes on him, moved swiftly away from the lighted door. The snow was coming down hard now, and she viewed the happenings below as though through a lacy veil. They might well be snowbound by morning.

She strained to recognize the second man. The archduke had come with so many servants that it was most unlikely she would know any except Fulke. But to her surprise, the man below, possibly aware of her eyes on him, looked up. And she recognized him!

Hard on the heels of her recognition came decision. She would put Reeves out of her mind tomorrow. But tonight she must warn him that he was not alone in the stable yard—that from somewhere out of the storm had come Emile, the squinteyed servant of the Comte de Pernoud!

She snatched up her dark blue cloak, threw it around her shoulders, and slipped quietly through the door. The stairs were in shadow, but from below came sufficient light from a lantern left on the table in the common room for her to see her way. Like a shadow herself, she descended swiftly, and in a moment stood on the step beyond the front door. Mindful of the chance of eyes watching from the building behind her, or more likely the vigilance of the two men she knew were already abroad in the night, she stepped away from the circle of light at the door. She was grateful for the Muscovy sable lining of her cloak. She pulled it close at her throat, for the wind-driven snow was cold and wet on her skin.

The yard was silent. The wind's keening was the only sound to be heard. She thought, with some apprehension, that a regiment might march across before her, and she would scarcely hear them.

Reeves had vanished into the broad band of darkness along the far fence. She had lost sight of the second man even before she had left the window. But she must first seek out the coachman and warn him that the enemy was stalking him in the night. Looking around her and seeing no sign of movement, she moved silent as a wraith across the intervening space. She found her breath again as she stood in the shadow of a great carriage wheel and believed herself hidden.

The coach beside her shone dull red and gold. It occurred to her that Emile must have arrived with Phrynie's Josef. Else how would it chance that the enemy, for he was that without doubt, could have emerged from the inn, moments ago?

Perhaps Josef Salvator himself was just such another as the Comte de Pernoud!

She must find Reeves. . . .

She looked around carefully, scanning dark corners, watching the snow swirl dizzyingly around her. Nothing moved. She took a step away from the gaudy coach.

A hand from behind was clapped over her mouth, an arm snaked from behind to close like a vise on her waist. Her involuntary scream was no louder than a sigh.

A voice spoke gutter French in her ear. "You know what I want, that bunchy package. Where is it?"

She twisted futilely in his grip, making strangled sounds against his hand. His fingers smelled of rancid grease and only a remote acquaintance with soap. Unpleasant as it was, she buried her teeth in his hand, satisfied to hear him grunt in pain. Her cloak was twisted around her hips, from Emile's grip on her waist. The wet snow found the opening, and her nightgown in only a moment became sodden, clinging clammily to her body. The cold stirred her to action.

She was indignant at the presumption of this base Emile, she was incensed by the fact that she could not travel as safely in Germany as in her own precincts and determined not to faint away like so many Rosamunds and Julias in those idiotic novels that had no relation to truth.

The garlic-breathing monster who had her in his grip now—that was reality!

She did not try to scream again. She bit the filthy fingers, she kicked backward to hit her attacker's shins—realizing with a start that she was wearing only thin heelless slippers. She bent double to take him unawares and writhed like an eel in his grasp.

He cursed in French. He grunted in exasperation. At

length, furious at her resistance, he lifted her up and threw her to the ground. She sprawled her length, her cloak billowing away from her. She was in a moment as wet as if she had fallen into a brook in spring flood.

The fall took her breath away. She saw Emile tower over her and then drop to his knees beside her. His hand hovered over her mouth ready to cut off her first scream as he demanded, "Where is the package?"

With guile she did not know she possessed, she said, quietly, "Why do you want it?"

"My master sent me," he said. She realized then that he was without wit, a mere automaton sent by the Comte de Pernoud, who must have surmised that the parcel would somehow act to discredit the Emperor. It would be a prodigy if she could not outwit the witless!

She must not give any hint to him that it was upstairs in her room. She dared not think of Phrynie's reaction were she to awake and find the man with the squint eye sorting through her personal affairs. She must think of something. . . .

"My brother has it," she told him. "It is already in Vienna!"

"You lie!"

"On the contrary," she said. "You must not believe I would keep it, when he was going to Vienna? I assure you it is in the hands of the English lord at this very moment."

He paused to allow the process that served him as thought to take place, and his attention left her for a moment. She saw her opportunity. The man's wits were not the peril. His brute strength was, for he could easily give one buffet to her head, like brushing off a fly, and she would have no further interest in the parcel—or anything at all.

She took her breath in silently. When she opened her mouth, her scream had all the force of a banshee's screech. At the same moment, she rolled away from him.

Emile grunted like a savage and raised his fist in threat. She was out of his reach. He scrambled for her on his knees, but she rolled over again. She attempted to scramble to her feet, but her knee on her wet cloak pinned her to the ground. Her nightgown bunched wetly between her thighs, and she fell back to the ground, knowing that Emile was a breath— perhaps her last breath—away.

But her scream had not gone unnoticed. She struggled to sit up, her eyes, wide and full of fear, fixed on her assailant. Suddenly it seemed to her that something jerked the man up to stand swaying, the snow piling up on his shoulders. She hardly had time to notice the odd phenomenon when its cause appeared.

Reeves was dealing effectively. A blow of seemingly insignificant force tapped Emile lightly, and the big man simply folded like a fan, to lie prone on the wet cobbles.

Reeves lifted her gently in his arms. "Are you hurt?"

"I don't think so!" She was breathless.

"Can you stand for a moment?" He set her on her feet, releasing her slowly. Assured that she would not slip to the ground again, he called into the shadows, and Fulke, Josef Salvator's factotum, emerged in answer.

"I don't understand!" she thought she wailed, but there was no sound other than the muttered conversation between the coachman and the archduke's man.

She was watching experts in their trade, she knew.

From somewhere Fulke produced a serviceable length of hemp, and Reeves tied Emile's wrists. After a short consultation, Fulke pulled their captive to his feet and shoved him ahead in the direction of one of the sheds beyond the stable.

"I don't understand," she repeated, this time aloud.

His hands touched her lightly. "You're drenched. Come. You'll freeze else."

How relieved she was, she heard herself thinking, to place her life in the competent hands that now led her to shelter! Muzzily she knew she had thought in error—not her life, of course!—but she did not feel able to come to more precise terms. She moved as he told her, took off her cloak as he commanded, all in a dream. She had no clear sense of time, nor of what had just transpired. He had brought her to an enclosed space floored with straw—in England it would be called a box stall, she believed.

She shivered and thought she could never stop. Reeves placed his jacket around her. Her teeth chattered. He paused only long enough to drape her cloak, fur side out, over the low partition that separated this stall from the remainder of the stable. Then he dropped down in the straw beside her.

"Where did he hurt you?" he asked. Not waiting for an answer, he touched her temples with fingertips delicate as butterfly wings. "Here? Here?"

"N-no, he didn't hurt me. But I think he would have."

"What were you doing out here? Can't you ever stay quietly in your bed at night?"

His voice was rough. Possessed of a strange insight, she knew he spoke not from anger but from anxiety for her. Even in her sudden satisfaction, she could not keep from shivering again.

His arms closed around her and drew her close. She could smell the strong unmistakable smell of the Scottish tweed of his jacket, mingled with the dry scent of the straw under them and the clean aroma of soap, by which she believed she would recognize Reeves anywhere in the world. He rocked her gently, and she gave herself up to warmth and comfort, as though she were a child, secure and safe. Some long time later, she became aware that he was humming. A simple little tune, oddly quieting. She could feel his heart beat and feel the faint vibrations of his singing.

Dreamily she murmured, "What is that air? Do I know it?"

"Most likely not," he said. "I learned it in Spain. In English, the words don't fit the tune. It's about what a man wants."

"And what is that?"

"The reflective life," he said, as though she had not spoken. "What a restful existence is that of the man who flees from the din of the world and follows the hermit's path, down which have passed the few wise men whom the world has known!"

"Restful? I wish I live to see that day. It occurs to me that the contemplative life does not include breaking into private castles? Nor being so very knowledgeable with your fists? I vow you hardly touched that man, and he dropped like a sack of grain."

"I never said I was wise," he told her. "I do not hesitate to admit that at one time such a quiet life had its appeal."

"No more?"

"A man, too, has a right to alter his thinking."

He put a finger under her chin and tilted her face up to his. His lips met hers, and totally of their own volition her arms went around his neck and pulled him closer to her.

There was one moment when she recalled, as though standing to one side in censure, that of all things she had considered to be altogether disgraceful, none of them descended quite as low as reveling in the close and wonderful embrace of the coachman.

The moment of hesitation, however proper, fled hastily, vanquished beyond recovery in the sheer deliciousness of her present situation, with which she was eminently satisfied.

Chapter Twenty-Six

Vienna at first sight was a city made of gingerbread, lavishly iced.

There were confection palaces, riotous with trimmings on roofs, eaves, doorways. The streets went in different directions, with a bewildering change of name at every cross street. Nell knew she would never feel at home in this capital. However, it seemed that everyone else in the world had come to Vienna and felt as much at home as though they had been born Austrian.

Within an hour only that morning, Nell reflected, she had seen the Emperor Francis, riding out through the great iron gates of the Hofburg behind armed postilions and outriders, his coachman driving six pure white horses. And Prince Clemens Wenzel Metternich, who considered himself the host of the glittering gathering of statesmen. The young Tsar Alexander, whom she had already met in London in the summer— he had recognized her and bowed most graciously.

Tom had pointed out to her the man who, above all others, was responsible for Napoleon's defeat—the eyes hooded like a hawk's hid all expression on the features of Charles-Maurice de Talleyrand-Périgord. "He's on our side," confided Tom, "at least for now. Although he can't be trusted—he was Napoleon's adviser not a year since."

Nell tried to pay attention as her brother pointed out the various notables whom he recognized. Her abstraction was obvious to him, and at length he gave up. "What maggot's in your head, now, Nell?"

"Nothing, Tom."

"Don't blame me, Nell. You've been moonish ever since you arrived last night."

"I am a little weary of traveling, I think. Pray, Tom, don't scold me."

He looked sharply at her. He had been on the lookout for Lady Sanford's blue traveling chariot since he had arrived himself three days since. Lord Castlereagh had generously set aside a suite of rooms in the palace allotted to the English dignitaries, and Phrynie professed herself delighted with the arrangements. Tom cast his mind back over certain remarks that his aunt had let fall, seeking some hint as to what had transpired since his own unceremonious but entirely necessary departure from the inn where Reeves had been recovering from the attack on the road.

Now, seeing that Nell had little interest in the traffic along the Ringstrasse—in fact, he was positive she did not even see what crossed before her eyes—he took her arm and led her back toward their quarters. "Who is this gentleman, Nell, that our aunt mentioned? The one who escorted you here?"

Nell forced herself to return a sensible answer. She had sunk low in her spirits, and the last three days on the road had been a trial, to put it mildly. "He is the Archduke Josef Salvator," she told her brother.

"Good God, an archduke? Trust Aunt Phrynie to fall on her feet even in a foreign country. He seems quite smitten, does he not?"

Nell smiled reluctantly. "He has promised to give a ball in her honor. In his palace here. He—he was most helpful, you know. When—when Emile, Pernoud's servant, you remember?—tried to steal that parcel. Tom, I must get that parcel to Lord Castlereagh!"

"He was busy all morning," said Tom.

"I know they would not let me see him. But dear Rowland will manage all."

"Dear Rowland," repeated Tom flatly. "Do I detect a certain lack of enthusiasm in your voice?"

"Not at all," she protested. "He is very busy. He has a great deal of responsibility here, you know. I am to see him later this morning."

"You did not tell me about Aunt Phrynie's latest conquest. He was helpful?"

"Oh, yes. You see, when that rogue of a servant attacked me, and then Fulke took him away—Fulke is the archduke's man, you know—and then the archduke had Emile put into jail, and I do not quite understand, but he told me that Emile would not trouble us again."

They had strolled nearly halfway back to the palace. Tom pulled her to a halt. "What of Reeves?"

"R-Reeves? What of him?"

"Don't pretend to be hen-witted, Nell. Where was Reeves while this attack was taking place? Why is it that Fulke captured the man?"

"Reeves—helped. Pray do not persist, Tom. If you want to know all, ask him."

Tom was as nearly set back on his heels as he had ever been. He had his own reasons for asking these particular questions of his sister. He had in truth never seen her quite so—he could not quite find the precise word to fit. Mooning in a dream—that was quite the habit of young girls, he believed. But Nell's dream was not a happy one. He was more troubled than he allowed her to see.

Nell had much to think about, and did not like any of it. Reeves had suddenly reverted to stiff remoteness. He had not once caught her eye on the journey from the inn to Vienna.

They had traveled tandem with the archduke and his three carriages, and there had been little opportunity for conversation. But he could have glanced at her. She found she had become accustomed to his habit of sharing amusement silently, the feeling of intimate conspiracy that lay between them. Now she sorely missed that.

But how could she have expected anything more? In truth, it should have been Nell herself who ignored her aunt's servant and put him in his place, as she knew well how to do. He had made insufferable advances, he had behaved as though they were equals, and he had even presumed to think that she would not object to the growing intimacy.

How dared he take her in his arms. . . .

Her brother said, "Your cheeks are flushed, Nell. What are you thinking?"

Tartly she snapped, "I'm cold, that's all. What else would one expect with snow on the ground?"

How dared he—but he had dared, as though he had no doubt that she would respond to him.

The dreadful thing, though—the knowledge that kept her from sleeping for three nights, the realization that sent her emotions into dizzying swirls—was that she had welcomed his embrace, and more than that, she ached to be in his arms again, and again.

The parcel in her hand, she followed a page through the bewildering passages that led from the suite to Lord Castlereagh's headquarters. The servant, chosen for his supposed fluency in English, chattered away as they walked.

She could not understand everything he said, but it was clear to her that if they had delayed one more day on the road, they must of necessity have spent last night in the Prater, the park across the street from the Schwarzenbergh Palace. "Never seen the town so full of folk," he told her. "A couple hundred families of royalty come to town to be in the swim of things. It costs a year's pay to rent a room on the Karlsplatz. That's the street that the church is on, the Karlskirche, I mean, not Saint Stephen's."

Fortunately they arrived soon at the white double doors that marked the entrance to the English minister's quarters. She had barely time to notice the rococo tables and chairs, in the style that more than ever reflected the Viennese tendency to decorate any surface, flat or rounded.

And coming toward her, smiling in welcome, was dear Rowland. He took both her hands in his and raised them one by one to his lips.

"My dear Elinor," he said, "I had never expected to see you here. But your brother of course told us you were on your way. I have been impatient, I must confess, for your arrival."

Strange, she thought, how one's ideas are altered. Just a month ago, she would have swooned had Rowland smiled down at her in such a way. Only four weeks ago, she had seriously believed that she would swim the Channel to be by his side, to gaze again on the handsomest face in England.

She was exhausted—that was all, she told herself. She could not quite summon up the enthusiastic response he waited for.

"Rowland, we are not alone," she said, glancing around her. "Can you bring me to Lord Castlereagh?"

The interview with Lord Castlereagh was short. A moment of explanation from Nell, a gracious word of thanks from the foreign minister, and it was over.

One month of peril, uncertainty, rough traveling, all for a moment's transaction. She could not explain the importance of the parcel to the peace negotiations, for she did not herself know. She did not quite know what she expected, but she knew it was not this simple handing over, as though she had brought a soiled shirt to the laundress.

She left the humming hive of Castlereagh's office, dissatisfied. She realized then that Rowland was beside her.

"Would you like some chocolate?" he asked. "Elinor, pray sit here. I should like a word or two with you."

Here it comes! she thought. Rowland will offer, and I don't know what I want.

In a moment a servant appeared with two small cups of chocolate, topped with whipped cream in the fashion that Phrynie recalled. They were in a large room, just outside Castlereagh's white doors. Surely Rowland would not choose such a public place in which to renew his attentions! It would be as inappropriate as receiving intimate addresses in the British Museum!

Rowland, however, had no such intentions. Instead, when he broke into speech, his question was on an entirely different head. "I must admit, Elinor, that I am in a way confused. This parcel that you delivered to the minister?"

"Yes, Rowland? Pray do not ask me what it contains, for I do not know."

"No, of course not. But it is the strangest thing. Your brother delivered a similar parcel—in fact, one might even suggest that it was identical—only three days since, when he first arrived."

She felt as though she had been struck in the face. There were not two parcels. There could not *be* two parcels. And yet there were.

"Tom did?"

"I fear I have startled you. Believe me, it is not my intention to cause you the least distress, Elinor."

"What was in Tom's parcel?"

Rowland looked sharply at her. Her voice had altered and become taut as a fiddle string. He was not overly sensitive as a rule, but his diplomatic training had instructed him to listen for nuances, and to interpret them.

His interpretation of Nell's demeanor was excessively unsettling to him. "I am not permitted to discuss the contents," he said warily.

"Nonsense! You have come so far with it, Rowland, you cannot stop now. What was in the parcel that my brother brought?"

"Certain documents," he said. "Of great value to our cause."

"Precisely."

If Tom had in truth taken the true parcel, then he had left her with a worthless package of whatever of an expendable nature might have been found at the inn. She scoured her memory to discover whether there was opportunity for him to make the substitution. There was indeed. He knew where she had hidden it, for she had told him. There was no reason why she should have secreted it away from him—and this was how he repaid her.

"I should not worry, Elinor," resumed Rowland. "I shall take it on myself to explain to Lord Castlereagh. . . ."

Her gray eyes turned steely. "And what exactly will you explain, Rowland?"

"Why, that you considered it sufficient . . ." His voice died away. She was not listening, however, and it was not until later that she understood what he did not say.

Just now, she rose from the brocaded settee. "Thank you, Rowland," she said absently and walked swiftly in the direction of her rooms. He rose belatedly to his feet and watched after her.

She hadn't even touched her chocolate, he marveled.

Moments later, she emerged from the rooms she shared with her aunt. Phrynie was, as usual, somewhere being amused by her new friend Josef Salvator. Nell was left lonely, but on the other hand there was no one to ask her where she was going. This was as well, for she did not quite know. She needed to ask some searching questions of her brother, wherever he might be.

Quite some time later, she caught sight of him in the distance. A drive from the street below curved around before the front entrance of the palace. Another, narrower road took off at a tangent to lead to the outbuildings spreading out behind the palace. Toward the back of the palace itself, on this

service road, she saw Tom and another man in close colloquy.

She hurried toward them. She had come within calling distance when Tom looked up. Obviously aware that she was
angry, for she had let her cloak fly out behind her and she
was walking in a determined manner, he left the other man
and in a moment disappeared behind some buildings.

She stopped short. She would have run after him shouting
his name had she been at home, but she was among
strangers. Even Tom's companion, watching her approach,
was a stranger to her, even though she knew him well.

"Reeves!" she said when she drew near. "I wanted to talk
to Tom, but the coward has vanished."

Reeves again wore the amused expression that she had
grown accustomed to—and sorely missed. "Coward? Any
man might flee if an avenging angel was bearing down on
him."

"B-but you did not."

"I did not see you in time," he said, his features impassive,
but his hazel eyes laughing.

"Nonsense!" She should have returned the way she had
come and caught Tom at another time and place. She stood
where she was, loath to leave.

A small silence fell between them. At length, the coachman
inquired, "Shall I wish you happy?"

"Happy?"

"You came to Vienna, as I believe, to be with your fiancé,
Lord Foxhall."

"Not quite affianced, Reeves," said Nell. "Not quite yet.
He wishes to speak to my brother."

"And your brother is here. So we may expect to hear the
good news at any moment, I suspect."

Her mind was far from Rowland and her delirious happiness at seeing him again. In truth, she had not yet come
upon the state of ecstasy. Instead, she inquired, "Reeves, you
remember that parcel."

He raised his eyebrows. "How could I forget it?"

"It was not the true parcel." She eyed him closely. She
could not discern any element of surprise in him.

"Then all our efforts were for naught?"

She suspected that he was more curious about the extent of
her knowledge of the parcel than he was about the item itself.

There was no need for secrecy any more. "I delivered the parcel myself to Lord Castlereagh not an hour since," she told him, "as I had undertaken to do. I am told—not by the minister, but by Lord Foxhall—that another parcel, that one containing the important papers, had already come to them."

"How strange."

"I am persuaded you do not find it strange at all, Reeves. I wish to know what part you had in deceiving me."

He thought for a moment. "Indeed, I should think that you should be expressing gratitude to your brother for his consideration of you rather than flying up in the boughs."

"Gratitude! For making me out the veriest kind of pea-witted fool?"

His mocking amusement vanished. "It was your brother's thought, Miss Aspinall, that your fiancé—or almost fiancé, whatever his status is—might take it amiss were you to arrive in Vienna, your heart on your sleeve. Indeed, while I could not quite believe that any man worthy of the name would resent such evidence of devotion, Tom claimed more intimate knowledge of Lord Foxhall. I, of course, bowed to his decision."

At the most inopportune moment imaginable, she recalled that sentence that Rowland had cropped short. He would explain to Lord Castlereagh that the parcel was considered by Nell sufficient to . . .

Sufficient to serve as an excuse to join Rowland!

Her anger was directed less at the vain Lord Foxhall, who considered her efforts as no more than his due, than at herself.

Rowland had read her own motives far too well!

Chapter Twenty-Seven

She came back to herself to see a pair of hazel eyes full of anxiety for her.

"Was Tom wrong?" asked Reeves softly. "Should we have told you that he was taking the genuine package?"

"I should not have worried so, if he had. It's no matter, truly, about the parcel. It was urgent to get it here, and that was of the first importance. It is simply that . . ." A sob rose in her throat.

"That no one trusted you. I see that."

She looked intently at him. Surprisingly he did see that she was hurt because no one thought her intelligent enough to know the truth.

"I'm sorry," he said. "It was all wrong."

She was recovering her usual good nature. "If I had not been so foolish at the start . . ." She remembered that Reeves had no notion of how the ill-starred journey had started, how she had cozened Mr. Haveney, how she had even persuaded her aunt against her wishes to set out. "No matter," she went on. "It's done now."

She could hear someone coming from the mews behind the palace. She turned to go. Reeves stopped her. "I am giving up my employment. It's back to the country for me."

She did not know what she answered. On the one hand, she could not wish him luck in a new employment as coachman, for there lay too much intimacy between them. Nor could she tell him that she would miss him, for there was the abyss between their respective conditions of life.

She did the only thing possible—she turned and, picking up her skirts, fled. If she had looked back, she might have seen Reeves watching her gravely, but she did not.

At the front of the palace, feeling tears stinging the back of her eyelids and longing only to fling herself on her bed and cry—cry for Tom's high-handed ways, for Rowland's satisfied vanity, for Reeves, for Reeves—she met Penelope Freeland.

"Miss Aspinall," said the light cool voice. "I heard that you had arrived in Vienna."

Nell looked up into the light blue eyes of the woman standing above her on the steps. "Yes, we did." The faintest stress on the pronoun was not lost on Miss Freeland.

"Wasn't that your coachman to whom you were speaking just now?"

Nell realized then that Penelope, like herself, was returning to the palace. "My aunt's coachman."

"There is something familiar about him. But then of course I must have seen him many times in London. One hardly looks at a servant of course."

Nell did not feel obliged to explain that this particular coachman had never driven them in London. Nor, she knew, would he drive them again. She said, in a lofty tone, "I was giving him my aunt's instructions."

"To carry you to the archduke's ball tonight, doubtless. It did not take long for him to open up the Salvator Palace, did it? I understand that he too arrived only yesterday, in your company. Your aunt seems to charm gentlemen to her own advantage, does she not?"

"Doubtless," said Nell sweetly, "because gentlemen find a woman with such feminine ways a rarity."

Penelope turned caustic. "I consider it beneath my dignity to flatter any man. I am no hypocrite. If a man cannot see what is for his own good, then he should be instructed."

Nell's eyes glittered. "One must certainly admire anyone who knows what is best, not only for herself but for everyone around her. What should we ever do without our self-appointed mentors?"

She swept up the stairs, leaving Penelope looking as surprised as if a kitten had clawed her. Nell's strong irritation was not soothed by finding Rowland in her own sitting room, waiting for her.

"Where have you been?" he asked, nettled at his long wait.

"Out."

"I can see that." He was on the verge of asking where but thought better of it.

"What did you come to tell me, Rowland?" she demanded. She was not in a mood to sustain frivolous conversation. "Have you looked into that parcel I left with the minister?"

He reddened. "The parcel is not relevant. I came in hopes of having a private interview with you. Not for the first time, as you know, but I venture to hope that this occasion will find all in order."

She looked at him blankly. "What on earth are you talking about?"

He smiled. "I must express my admiration for your quite proper reticence. But I assure you that it is quite unnecessary for you to pretend not to understand the purpose of my visit, especially when your brother has quite kindly put himself in the way of my approaching him to ask his approval of my offer."

She sat down abruptly. This particular moment had been the goal of her privations and her acceptance of unexpected perils. She had longed for Rowland to make his offer, for Tom to accept the desirability of Lord Foxhall, heir to an earldom, as a brother-in-law, and for the inevitable result of such a felicitous circumstance—a lifetime of bliss.

She contemplated, as though she had not previously seen them, her hands folded in her lap. Now that the exalted moment had arrived, she could not properly concentrate on it. She was well aware that a young lady's first offer was one which should be enshrined in memory. Just now she could not recall what he had said.

She hesitated too long. Rowland, disturbed at her lack of beatific response, was moved to speech. "Surely you were aware of my intentions. I told you as much in London, that as soon as I could gain your brother's approval, I should offer you marriage." He eyed her warily. "As well as my prospects, you know, being in the direct line for the title and a sufficiency of income of which I have already satisfied your brother, I dare to hope that you will find the life I have chosen—as a diplomatist, you know—one of constant satisfaction to you."

His life as a diplomatist aside, she thought, she could not but look at dead dry years ahead, without humor or wit—of which Rowland was deprived at birth—but with an oversufficiency of self-satisfaction, long-winded prosing, and overweening dignity.

"Rowland, we shall not suit."

"Not suit!" He was aghast. "Not suit? What then do you want?"

She could not tell him what she wanted. She wanted someone who would sympathize and share her troubles—like climbing in illicit windows. She longed for someone to be tender of her welfare, keeping watch, if it were required, on the landing all night.

And above all, she ached for someone who could be swept away by sheer desire for her love to forget his status in life and deal with her like a woman and not a diplomatic treaty!

"I am sorry, Rowland. My affections have altered."

"Altered!"

"Pray, Rowland, do not repeat my every word. Just understand—*try* to understand—that I can never marry you."

"Then—then you didn't come with that ridiculous parcel just to—to marry me?"

"Indeed, I did not." What was truth, after all?

He gathered his dignity around him almost visibly, like a Roman toga. At the door, he paused to deliver one more pronouncement. "I am grateful that at least I had sense enough not to put a premature announcement in the *Gazette*. I should not like to look the fool."

"But," said Nell, aroused, "you were willing enough to brand me an idiot for so far forgetting decorum as to chase you across Europe with a parcel of nothing as an excuse? What kind of fool do you take me for?"

"But," said Rowland with every appearance of reason, "you are female. And no one expects logic from a woman."

She seethed until late afternoon and time to dress for the archduke's ball. She was sitting in her dressing gown staring into the mirror when her aunt entered.

"Whatever is the matter, Nell?" she cried. "You haven't begun to dress. What are you to wear? I'll send Mullins to you!"

"No need, Aunt. I am ready but for my gown."

"Do not delay, child. We are to be there early. Josef is sending his coach for us, and I do not wish to keep the horses standing."

Nell looked sharply at her aunt. An odd note in Phrynie's voice was reflected as well in an unaccustomed expression of doubt. "You, worried about keeping cattle standing, Aunt? This is not like you."

Phrynie laughed, not merrily. "I know it isn't. In truth I do not quite know what is like me anymore. You know that Josef is related to the Emperor? His wife—I mean Josef's—died several years ago, about the same time as Sanford, isn't that an odd coincidence?"

"Quite likely several hundreds more died at the same time, Aunt."

Phrynie took a turn around the small bedroom. "I declare I never—" She whirled back to face Nell. "Nell, do you think I would like living in Austria?"

Phrynie's vulnerable expression moved Nell to the verge of tears. "Aunt, really? Is it something you would like?"

"Oh, Nell, I'm so fuddled I can't tell what I would like. But he is so kind, and so considerate. . . ."

Nell sprang up to hug her aunt. "Oh, I am delighted for you, so happy, you deserve everything. . . ."

Wiping a tear from her cheek, Phrynie said, "What about you? For I shall not dare to be happy until I have you settled!"

Nell kept silent. How could she dash her aunt's visible happiness by telling her that her own marriage would not now take place? The answer was evident. "I'll tell you later," she said. "I shall not wish to be the cause of the archduke's cattle standing in the cold!"

Phrynie returned to her room, and Nell proceeded to put on her ball gown. She wore her new white lace and fastened her mother's pearls around her. How virginal she looked! she told herself. An omen of some significance, more than likely.

A tap on the door heralded another caller, this one more than unwelcome. "Tom, I am surprised to see you," Nell told him, frost edging her words. "When I saw you last, you could not escape quickly enough."

"I am sorry, Nell. But I must tell you—"

"Nothing I wish to hear, I am sure."

"Quite likely." She saw that his lips were set in an unaccustomed grimace. Clearly his message was not expected to be a popular one. "Nell, I'm not giving my approval for you to wed Foxhall."

She gaped at him. "But you already did!"

"I will rescind it. Nell, you cannot be happy with that windbag."

Irritation turned to full-fledged anger. "I suppose you are doing what you think is best for me? My dear brother, I beg leave to take exception to your misguided authority. It is entirely your fault that we came here to Vienna. If you had been where you were supposed to be, you could have made your decision at once, instead of weeks later, after that odious journey! You could have brought the parcel yourself to Vienna, and I would now be preparing for the Christmas holidays in Essex. And I would not have made myself a complete idiot, for you must know that Rowland has explained to me the contents of that parcel I guarded with my very life!"

Tom's mouth dropped open. He was stunned by the fury of her onslaught. He caught hold of only one of the accusations hurled at him. "But you thought Foxhall wouldn't believe you, without that parcel for an excuse!"

"That doesn't matter. He offered for me."

"He did?" Tom's eyes narrowed to slits. "Then I shall have to seek him out, to tell him—"

"Oh, tell him nothing!" she raged. "I have turned him down. You may call me ape-leader, for you will never call me Lady Foxhall!"

For once, and wisely, Tom held his tongue. He was rewarded by his sister throwing herself in his arms and sobbing violently on his shoulder. For perhaps the first time, he felt some sympathy with Foxhall. He had a shrewd idea that the man was just as bewildered by Nell's about-face as he was himself. *Women!*

The Archduke Josef Salvator's ball was a huge success. Everyone said so. The Duchess of Netwick screwed up her malicious little face, cast a significant glance at Phrynie, and remarked that the archduke was coming out of mourning, wasn't he?

Penelope Freeland entered, triumphantly smiling, on the arm of Lord Foxhall. Nell, her dress as innocent as the one she wore when her aunt presented her to society last April, was escorted by her brother, to whom she seemed to have little to say.

The evening seemed to her to have no relation to time. She

could not tell how many sets she danced, how many partners she had, for they all flew by in a blur. At length, when Tom came to her, perhaps an hour after they arrived, she was dizzy with the noise and the insufferable heat, more suitable to a conservatory than a ballroom. The Austrians knew how to keep warm, without doubt.

"Tom, please, let us not dance. I have the headache, and I am so thirsty."

Relieved, he said, "Let me get you something to drink. Not alcoholic, of course, but I expect they have lemon squash."

The small room to which he led her was a quiet haven. The door stood open, of course, but the insistent hum of many voices receded, like the distant hum of bees in the meadows in high summer at Aspinall Hall. Would she had never left it!

Her brother had been gone a very long time, so it seemed. She could hear voices outside now, someone sounding very much like Rowland, saying deferentially, "Your Grace—"

The door opened, not to admit Rowland. Instead a man dressed in a colonel's uniform, resplendent with medals, came in and closed the door behind him. He advanced to her and bowed low over her hand. "Miss Aspinall," he said, "I hope I see you in good health?"

"Reeves! What are you doing here? Where did you get that uniform?"

"I admit," he said looking down at it, "it is not the precise fit that Weston would furnish. I did have to borrow it."

"Borrow! Stole, more likely. Reeves, Rowland is coming back in a moment. You've got to leave!"

His hazel eyes quizzed her. "You want Foxhall?"

"No, no, but you will be caught! You'll be in jail!"

"I think not." He still held her hand tightly in his.

"There is nothing amusing about being in jail!"

"I have been imprisoned before," he said. "Does that make a difference to you?"

"That was when you were in the war. And it wouldn't make any difference anyway!" Her fear for him loosened her tongue and swept away discretion. "I'll get Fulke. He must be nearby. He'll help you get out of the palace."

His smile was odd. He pulled her to him and held her close. He bent to touch her lips gently with his. She moaned in frustration, and some real irritation.

"My dear, I do not wish to leave the palace. I came here purposely to see you."

"Very well, I'll go with you. It's not safe to be here."

He seemed heedless of any danger to himself. Instead, he seized upon her remark. "You will go with me? How far?"

"Out of the palace—"

"How far are you prepared to go, to be with me?" he persisted.

She was shaken. He was demanding of her more than she could give. She could not see herself as a coachman's wife, or even the wife of a man who had behaved so badly that he had to wander through Europe, picking up employment where he could.

But, to be quite honest with herself, she could surely see herself as the wife of this man with the hazel eyes, usually so full of amusement.

He was not amused now. His eyes seemed to bore into hers, to pull out of her the truth she did not wish to admit. "I cannot tell," she said at last, in a pitifully forlorn tone. "I do not know how to do so many things that you would need. I cannot sew or cook, and you would soon detest me. . . ."

"You intend then," he said harshly, "to marry Foxhall for the advantages he can give you?"

Incensed, she drew back. She lifted her open hand to slap him, but he caught her wrist.

"Shall I bring him back?"

"No. I have turned him down. I cannot marry him."

The moment was tense. He waited, silently demanding, and she could not answer him for a bit. Finally she looked away. When she spoke, he had to bend to hear her. "Without you, I will go sadly all the rest of my life."

"Then?" He was still, waiting for her.

"I should not like to be forward. Do you want me?"

His answer was swift and wordless. Gone for the moment was the gentle touch, the sweet tenderness she had known once before. Now his embrace was the exultant expression of a man who had been given his heart's desire. "Do I want you!"

He released her at last. She caught her breath tremulously and smiled up at him through teary eyes. "I don't know what will happen, Reeves," she said, "but I don't care, if you are with me."

The door opened with a bang. She would have sprung away from his embrace, but he would not let her go. "Here is your glass of squash," said Tom. He surveyed them both, grinning. "I thought you had the headache, Nell."

She looked from one to the other. She had an impulse to stand between her aunt's coachman in his stolen uniform and retribution in the person of Lord Foxhall. The coachman glared at the intruder. "Tom, I thought I told you to stay out."

"Doesn't Nell want her drink? She is thirsty."

"Are you, my love?" said Reeves, laughing at her appalled expression.

"Tom . . ." she said faintly.

"It's no good, Nell," said her brother, unaccountably chuckling. "No need to ask me to approve this marriage. With what I have just seen—"

"If you had obeyed my instructions, you would have been spared such a sight," retorted the other.

"Duke," said Tom, smothering his amusement, "do you wish to ask me something?"

"Very well. I shall ask for your sister's hand in marriage, you rogue. And I do not scruple to tell you that a refusal will result in your head-first immersion in the nearest horse trough."

Nell chose this moment to interrupt. "I do not know quite what you two are talking about. Schoolroom japery, no doubt. I have not agreed to marry anyone in this room. Tom, I shall ask for your escort back to our aunt."

"Now wait, Nell . . ." began Tom. Upon a gesture from the other man, he slid through the door and closed it firmly behind him.

"Now then," said Reeves, "my little love, what is amiss?"

"I collect that you and my brother have combined once again to show me up as the fool that I am." The tears in her voice strangled her. She put her hands to her face. He came to her, but she shrugged away from him.

"If you were willing to come with me into what you supposed to be a life of exile, then I cannot understand why you are unwilling to be my love in a civilized life." He laughed a little. "I cannot help it, my dear, that I succeeded to the title. It was no part of my plans to become the Duke of Whern."

She whirled in astonishment. "The Duke of Whern?"

"You did not guess? I fear I was not a very convincing coachman. Does it truly matter what I am?"

She could not answer. Shock held her in its grip so that she could not move, or even speak. She could only look at the floor. After what seemed to be a long time, she heard him say, in a dreary tone, "Very well, my dear." She heard his footsteps retreating to the door. She must not let him go!

She called out, "Reeves—I mean, Your Grace . . ."

He turned back to see an expression he would never forget on her face. Her eyes brilliant with tears, a pinkly radiant flush on her cheeks, her hands out in an arrested gesture of appeal—he reached her in two strides. "My love, my dearest, my beloved . . ."

The rest of his words were lost in her hair.

She drew away at last. Shakily she whispered, "Reeves? Truly I do not know what to call you."

"John will do. If I may make a suggestion?"

"Oh, yes."

"John *darling* would suit."

She repeated it prettily. "I shall be easier with it," she added, sweetly shy, "as I become accustomed to it."

"You will have every opportunity to practice," he said, and kissed her again, even more thoroughly.

Phrynie, having been brought *au courant* by her nephew, was consumed by impatience. Imagine, the Duke of Whern her coachman! And she had thought him a product of Newgate prison!

She placed herself now in a position to watch the door behind which momentous events were taking place. While she watched, Tom had gone in and soon emerged, winking at her before he moved away.

Her little Nell a duchess! It was quite beyond belief.

But as the time wore on, Phrynie began to wonder whether it would all turn out right in the end. Always one to turn first to the last page of a novel to see how it came out, now her impatience prodded her unmercifully.

On tiptoe she crossed the carpeted hall and put her hand on the latch. She glanced about. There was no one in sight, since all dear Josef's guests had gone in to supper. She put her ear to the door and listened. There was no sound. Not even a murmur.

She could no more have resisted her next move than she could have waltzed on the rooftop. She pressed the latch and silently opened the door.

What she saw within the room caused her to retreat at once, entirely satisfied. Now she could look forward to her own concerns. The Emperor was giving a ball on the weekend, and Josef planned at that time to seek permission of the head of his family to marry. If he played his cards right, he had confided in her, there might even be an ambassadorship to London sent his way, and he could take his bride back to her homeland in style.

Coming to Vienna had been the most superb idea, and she was most pleased with herself for thinking of it. She must remember to point out to Nell how well things had turned out after all.

She smiled to herself. She was quite sure that Nell already knew that.

About the Author

Vanessa Gray grew up in Oak Park, Illinois, and graduated from the University of Chicago. She currently lives in the farm country of northeastern Indiana, where she pursues her interest in the history of Georgian England and the Middle Ages. She is the author of a number of bestselling Regencies—*The Masked Heiress, The Lonely Earl, The Wicked Guardian, The Wayward Governess, The Dutiful Daughter, The Innocent Deceiver,* and *The Reckless Orphan*—available in Signet editions.